# SUNSET

# SUNSET

## Jessie Cave

WELBECK

Published in 2021 by Welbeck Fiction Limited,
part of Welbeck Publishing Group
20 Mortimer Street London W1T 3JW

A CIP catalogue record for this book is available from the British Library

Hardback ISBN: 978-1-78739-529-9
Waterstones edition ISBN: 978-1-78739-791-0
Trade Paperback ISBN: 978-1-78739-533-6
E-book: 978-1-78739-530-5

Typeset by Palimpsest Book Production Ltd., Falkirk, Stirlingshire

Printed and bound by CPI Group (UK) Ltd., Croydon, CR0 4YY

10 9 8 7 6 5 4 3 2 1

*For Bebe*

# PRELUDE

We're holding hands and walking up a hill. Our hotel sits at the top. A messy red plait hangs down her back and her summer dress is too short so it keeps riding up. She doesn't notice, or maybe she doesn't care because we're on holiday. She's pulling me along, and as my heart starts pounding I regret not keeping up with swimming, keeping up with anything. I wish I had her discipline, her strength. My pink flip-flops are digging into the sides of my feet and sand nestles in a new blister; my calves ache from walking on the beach today. I'm so full of pizza I beg her to sit down.

We sit on the edge of a grassy mound and catch our breath as the sun goes down. The sky is splashed with neon pink and orange like a painting. She points to the setting sun.

Her: That was lucky —
Me: I planned that.
Her: Come on, up we go —
Me: Hannah, I can't, please —
Her: You can —
Me: Let's just stay here for another minute and watch the sun go down —
Her: It's gone. But there's always another one tomorrow.

She sprints ahead in the dark, laughing. I sit still, unable to move without her, refusing to move without her. She comes back. Of course she comes back.

★ ★ ★

List of weird things I've done<br>in the last eight months:

- Severely burnt my tongue on microwaved lasagne and got so angry that I threw it out the window. It landed on top of a bus stop and was eaten by pigeons for days and days.
- Stuck gum on my wall as I went to sleep each night because I couldn't be bothered to get up from bed. Slowly I accumulated a 'gum mountain' which is now home to six dead flies.
- Bought ingredients in the middle of the night for carrot cake even though I hate carrot cake. I tried to give it to a homeless person, but I couldn't find one who'd take it.
- Fell asleep in the bed department of John Lewis. Had a graphic nightmare and woke up screaming, surrounded by three sales assistants and an uninterested policeman.
- Incorrectly completed multiple Sudoku puzzles in newspapers and wrote slightly aggressive and cryptic things like I STILL KNOW WHAT YOU DID LAST SUMMER next to them.
- Masturbated to *Location, Location, Location* with an expensive vibrator that I stole from my sister.

# 1

Heathrow Terminal 5
2019

We're in Departures and I'm waiting for her to get off the phone. I know she's speaking to him because her lips curled up at the sides when she saw who was calling. She knows that I find the 'in love' version of her annoying, so she slides off on her own for the call. I watch her leaning on a metal rail. She got Mum's legs; I got Dad's thighs. I pretend for a second that she's not my sister and I wonder if I would look at her and find her attractive, from behind, at first glance. I think I would.

I'm in an old grey Adidas tracksuit, huge pants and no bra. My usual travel attire. My sister is wearing a short brown skirt to annoy me. She always wears tight skirts on flights, and says she doesn't dress intentionally sexy to annoy me, but she absolutely does. She's also wearing a tight ribbed white T-shirt and thin grey tights. It's slightly too early to ruin the holiday so I won't say anything about her outfit. I'll just wait until we board the plane. We'll get settled in our seats, then she'll look around sheepishly and undo the top button of her skirt. I'll turn to her and say, 'If it's uncomfortable then why are you wearing it on a flight?' She'll insist she's totally comfortable. She's a liar, but then I am too.

I don't have a person to call like she does, so I go and get our coffees. We have this ritual now of getting to the airport early and sitting with a coffee and watching the planes. She makes me guess the place we're going. I always guess wrong, and then feel surprised about where we're going because it's never that cheap. She insists on paying for everything, and I protest, even though I have no money. She insists that she's the big sister, she's the one with a salary, and that she loves me. I don't know why she loves me – I'm an awful person.

I slept over at Hannah's last night. She has a spare room for me but I never use it, I always sleep in her bed. I had a bath while she read an article to me – an article I didn't understand but pretended to – then she got in the bath and I got out. It's gross, but she gets a kick out of saving water. I wrapped a towel round my bottom half and lay on the floor, pretending to be a mermaid. No one laughs at me the way she does, it's like a superpower I have which only works with her.

As kids, we pretended to be mermaids by squeezing both of our legs into pyjama bottoms and swivelling and swishing along our bedroom floor, like we were trying to escape. I think it was an amalgamation of *The Little Mermaid* and a heist film. We made each other laugh, our parents less so, but at least they would watch for a second before going downstairs to start their evening. I only realised relatively recently that quite often they would leave to go out as soon as we were quiet. We wouldn't be asleep though, we would still be giggling softly in the dark, unable to stop.

In adulthood, I tend to go through phases of becoming

4

a new person for about five days at a time before I get bored and give up and stop trying to be better. I go over to Hannah's to lie in bed with her and she tells me what I need to do to get my life in order again: who to stop texting, what foods I should eat to give me more energy, and which conditioner I should be using. She draws bullet points in the air in soft strokes and I follow the path of her fingers.

Her flat is way too nice for her age, in a converted warehouse in King's Cross. She's four years older than me, and although I hope that I'll have a flat this nice by the time I'm her age, when I've got my shit together, I highly doubt it. Her pictures are in frames, not just blu-tacked or taped to the wall. She has mirrors to make the rooms look bigger, vinyl records, a weird cactus and a fireplace with real wood which scares me. She's even got her own lamps – fancy ones with light bulbs so specific that you have to order them online, not just shitty lamps left behind by the previous tenants, like mine.

My flat is quarter the size of Hannah's, nearby in Caledonian Road. It's an ex-council property that our parents bought when they had some extra money in the nineties – the one sensible investment they've ever made – and it was supposed to be insurance that we would have somewhere to live when they became extremely rich and famous and had no time to worry about us as adults.

I never think about money. Hannah does. She plans and she saves but she isn't anal about it. She doesn't buy new clothes very often except fancy power-suits for work. She goes to charity shops, and she gives to fucking charity shops, to homeless people. Sometimes I tease her by saying she only does that to seem benevolent, but then secretly goes in the next day in disguise to buy her stuff back.

She doesn't like it when I say that. We have a very different sense of humour when it comes to moral integrity.

While she snored soundly in a giant T-shirt she's worn for a decade (the faded Betty Boop one which used to belong to our mum), I sat restlessly in the bathroom and stared at her endless collection of products. I was bored so I tried some of them out. She has so many hair creams and stylers and serums for curly hair, which I find funny because I know that her hair is naturally quite straight. As I was inspecting the ingredients of a bottle labelled 'Eternal Radiance Goddess Hair Oil' I noticed that there was a man's deodorant in the bottom left shelf. This is the first time any of her boyfriends has left a trace of himself behind.

I order our coffees at Costa – the barista doesn't speak to me, he just turns the iPad towards me to pay. I look at another Costa employee hanging up wall art above the bit where you can get sugar, sweetener and those little sticks that hurt your tongue. The picture he's hanging is a generic shot of London. Black-and-white apart from a bright red post box. It's devoid of meaning and ugly, but I kind of like it.

I sit down and wait as Hannah's decaf oat latte gets cold. I'm having a mocha with an extra shot, the grown-up's hot chocolate. I start drawing on a Costa napkin. At art school, they told me I should try drawing something other than my sister, but I said I wanted to keep trying until I got her just right. She finally gets off the phone and sits down opposite me – I wait for her to glance at my cup and tell me off about my choice of drink. So much sugar, she'll say, after which she'll google exactly how many grams of sugar there are in a large Costa mocha with an extra shot because she genuinely finds that kind of thing fun. But she doesn't. Instead she looks at my doodle with a glowing smile, takes my pen and draws me in less than a minute, on another napkin, capturing me perfectly. I'm enraged by the ease of it.

I don't ask her about the phone call. She gets out a bunch of plastic folders with our passports, boarding passes and travel insurance as well as everything else we need. I let her keep my passport in her bag because I lost it once before boarding and we missed our flight. She didn't get angry, and we found it in the toilets an hour later, but she hasn't trusted me with my own since. We have to get them renewed soon. They will expire shortly after this holiday and Hannah will put them safely in her collection of our old passports. She likes collecting things.

We watch the planes in contented silence. The sounds of the airport soothe and excite me.

Her: I need my books!

She likes crime novels. We go into WHSmith; some pop music is playing and she's bobbing her head and humming as she reads the backs of books and puts them down again. Finally she picks two. I've forgotten to bring the book about philosophy I've been pretending to read for six months, but I don't think I'll have time to read anyway. I'll be having too much fun.

She goes to the self-service counter to pay and I try to add some sweets for the plane, a bag of fizzy Haribo. She holds the bag up with her thumb and index finger, like it's a mouse, and doesn't let me buy them. She pointedly pulls out a huge bag of almonds from her tote bag.

Hannah: They're good for you, vitamin E is great
    for your skin.
Me: Vitamin E! Wow, thank you.
Hannah: You'll thank me later.

I really regret not wearing a T-shirt and not wearing
a bra. I'm already boiling like an idiot and don't know
what I was thinking, getting dressed so early. Why didn't
I put on a T-shirt? Hannah tucks her hair behind her
ear and I see she's wearing the faded gold hoop earrings
I got for her from Claire's years ago. We both share a
taste for cheap hoop earrings that look slightly dirty.
As she bends down to put her books in a bag, I see a
man look at her bum. I scowl at him but he doesn't
flinch. I am used to feeling invisible standing next to
Hannah.

I know people see us together and assume we're sisters
because we have similar faces, lips and eyes, though all of
her features seem more pronounced, fuller, more finished.
We even have similar voices though hers is more high-
pitched and nasal, which I like to tell her often. I look
like the one who hasn't tried. Hannah sometimes buys
me clothes in an attempt to get me to dress more 'for
my shape' – but I insist that I have no shape. I'm slim
but somehow still formless. I tie my mousy hair back up,
and a strand of hair sticks to my sweaty forehead. Hannah
turns around and unsticks it for me.

Her: Have you got the factor fifty?

I nod. I have it in my bag, the same bottle I took with
me on our last holiday. We'll have to get a new one for
our next holiday, probably later on this year – as long as

Hannah isn't pregnant or married by then. I feel bad that I hope she won't be. I don't need the factor 50 as much as she does. She'll have gained a hundred freckles by the time we're home.

# 2

1999

I suddenly realised I wasn't wearing any pants. Mum and Dad had just started letting Hannah take me to school on her own, she was in Year 5 and I was in Year 1. It was a sunny day, but really windy. I knew we were already late and there was no time to run home. I burst into tears and told her I was scared that I'd get found out and be told off. Hannah led me behind a tree, checked no one was looking, took off her knickers and gave them to me. They were too big and had purple butterflies on. Then I held onto on her backpack string (we called it a 'lead') and she started running, towing me along all the way to school. It felt like I was on a fairground ride.

I waited for her to pick me up at the end of the day. Her classroom was on the other side of school, so I was usually the last to be fetched, waiting with a teacher who had glossy black hair with a white streak in a tight bun. I don't remember the teacher's name but I remember that she wore the same long blue skirt every day and smelt of lavender soap. When I saw Hannah running towards me, I held my arms open, lunch box in one hand, ready to be swooped into her arms.

Her: Did they stay up?
Me: What?
Her: The pants. Did they stay up?
Me: Yes.
Her: Good. I was so worried.


We could see cigarette smoke clouds and smell bacon when Mum opened the front door in her fancy sunglasses, with a teacup of wine in her hand. She'd wear these sunglasses most days, and liked telling the story of how she'd stolen them from a shop when she was twenty, and felt so terrible about it that she wore them every day to make up for it.

My parents were having one of their afternoon parties, full of actors, writers and people masquerading as producers or casting directors. People in flamboyant flamingo shirts were sitting on the piano or sprawled on our sofa. The TV was covered with one of Mum's headscarves which confused me – why hide the TV? Even though I was only about six, I sensed that these people were dead behind the eyes when I was forced to say hello to them. All they wanted to do was keep telling everyone their audition anecdote rather than be interrupted by an un-interested child.

Mum only kept us downstairs when she wanted us to perform for her guests. Hannah would be much keener than me to sing a song. I got nervous and watched her from the stairs. After she had done her duty we'd rush upstairs to our bedroom to make a fort. We liked it when they had parties because we had hours to play and no bedtime.

Hannah would make us a 'magical kingdom' – bedsheets hung over high-backed chairs stolen from the kitchen, and piles of pillows stacked in every corner. Inside the kingdom we'd tell stories with a torch under our chins, distorting our faces. Or Hannah would get us to leave the fort and come back in, each time pretending we were in a different country, an exotic foreign place full of exciting things, putting on funny accents and describing the sights. She made me see these places, really see them. By the time we went to bed and Dad stumbled in to turn our light off with a drunken mumbled goodnight, we had travelled to faraway lands, told hundreds of stories and barely noticed that we'd forgotten about dinner.

The next morning there would be a random man or eccentrically dressed couple asleep on the sofa as we ate a huge breakfast – two bowls of mixed-up cereal was our favourite. Crunchy Nut corn flakes and Coco Pops. Hannah tidied up while I took Mum's headscarf off the TV and watched cartoons.. When we said goodbye and looked in on our parents, Mum would most likely be gone already. Dad would sleep until we got home from school. When we asked how his day was he'd say he'd spent it 'thinking'.

I went to do an art foundation the year after sixth form. I got in easily, because my entrance portfolio included life drawings I had stolen from Hannah's sixth-form artwork, which were amazing. She could draw better than me, paint better than me, but didn't want to be an artist like our parents. I always had good ideas, I just didn't know what to do with them so I let them disappear, let myself forget. Occasionally when I told her an idea late at night, she'd make me stop talking until I got my notebook and pen out.

Her: You won't remember if you don't write it down.

After my foundation, which apparently I excelled in, I started my fine art degree with hope, but I was quickly derailed by myself. I became obsessed with boys who weren't obsessed with me. Rich boys who tried their very best to appear poor, hands and faces smeared with paint, charcoal fingernails. At the beginning this was basically every girl's 'type' at art school, but gradually all the boys became tragic tattooed clones of each other, and most girls came to understand (as they thought more realistically about their chances of becoming the next Tracy Emin) that it was neither hygienic nor beneficial to their health to be fingered by one of these wannabe tortured souls. They moved on. I stayed behind.

# 3

## The Mediterranean

I wake up early because of the light. I see her by the window looking out to the sea, tying the curtains up. I can tell she's already got her make-up on – I never catch her without gold eyeliner. She's doing her chirpy morning yoga routine.

> Me: You're just doing that to annoy me –
> Her: No, I'm energising my soul.
> Me: Your soul doesn't need energising.
> Her: Let's go and find a good spot –
> Me: One more hour, please –
> Her: All you have to do is get on your swimming costume and walk out the door –

I'm not ready to leave my pretend bedroom for the week. I want to stay in bed for a little longer, to take my time. I'm not a morning person like she is. On her way out, she closes the curtains again for me and strokes my cheek.

I fall back to sleep and I wake up feeling anxious and want to rush to her. On the way to the beach, down the big hill, I text her some emoticons which I know she'll understand are my way of saying 'sorry for sleeping in'. She replies quickly with some emoticons to say 'no worries'. Her happiness since she met him, even via text, is outrageous.

I notice some beautiful flowers on the side of the hill. Bright pink and red; everything seems so much more colourful here. I crouch down to smell them but all I catch is the salty tang of the sea. I feel self-conscious that somebody will notice me trying to smell the flowers so I stand up and scan the beach below.

I spot her immediately, wearing her fuchsia pink swim-suit which is a size too small, so that her bum pokes out of it slightly. She's laying a towel on a beach chair. It feels urgent to shout her name, so I do, doubtful that she can hear me from up here:

HANNAH!!!!

But she does hear. She looks up and waves. I wave back and we stand there stupidly waving and laughing for a moment. She turns her back to me as soon as I arrive at the deck chairs she's specially selected. This is my cue to spray factor 50 all over her.

Her: Nice sleep?
Me: I don't know what happened, sorry. I had weird dreams.
Her: They're always weird when it's bonus sleep.
Me: Were you bored without me?
Her: No. I had a nice little walk. Can you see those people jumping off that cliff over there?

15

She points to the huge cliff to our right. As I look I see a little person diving off it, so small it's like watching a mini Lego figurine tumbling off the side of a table.

Her: Let's do it!
Me: What?
Her: Do what they're doing, look –
Me: I am not jumping off a fucking cliff – are you mad?

I buy one of those mini iced coffees you can only get on beaches, served in plastic shot glasses. It's the most delicious thing I've ever tasted.

Her: You should stop surviving on sugar and caffeine –
Me: Have you tried one of these, though?

I make her take a sip. She smiles.

Her: OK, I had one earlier. They are amazing.
Me: Ten of these would be my last meal on death row.
Her: You think about your last meal on death row too often.

She gets up and runs to the sea. I dig a hole in the sand with my hands, put our phones in the little plastic bag we used for toiletries at the airport and bury it. Our own makeshift safe. I run after her and we swim out together. I swallow some seawater and start coughing. She gives me a piggyback, standing on a big rock while I recover. We see a jellyfish as we race to the buoy bobbing in the distance, about twenty-five metres away. I win, for the first time ever.

Me: Did you let me win?
Her: Maybe.
Me: Why are you being so nice? It's disconcerting.
Her: I'm not –
Me: You are.

She splashes at me to shut me up, and then tells me some semi-interesting facts about jellyfish – 'Did you know that the jellyfish's mouth is in the centre of its body?' – and I mimic her in a geeky voice. She loses her sunglasses under the water. We both try to retrieve them but fail. Usually she gets very upset about things like this – she hates losing stuff – but today she's carefree. She gazes over at the cliff again, like it's calling out her name.

We breaststroke back to the beach. She is humming, her usual song which I don't know the name of. I hum along with her, off-key as usual. People on the beach are asleep in the lunchtime sun, burning obliviously. I observe the books people are reading, and notice that three women have the same one.

Hannah holds my shoulders and stares at me with a wild look in her eyes that I'm not used to. The light from the sun is making the green that she insists is in her eyes (I maintain they're just plain blue) glint beautifully. She looks like a goddess. I would hate her right now if I didn't love her so much.

Her: I have something to ask you, and I want you to know that if you say no, I'll be totally OK with that.

17

Me: Oh God, what?

Her: Well . . . I was wondering if you would mind
– please don't be angry – if Rowan came out?

Me: What the fuck?

Her: I honestly don't mind if you say no –

Me: 'What the fuck' kind of implies no, surely –

Her: But can you just think about it. Please?

She lets go of my shoulders and smiles. She's unravelling slightly; she needs me to say yes. I like the power shift. But the idea of them all over each other in front of me is unbearable, sitting on each other's laps, kissing tamely out of politeness, whispering to each other in their secret language – even playing that out in my head is infuriating.

Me: No. I don't want to have to make him like
me –

Her: He already likes you –

I collapse in a huff onto the beach. She sits next to me and puts her hand on my sandy knees, which are bony next to hers.

Her: Look – he's already coming. I'm really sorry
– I genuinely thought you'd be fine with it. You
seem so great at the moment –

Me: What's that supposed to mean? 'At the moment'?

I flip too quickly.

Her: Please? We still have today, just us. Let's get
some lunch and go on a walk or something. I'll
buy you stuff.

She's chewing her lower lip.

Me: You'll buy me lots of stuff.
Her: Is that a yes? It's a yes.
Me: I need to eat.
Her: I knew I should have waited to ask until you'd
    eaten –
Me: We both know you were never actually asking
    me, bitch.

As she hugs me she lets out a contented screech. We
walk along the shore. She points discreetly at a tall brunette
woman. Her body, a perfect hourglass, looks like it's been
moulded for her neon pink bikini. She has a deep tan,
muscular thighs and such a round bum she could be a
Kardashian. Men are staring at this woman from the other
side of the beach. Hannah and I stop and stare too.

Her: I don't concentrate on my bum enough.
Me: I think you have enough to concentrate on –
Her: But I'm thirty. I need to start doing more lunges.
Me: You're not thirty yet –
Her: I'm almost thirty, which is basically thirty.
Me: True. God, I can't imagine being that old.
Her: You will be. So you've got to get your shit
    together, OK –
Me: It's too early for a pep talk –
Her: And I'm going to get a bum like that woman.

She starts doing walking lunges in the sand, looking so
silly. I imagine what it must be like to have a sister you
have debates with about philosophy and politics, serious
conversations about ways in which the world is ending.

I'm sure she'd be well equipped to have those debates with someone else. But with me, she reveals her true self. My Hannah loves shitty reality TV, likes gossiping about celebrities and knows the exact calorie contents of a Twix, KitKat, Twirl and Mars Bar. I like being the one with whom she chooses to have the Mars Bar chats.

We continue to walk normally again as the woman with the good bum starts wading in the sea taking selfies. Hannah checks her phone and lets out a sigh.

Her: I've never felt like this before about anyone –

Oh but she has, she definitely has. She gets swept away and then forgets that she's been swept away maybe nineteen or twenty times before. I don't mind that she rewrites her history.

Her: Honestly, this time it's different. I love him.
Me: You loved the other hims –
Her: He's so, so different though. He's vulnerable, he's kind. He's creative, he texts back straight away, he has a big –
Me: You said Brian was 'vulnerable and kind', you said Francis had a big –
Her: Yeah but I didn't realise that his was actually average – really average –
Me: You said –
Her: No, Ruth, this time, seriously, I think that's it. I'm done looking around. He's the One.
Me: You said there's no such thing as the One –
Her: I know, I know. But now that I've met the One – I know he's my One.
Me: Jesus.

She points at the cliff again and we see people jumping off, one after another, some in pairs holding hands. They get separated as they fall.

Her: I feel like doing something to challenge myself.

The cliff would be good to draw. I like the sandy colour and its little splattered patches of grass and flowers; it already looks like it's a painting. I promised myself I would try to do a drawing a day on this trip. She puts my hand into hers.

Her: Come on. Don't be boring.

She knows that 'boring' is one of my trigger words. So she wins. We go back to our deck chairs. We dig our phones out of the hole again. As I'm tipping out some sand that's crept into my phone case, I turn to tell her how hungry I am – but she's already on a call. From the way that she's walking I know she's telling him that I've given them the romantic green light.

I get another coffee shot and down it quickly before she can tell me off. She's moving quickly, looking out to the sea. I try to catch up with her, but there's no point. She's too far ahead now.

# 4

As we start walking up the cliff, the blister on my foot begins to really sting. I must find a pharmacy later. When we get to the top, I'm weak and lightheaded and need to sit down. I notice a faded sign which someone has hung their bag on. The sign says something in Italian which I can't be bothered to google translate, and it stands wonkily, like it's been hit.

A wet young woman in a swimsuit goes up to the sign and unabashedly takes a photo of herself in front of it with a selfie stick. She has a bit of seaweed stuck to her calf. I watch Hannah look over the edge of the cliff and retreat. She's scared. I realise this is my chance to get us out of here, to get us some food, to go back to our lovely air-conditioned room, away from the selfie sticks.

Me: Please – let's just go, Hannah. It's too risky –
Her: Risks are good.

She studies the people getting ready for their jump. Her competitive streak begins to show itself as my killjoy instincts flare.

Me: What if we hit a rock —

Her: No one else has. Some people have done it two or three times. I've been watching this cliff all morning —

Me: Well, I'm not fucking doing it. I'm just not.

Her: Ruth! Relax. Everything is going to be all right.

She grabs my shoulders and hugs me. I love it, I love her, and I let her down this morning by being lazy. I let her down too much.

Hannah starts doing star-jumps. The way she's acting now reminds me of the slightly unhinged Hannah of her early twenties. I quite like it. I haven't seen her like this since she was dumped by someone who looked like Brian from the Backstreet Boys. She went through a phase of sitting on the top deck of night buses with her head between her knees. I would stroke her back and look out of the window, glad I was on the night bus with her and not out there.

She takes a sip from the communal water fountain, which surprises me because she's a germ freak, and wipes her mouth with the back of her hand. She suddenly seems so young with her red cheeks, which are freckling already.

Her: Come on! Fuck it! Think of the photo!

Me: We aren't taking photos.

Her: Everyone takes a photo, you just stand down there. See?

She points to a ledge just below the top of the cliff. We watch as someone takes a photo of his girlfriend mid-jump. We see her land in the water and wave up at him as he takes another. I wonder how different my life would have been so far if I was a boyfriend type of girl? How different would Hannah's life be right now if she wasn't?

She's now doing side stretches as if she's about to take part in an Olympic sprint. I taste salt in my mouth. It makes me think of our mum, who used to carry a little bottle of salt in her handbag because she liked everything to be 'extra extra salty', which made her sound like a fussy child when she said it. In her extremely superstitious actress phases she would throw salt behind her left shoulder on the street if she saw a magpie. Once it went into my eyes.

The woman who's just done the jump runs up the rocky path to her boyfriend. They kiss and then look around for someone to take a photo of them. They ask Hannah because she looks more approachable than me; she looks like she could be friends with this woman, with her similar swimming costume and real-life boyfriend. She takes the photo of the giddy couple, both recovering from their epic jumps, and then another and another, just in case they want variation. They all have a conversation in Italian and I remember my sister can almost speak five fucking languages. Only the basic vocabulary but she's amazing at improvising.

Her: You go first? Or I'll go first?

It's happening and I can't stop it. The caffeine and sugar are just hitting optimum levels in my bloodstream, and suddenly I feel like I could run a marathon, or maybe a half-marathon. I'm not boring, I can do this, I can do this.

Me: I'll go first. But I don't want a photo of me –
Her: But you look beautiful –
Me: I just don't want a photo, OK?
Her: OK.

I'm snappy, hungry and scared: a terrible combination. I step towards the edge of the cliff, I lift my arms out wide, feeling the sun on my face. I wave back at Hannah and for a moment I do feel beautiful, because she told me so. She shouts as I jump off –

Her: GO, RUTHIE!

I love it when she calls me that, though I pretend I hate it because I don't want to seem babyish. As I fly through the air I think of doughnuts, I don't know why. The sugar in me is calling out for more. Once Hannah has jumped, we should find a place that does doughnuts. She won't have one, but she'll let me because I'm letting her boyfriend come on our fucking holiday, intrude on our time.

Then I'm crashing into the sea and feeling nothing. It doesn't feel euphoric, I don't feel giddy. I just feel like I jumped off a cliff. I try to open my eyes underwater but my body comes up too quickly. The first thing I hear is Hannah screaming for me.

Her: YOU DID IT!

When I reach the top of the cliff again, panting and wet, she jumps me up and down and hugs me close. She smells of factor 50, which she's just applied to her face. I rub in a patch she's missed. She hands me our phones and the little plastic bag.

25

Her: You were amazing! So amazing!

Me: OK, your turn now, bitch.

Her: I've changed my mind. I've seen you do it which is enough –

Me: What? You made me do it!

Her: You wanted to do it! You made it look easy! Let's just –

Me: We are here because of you. You're doing it. Go.

Her: Let's just get some food –

Me: After. Come on. It's not fair.

Her: OK. OK. Jesus, why am I so scared? OK. The photo better be fucking amazing. Take a few –

Me: Hurry up, I'm hungry.

She tries to hug me but I push her away and point to the cliff edge.

Me: Go on, stop procrastinating.

She does some more funny stretches as I go to the photo-taking ledge. I wave.

Her: Love you!

Me: Love you too, stupid. Just jump!

She tucks her hair behind her ears and blows me a kiss.

Then she jumps. She seems to float in the air for a second. I take the picture. She's smiling, she's flying.

She crashes into the sea and I wait for her to come up, joyful. I check the picture I took of her, which is perfect; she'll be happy. Now we can go back to the hotel, I can get a doughnut and savour the rest of the day. I remember about Rowan, and my happiness morphs into anger that he's arriving so soon. Why couldn't it be just us?

I get so angry I don't notice how long she's been underwater.

# 5

It became clear that I was avoiding meeting her new boyfriend, so one day, she tricked me.

I woke up to condescending notifications that my fertility wasn't being tracked properly, because I failed to put in some vital information about my vagina. I never meant to track my fertility in the first place, I just wanted to know the days I could have unprotected sex. I didn't want to go on the pill because Hannah went on it once and she became an actual demon, and I have a deep-rooted aversion to condoms.

I feel insecure about asking a man to use one, because I fear that the condom-finding-and-putting-on-pause will make him think twice about why he is having sex with me in the first place. I would forget about the app in my frequent bouts of no sex, so when these sporadic notifications popped up, it felt like it was taunting me.

It was early morning, my neck was sore, and as my eyes readjusted in the light I quickly realised that I was not at my flat. I needed to leave before the man next to me woke up. He'd been hugging me all night and would have woken up, embarrassed by the intimacy and insistent on having sex again quite roughly from behind to regain some sort of power. I tried not to disturb him as I pulled my bra from under one of his feet and got dressed. I looked back at him as I opened the door. He flinched and opened his eyes for a second, then chose to pretend he was still asleep. I was insulted and relieved.

I met this one – Alexis – on Tinder a few weeks ago. Alexis was into strangling and so I pretended I was into it too to make things simpler. He was very polite and had a big dick, which was a relatively new experience for me. I didn't exactly enjoy it and it was quite painful, so I thought of it as a night of exercise, something that could be worthwhile in the end, if I stuck to it. He lived above a Starbucks so I always had a Frappuccino for breakfast. This was the fourth time I'd seen him and likely the last. It was a 'less than five times' silent arrangement.

As I walked out of his building, ashamed of how compliant I can be, I wondered how many women from Tinder he strangled a week; how many women have come round at 2 a.m. for a five-minute blow job? Alexis will probably get married and have a baby one day. Will he strangle his wife 'for fun' with the baby in the cot asleep nearby?

I am not equipped to have a baby. Hannah has always been ready, having already had enough experience with looking after me. For years now, whenever we saw a baby, she would make me stop and look at it as it passed us by. It's like she knew I didn't have that natural instinct and wanted me to develop it.

Me: I'll just be the weird auntie to your kids, I'm fine with that.
Her: A child would help you to be more –

Me: Normal? Ha. Fuck you –

Her: You know what I mean.

Me: Who would want to have a baby with me? They don't even want me to stay the night.

Her: Oh God, it's too sad.

Me: I like being alone –

Her: No you don't, you're with me the entire time. Good men are out there, you know.

Me: Just because you think you're with a good man, doesn't mean he is.

Her: You need to meet him. Please?

The person I might lose my sister to? No, I absolutely didn't want to meet him.

Hannah said she wanted to meet for breakfast before work, so I walked from Alexis's flat in Farringdon with my Frappuccino. We met at a nicer-than-average Pret in Old Street. She was already there when I arrived, drinking a coconut latte and eating a dainty granola-and-yogurt pot. She looked beautiful in a new scarlet power-suit. I don't know if it was actually a power-suit but she definitely looked powerful. She had a proper job I didn't understand – something in the business sector involving the occasional conference in Germany and a swish lanyard.

She had her own office I had only been inside once. It was strikingly bare, no evidence of her. I think that was because she was not really being herself in that job; her heart was in helping people, in her second job/vocation – PaperbackKids. She set up the charity scheme for kids while she was still at university, but still didn't have enough money or influence to do it full-time. It was part of her much-hyped five-year plan before she wanted to go full steam ahead into philanthropy. I was not allowed to make any jokes about her philanthropic aspirations.

In her office she had a framed photo of Bill Gates, who she idolised. She loved that he was known to carry around a big bag full of books wherever he went, so she would try to do the same. Her bag contained titles on business at first, but then she began to keep children's books in there. I was with her a couple of times when she saw a child on the Tube and left one for them on her seat when we got off. I called her a 'Modified Mary Poppins'. We would stand on the platform and watch the child reach for the book as the train blasted away.

She was quieter and less smiley inside the City office. I was wearing my Adidas tracksuit the day I visited and that's probably why I wasn't invited again. She insisted it wasn't because of the tracksuit, it was because they weren't actually allowed guests due to the security risk, but I knew she was lying. One day I tried dressing up really smart, in one of her power-suits and her heels which were too big for me, and meeting her outside the building without warning when she stepped out for lunch. She found it really funny but maintained the lie and I wasn't allowed in. I walked home in my socks, holding her heels, feeling silly.

She went to get me a coffee and another granola-and-yoghurt. I didn't tell her I'd just had a Frappuccino. I watched her engage happily with a barista who had a chin piercing. She was so skilled at banal small talk, with everyone and anyone. Rowan arrived and I knew it was him from my stalking online and the odd photo she had sheepishly shown me. He snuck up to her and stroked her back. She didn't turn round – she was still chatting shit – but when she took his hand behind her and squeezed

31

it in such an intimate and familiar way, I suddenly felt embarrassed for looking. He picked up the coffee and granola and looked around to find me sitting there, watching him.

Him: Ruthie?
Me: Yeah. Well. Ruth.
Him: She always calls you Ruthie, sorry –
Me: It's fine.

I tried to smile but I was insanely, repulsively tense, and annoyed by how handsome he was. Brown skin, black curly hair, dressed entirely in shades of navy. Skinny jeans rolled up to show his white sports socks and black Converse. A T-shirt which was shrunken and showed the top of his boxers. He held out his hand for mine, and I shook it limply on purpose. She joined us.

Her: Sorry, sorry. I know you'll be angry –
Me: I'm not angry –
Her: I just wanted you to meet each other.

I was angry already with the trickery but tried to sound upbeat. Rowan went in to kiss her and she kissed back with one eye on me. He looked her up and down.

Him: Never seen you in a suit –
Her: Oh God, I know. I have to present to investors today and need to look – professional.
Him: I love it.

She went red. Beads of sweat were forming on her top lip. I could tell she was wearing more foundation than usual by the fuzzy orangey line at her jaw. Her gold-lined eyes were so wired, flashing back and forth between me and him. She wanted so much for us to get along.

Him: So, what do you do, Ruth?
Me: Ummm – well, I –
Her: She's finding her way –

Hannah liked to say that 'finding my way' was my job. It was infuriating. I rolled my eyes at her.

Me: No, I've found my way. To Wahaca.
Her: You're too talented to work in a chain restaurant –
Me: Why do you always have to mention that it's a chain restaurant? Why do you find chain restaurants so –
Her: They're just bland, unlike you.
Me: Maybe I like blending in. Are you the kind of cool person who hates chain restaurants too?

He didn't answer and I could tell he was uncomfortable with our critical yet sisterly dynamic – I think he thought we were actually fighting. Hannah hated that I worked at Wahaca. She hated it so much. And that's probably why I stayed working there for so long. I know I could have done things, even if they weren't the things I wanted to do like painting and drawing; I could have done something meaningful and efficient, like her. But I just wasn't ready to make the leap yet, to expose myself and seem vulnerable by trying to do something I cared about. And there's something wonderful about just fitting in sometimes. There's safety in blandness.

She checked her phone.

Her: OK – well – I have to go, sorry. They need
   me to help set up the room –
Me: You can't be going already?
Her: You were late, Ruthie –
Me: Ruth –
Her: Ruth, stop it! Get better at time management.
Me: Stop –
Her: Where were you last night?
Me: I was being strangled –
Her: God, not again –

Rowan took an awkward sip of his coffee.

Her: Look, I'm sorry. Stay, please – finish your coffee
   with Rowan. Do you want to go for dinner on
   Saturday with us?

This was an ambush. Rowan kissed her again, on the
cheek, as he caught my studying eyes. Hannah got out
of that Pret as quickly as she could. She didn't hug me
or look back at me because she knew. She knew how
she'd played me. I watched her run away, her big, beautiful bum in the scarlet power-trousers swishing from side
to side. I saw Rowan staring at it too.
   Then he sat down. We were at one of those tall tables
with uncomfortably high seats. He began finishing her
granola and her coconut latte as if it were his to finish.
I sipped my flat white and looked at him. He had yoghurt
around his mouth, which relaxed me a little, so I ate some
of mine. We sat there just eating fucking granola for a
bit. He didn't seem to find it weird at all.

Him: What are you up to today?
Me: I don't know yet. I might just – go for a walk
or something. It's weird being in the City so early.

He smiled in agreement. A lovely smile, white teeth
– good, straight teeth. Lucky Hannah. A large percentage
of the men I slept with had awful teeth. I smiled back.

We walked through the City afterwards, past Chancery
Lane, towards the river, largely in silence. I remember
that I liked him a lot by the end of the walk, and felt a
tiny bit jealous of my sister. More jealous than usual,
anyway.

# 6

On one of the first nights after we came home I got incredibly drunk and bought twenty lasagnes from Tesco.

When we were kids our mum rarely cooked, but once she went to the effort of making us a lasagne from scratch. It was disgusting; oil was gathered in little cheese holes, and there was too much tomato sauce so it was more like a lumpy soup. But Hannah ate it all – she wanted Mum to think she'd done a good job. When she wasn't in the kitchen I crept away and poured mine into the bin. I didn't realise at that moment there was no bin liner in the bin and when Mum found out she was so angry and rarely cooked for us again.

A couple of nights ago I microwaved the first of the frozen lasagnes. I took a bite too soon and it burnt my tongue so badly that I considered going to A&E, but I didn't want to go into a hospital again so soon. I was so upset I threw it out my window. Luckily it landed on top of the bus shelter, rather than on a passer-by. Pigeons immediately swarmed to it, and have continued to peck away at it since. I took photos of the pigeons eating the lasagne – I don't know why. It's still not finished. My tongue still hasn't healed.

I go to her flat in the early hours, when the world is

quiet and no one can find me, and I water her plants. I check that her fridge is working. I lie down in her bed, or on her sofa; sometimes I have a long shower there too. I use her hair products and put everything back exactly as she likes it. I can't stay there for long before I start thinking too much, so I walk home listening to my Disney Princess playlist.

I mainly just sleep, through most of the day and night. I am moving so little that I've gained weight, I'm slower. I don't remember when I last had a glass of water. I bulk ordered five hundred Diet Cokes online one night when I was half-asleep, so that's my main liquid now. The cans are littered all over my floor, a habit inherited from my father. I stepped on one as I sleepwalked to the toilet the other night and now I have a huge cut on my left foot which I've done nothing about.

Hannah would leave her cuts until they got infected. It was confusing because she was so organised and meticulous in all other aspects of her life. I made her wash them, tried to get her to see a doctor if necessary, but she said she didn't have the time. I pretend I can hear her talking.

Her: These things get better on their own.

I feel silly that I can actually hear her. She had faint scars speckled all over her legs and arms from years of picking at scabs, scars that only I could see.

# 7

I found myself in King's Cross St Pancras at 5.00 one morning, just before the sun came up. I had spent the night eating Kettle crisps, drinking wine and walking aimlessly around London. I'd somehow walked over forty thousand steps to Ealing, where we grew up, and back. I had spilt wine on my ballet pumps. I looked at the train boards and felt comforted by the monotonous tannoy announcements, like they were giving me instructions, ideas about where I could go. I decided to go to Edinburgh, to visit Evelyn. We hadn't spoken in a while and I didn't know where exactly in Edinburgh she lived, but it felt like a good idea. I texted her as the train left to say I'd be arriving that afternoon.

Evelyn was in my year at art school. On the first day she told me she wanted to be a portrait artist and that she was asexual, and she was so nice to me that I just clung to her. She had extremely long hair and a completely flat chest. She didn't drink or smoke and could draw and paint beautifully. She intrigued me, and I tried for a while to be as pure as her. Hannah didn't like my friendship with Evelyn; she couldn't believe someone so young and so beautiful could be asexual. She didn't trust her; she said that she must lead a double life when she went home at the weekends.

I fell asleep on the train and woke up with coffee spilt all down my front. I didn't even remember getting coffee, and for a moment I thought someone might have poured it on me while I dreamt of the sea. I checked I wasn't burnt. I texted Evelyn again to say it would be nice to see her. She immediately replied saying she had a break from work at 2 p.m., and sent me an address. I was prepared to find her at a gallery, hanging her new portrait. Instead the address she gave me led me to an EE phone shop. Evelyn came out to greet me coldly, and it was impossible not to notice that she now had a shaved head. It highlighted her new tattoo: Jesus on the crucifix at the base of her neck.

She had a thirty-minute lunch break, during which she took me to the Costa coffee shop next door. I hadn't been in a Costa since the airport with Hannah. She ordered a panini and some crisps and I had a mocha, but I couldn't drink it. I liked the familiarity of the Costa, I felt safe. Our conversation was generalised and uninteresting; she wasn't particularly friendly to me and didn't offer me a place to stay. She told me she'd met her new boyfriend at church, that he was an estate agent. They were saving up to buy a house in Leith and planning to have children in the next two years, after their wedding, which I wasn't invited to.

I asked about her art and all she said was that she didn't want to paint any more. I didn't ask why. She didn't ask me about Hannah and I didn't tell her.

We hugged and I walked back towards Waverley station, past the Edinburgh Dungeons. A girl kitted out as a maid with blood down her dress beckoned me in, and she seemed so desperate to perform that I followed her inside and paid £19.95 for a ticket. I was the only person in there that day, so the horror show felt more personal. I cried in the dark during the Jack the Ripper bit. I asked for an application form on the way out, which I filled in on the train home.

That night I decided to apply online for a job at Costa too, the Heathrow branch. I also applied to Boots and Accessorize but they never got back to me.

# 8

Costa, Heathrow Terminal 5

Costa boss: Tell me, what makes you want to work
 at Costa, Ruth?
Me: I feel safe here.
Costa boss: Right, that's nice –
Me: I like the artwork. I like the coffee, I like the
 iced coffee. I like watching people.
Costa boss: Watching people?
Me: It's nice seeing people who are about to go away.
 They look so excited. Most of them, anyway.
Costa boss: Yes, that is the nice thing about this
 branch –
Me: The team? Is that what I'm meant to say? That
 I like being part of a team?
Costa boss: Excellent. It's a friendly group, the
 Heathrow group.

Before I can stop it, a single tear drops onto the iPad
in front of me. The weight of it presses the touchscreen
– the button for whipped cream. An additional 35p.
Undo. More tears start to form and I wipe them away
roughly.

The artwork on the walls has been updated. Now there are huge blown-up photos of New York, Italy and Paris to join the London one I saw being put up months ago. Splashes of colour on a monochrome background. If you go up close, you can see how pixelated the images are, like someone has just taken a photo on an old iPhone and stretched it onto canvas. Sometimes we have to clean them with special wet wipes. I don't think that anyone really looks at the wall art in here apart from me. They're too busy planning and waiting, double-checking that they have their boarding passes, or having fights with their families about what's been left behind.

I have five more hours standing in this spot. I've managed not to speak at all for the first two hours on the clock. People just tell me the coffee they want, and I turn the iPad towards them. They tap, they move on. I haven't graduated on to making coffees yet. I'm afraid that's beyond my capabilities right now.

My brain feels like it's shutting down. I have dry skin on my cheeks, in little patches that I can't stop scratching, and a new eye twitch. It's like I became a new person that night, with new skin.

My hair was cut into a bob last week, the day before I started this job. I didn't want to get it cut but I fell asleep with gum in my mouth because I couldn't be bothered to go to the bin. When I woke up the gum had fallen out and embedded itself in a clump by my shoulder, a sticky nest. Another irretrievable situation. The hairdresser tried to chat about idle things with me, as if I wasn't an adult woman who'd managed to get chewing gum stuck in her hair. I pretended I was deaf rather effectively and avoided her gaze in the mirror.

A large woman with large boobs and a brightly patterned bandana around her head is next in the queue.

Woman: Large cappuccino, please.

I turn the iPad towards her and she smiles at me, revealing yellow teeth. The bandana has pineapples on, and she's pinned a breast cancer ribbon to her T-shirt. I notice that she's wearing a Carrie Bradshaw style necklace which says her name, Linda. I want to know where she's going. When Linda's large cappuccino is ready, I watch her as she tips two sachets of sugar in. She takes a selfie as she leaves Costa. I bet her caption will be something like 'Up, up and away! <plane emoticon>'. I want to hug her goodbye. She takes a sip of coffee and wheels her floral suitcase towards Security. This could be her final holiday. I hope it's not.

# 9

## Costa, Heathrow Terminal 5

It's 11 a.m. I'm on my break in the back room, drawing a unicorn because I just saw an American woman wearing an 'I believe in Unicorns' T-shirt. Doodling stops me from eating my nails and chewing the insides of my cheeks. It's one of the few things that alleviates pain for a few seconds. I sit on a bag of coffee beans and drink a latte with an extra shot and three sachets of sugar.

Caffeine and sugar: my most loyal friends.

We share the back room with WHSmith. As you open the doors it first smells of magazines. Boxes are everywhere and it feels like I'm in Ikea quite a lot of the time. This is where employees leave their coats and bags in tiny little lockers. I don't lock mine because I don't have anything to steal apart from my phone, which is always in my pocket, always waiting for a text. On my first day here, I opened my locker to find an abandoned apple core. It must have only been a couple of days old, it wasn't rotten yet, so the person who previously used the locker must have only just left. Where did they go?

Sometimes I catch people in here skiving. I saw a couple fucking once. They work at WHSmith together. They are young, late teens maybe. She has long ginger hair which she always scrapes into a high ponytail, and he has brown greasy hair which he parts in the centre. The sex only lasted around six minutes, which I noted because I had six minutes left of my break. She pushed him downwards with her back against a trolley. He pulled down her tights and his head disappeared up her skirt for about one minute. Then she pulled his trousers down and went down on him for exactly two minutes. Then he stood and they tried to fuck standing up but he couldn't lift her properly. They lost momentum and seemed worried that she was going to fall. Then I had to cough which made them abort the whole thing. They kissed functionally, straightened their uniforms and went back to work, seemingly satisfied.

They didn't even look where the cough came from.

I was so impressed by their routine. It was considerate and equal, and they used their time so efficiently. They weren't exactly sexy-looking people, either, which made it even more impressive. Sometimes I look at a person and think, 'That person has sex a lot,' but with these people, I would have thought the exact opposite, which is mean of me. But I am meaner now.

Every day I hope they come back and attempt the routine again.

When it's quiet I can watch them at work. Today she's working the tills and he's overlooking the self-service machines, checking that people have scanned their items. They occasionally joke with each other, but you would never know they're a couple, that his head disappears beneath her skirt and they fuck in back rooms near boxes of magazines and bags of coffee beans. Sometimes I see them on the Piccadilly line on their way home, holding hands and chatting to other Heathrow staff.

It's a friendly group, the Heathrow group.

# 10

Our parents split up when I was eighteen and Hannah was twenty-two. Dad moved to Edinburgh because the rent was cheaper, and our mum moved to California to chase her American dream. She sold our family house as soon as she could, and got rid of all our childhood and teenage possessions without warning. I'd not liked the house much anyway – it had no carpets and I got a splinter a day from the wooden floors. Mum was forever planning to reclaim and varnish the wooden floors but she never got round to it.

Dad's study was full of books and incredibly dusty. He rarely let us go inside the office, so we wouldn't disturb his writing. He drank Diet Coke all day and crushed the empty cans with his foot. The crushing sounds scared me at first, but then I grew to like them. He was obsessed with crime novels, which is how Hannah got into them, and often I'd peek in through the gap in the door and see him reading one, with balls of scrunched-up paper all around him, having given up writing for the day.

Our parents' bedroom was decorated in shades of maroon and burgundy, with curtains that were always drawn. Mum loved dark red colours, and hung garish gothic art on the walls, which only she liked. I don't think Dad even noticed the walls and how often the artwork around him would change. Hannah and I shared a bedroom. We both had single beds, and we stuffed the accumulated junk from our childhood underneath them, making way for our teenage desks and rails of clothes and a mannequin we found in a skip and named Lisa.

Hannah was very upset about the mannequin when Mum threw it away because she had been planning to hang her wedding dress on Lisa one day.

Meryl would start the day with jewellery on, but get annoyed by it as the hours went by and discard pieces around the house. Once I found a ring in the fridge. She liked wearing oversized T-shirts and leggings, but the look was misleading because the T-shirts usually cost hundreds of pounds and the leggings were made of some kind of expensive rare animal. We were embarrassed by her clothes because she stood out so much at the school gates, in her stolen sunglasses, bouffant bun and dark lipstick. In the winter she wore a massive blue fake-fur coat. She'd keep Wrigley's gum in one pocket and thin French cigarettes in the other. She dressed like someone who was famous, which I guess she almost was.

She carried a huge bag around with play texts spilling out. Pinter, Ayckbourn, Brecht. Once I found a random page from one of them, brown and old, and thought it was rubbish so scrunched it up, like Dad did. She found it on the floor and told me it was a beautiful monologue, not rubbish, and for punishment made me learn it off by heart. She put a T-shirt over the page so it wouldn't burn and ironed the scrunches out.

Mum split her days into scenes. Me learning the monologue. Ironing the page. These were just little scenes.

For Mum and Dad's wedding day they were given their

names, 'MERYL & MICHAEL', in letters sewn out of white lace. They pinned them onto the maroon wall haphazardly and they remained there until we were teenagers. One day, I came home from school and saw that the L in Michael had fallen. I tried to pin it back up but accidentally pulled down all of my dad's name. He was away, so I ran up to Mum and told her, thinking she'd be livid, but she said Dad would pin it back up when he got home. The L stayed on the floor.

When we were teenagers I foolishly asked Mum if she would ever get a 'real' job. She stormed out, and didn't come back for two days. Hannah got so emotional when me and Mum fought. Once when we were slightly drunk, Hannah told me that Meryl was cast in a good acting gig when she was pregnant with me, but didn't take it. She thought that's why we clashed so much – because she resented me for her lack of career. I don't think this was true.

Hannah would urge for me to be gentler with her, say that my mum was talented, that she would get a big job one day. Hannah had faith and never spoke badly of Mum until she had left for America, for pilot season. She'd been trying to contact her for months and months when she woke me up one morning, as would become routine with our future holidays, and said we were going to Los Angeles to visit her. Hannah had just started her job in the City and was knackered – she slept on the plane, the whole ten hours, and snored for about nine of them. I watched four films but the only one I remember was *A Bug's Life*, which I enjoyed too much.

We got to LAX airport and Hannah told the taxi driver to take us to Hollywood. We got out on Hollywood Boulevard, our eyes squinting in the sun, and we were

49

barraged by cartoon characters and superheroes on all sides. Homer Simpson came up to us first, and I noticed his costume was splattered with dirt. He said it was $10 for a photo with him, but Hannah gave him $20.

Her: Poor Homer.

We found a cheap hotel with a neon sign and booked a room. Hannah called our mum again to no answer. We took a nap and when we woke up it was the middle of the night. Bored and restless, we went to a nearby CVS to look at the incredible range of cereals and all the different pills and vitamins. I took a photo of Hannah in the hair-product aisle, studying the ingredients of a big purple bottle. She could have stayed in there for days.

We bought loads of stuff we didn't need, ate our snacks on the way back to the hotel and stayed up watching American TV all night. In the morning, our mum finally called back. She gave us an address and we got in a taxi. She was staying in a cheap motel way out of Hollywood. She opened the door to reveal her face smothered in make-up which was melting in the heat, and looked even thinner than usual. The room was small and grotty, and scripts and make-up were scattered all over her bed. There was no small talk.

Mum: I don't like surprises.

She wanted our help with an audition she had later that day, someone to read the other character's lines.

Mum: This is a big audition for me, girls. It could be huge.

I tried to read the lines first, but I couldn't stop laughing – the script seemed so silly. It was some sort of show about an apocalypse and human-animal hybrids. She was auditioning for a character who was meant to be forty. My mum quickly got angry with me and said she'd prefer to read with Hannah, who tried her best to keep a straight face. Mum was struggling to remember the lines, and kept getting it wrong, but when Hannah corrected her she would get shouted at. I glanced around the room and noticed several miniature alcohol bottles in the bin. I was worried about her, but didn't say anything.

I was angry that she was being so abrupt with Hannah, who had looked forward to seeing her so much, who'd been reduced to stalking her own mother in a different country. Rather than focusing on her own lines, Meryl kept getting Hannah to redo hers. Hannah was good, really good, and she didn't let herself be rattled. Suddenly Mum said she needed to shower and that we should leave, which was odd because she was fully dressed up and ready to go out. We arranged a place for her to meet us after the audition. She didn't turn up.

We attempted to have a nice time despite the overwhelming heat and Meryl's rejection of us. In a diner called Shake, Rattle and Roll! we shared a huge plate of fries and a giant chocolate milkshake. I wanted to cheer Hannah up, so I hailed a cab and asked the driver to take us to Santa Monica Pier. We could hear people screaming as we got out of the car. We walked fast, aiming straight for the most horrifying-looking ride. Hannah was so excited. It wasn't that busy so we were able to go on everything, and stayed there for hours and hours. We were exhausted and sweaty and starving by the end of the day. Before we left she begged to go on one final ride so we chose the Sea Dragon, which looked like a pirate ship swinging side to side.

We were the only people on it, and it became so terrifying so quickly that I almost vomited. I felt seasick. Hannah couldn't stop screaming and laughing, which made me laugh too. Then the ride suddenly stopped, followed by a loud creaking sound. The jaunty pirate music stopped playing. We were just hanging in mid-air. I looked at Hannah and she had gone white.

Me: It's fine, don't worry, this is probably meant to
    happen –
Hannah: It doesn't feel like this is meant to happen –

We stayed silent and rigid in a state of frozen panic, gripping each other's hands. In reality it must have been only a few seconds, but I truly thought that was it – that we were going to be the girls in one of those stories you see on the news about theme park rides and people losing their legs. But finally the Sea Dragon started moving again. We were silent for the rest of the ride and we got off wobbling. I threw up in a trash can as she stroked my back and talked softly about where we should go for dinner.

We saw my mum once more on that trip. She wanted to meet in a farmers' market and was holding a basket full of oranges when we found her. It jarred with me to see her with a basket like that, and I realised I had never seen her eating an orange. She said that she was sorry but she just had too many auditions, and that it was a mistake for us to have come out. Hannah said she was sorry for surprising her, and looked sad.

I took an orange from my mum's stupid basket and started squeezing it. I wanted the orange to burst.

# 11

On Friday nights I go to the launderette, and as I wait for my clothes I read. I can only read about death now. The whirling and thumping of the washing machines and tumble dryers drown out the sounds of people having fun outside. I don't feel like a loser in here, and I find folding my clothes cathartic. I see strangers' ugly pants and I feel better about my ugly pants. I'm not sure why but the combination of heavily scented cleaning products and loud noises has a numbing effect on me. I feel a little safer in here.

No one talks in here. The faded seventies decor and handwritten signs would make this a fashionable place to do a photoshoot if it wasn't for the owner. She's a moody elderly woman who never smiles and always has a line of £1 coins on the fold-up table she sits at. I like that she's so unfriendly and doesn't even acknowledge the fact that I'm here.

Today there is a man here with his young daughter. I reckon she's about five or six, though she could be eight or nine – how the hell would I know. She's wearing a top that is similar to one Hannah wore as a girl which was handed down to me. Red with black polka dots. The little girl is reading a kids' magazine obediently as her dad reads what looks like a dictionary, though I realise it can't be. I want to know where the mother is, and I berate myself for hoping there is a tragic story behind her absence.

I have a washer-dryer at home but a kirby grip broke it. Hannah would usually call her plumber for me in these situations. She had a number for everyone. A plumber, dentist, physiotherapist, therapist. She wrote it all down by hand in a little purple Filofax. I keep the Filofax in my bedside drawer now but haven't been able to look inside.

I sit and read my book. Magic FM plays. I remember when Hannah and I phoned in once as teenagers and requested our favourite song.

*Now we have K-Ci & JoJo's 'All My Life' for Hannah and Ruth in Ealing.*

The launderette sits opposite the pub I used to work in when I was at art school. It's where all the art students go. Sometimes I look up from my book to see if I recognise anyone, but all the people I knew would have graduated by now, moved on to a new pub, reaping the rewards of a completed art degree.

I think of Fred. He was in the year above me and well known on campus because he looked and acted like a rock star. Long hair, tattoos, motorbike, tick, tick, tick. He did such bizarre and basic installation art that people mistook him for a genius. One of his pieces was an extremely long video of him picking the petals off a flower, gluing them back on, and then spray-painting the flower black.

He didn't notice me until I served him at the pub. It really was a cool pub. I liked that the cool people needed my attention in order to get what they wanted, usually a cool craft beer I couldn't pronounce properly. I was in a position to be selective with my audience, ignoring or charming them. I guess it's one of the only times in my life I've been similar to my mum, because I enjoyed the acting, playing my role of 'ice-cold barmaid'. It was easier than being myself.

I served Fred a beer and we fucked in an alleyway behind the pub that night. It was freezing outside, and afterwards he didn't ask for my number but I didn't mind because I went home with him every night after my shift for the next few months. He could stay up all night having sex, which I was flattered by, but now I suspect that he must have been taking something.

He didn't like me staying over, so I would walk home along the canal in the early hours each morning, which was irresponsible. I became exhausted, unable to focus, but nothing mattered unless Fred was focusing on me.

Hannah refused to meet him for longer than five minutes at a time, urged me to stop seeing him.

Her: He will hurt you.

And he did. Of course he did.

One night, after the longest stretch of nights apart, I asked him – too timidly – if I was coming back to his. He said he was going to a friend's studio to do some work. I pretended I had a bad headache to get the pub manager to let me finish my shift early and I followed Fred as soon as he left the pub. He went into a Sainsbury's Local and bought some cigarettes. He smoked as he walked to a block of flats nearby. I was so close to him I could inhale his smoke. When he was buzzed in, I looked up and saw a woman come out of her flat and wait for him on the walkway. He looked down and saw me. He didn't stop. His face didn't change. He went in.

For the next few weeks I still slept with him occasionally, and on the nights he said he was 'working' I continued to follow him. Six different flats. Six different women. I never asked, he never told. I was still grateful that he wanted to fuck me. It ended when he turned around on his walk from Sainsbury's Local one night. I told him I was following him. He said he knew what I'd been doing, and that I should stop.

Me: It's over, then.

I said it more as a desperate question. He laughed at me for a second before walking away. I stood still for a while, watching him until he turned a corner. Then I went into Sainsbury's and wandered around for a long time. Eventually the security guard asked if I was going to buy anything, so I chose a French baguette.

Hannah was working abroad for six months on a placement, and so at this point our main form of communication was long weekly emails. She listed the things she had done that week, what she had learnt, and I would list the things I hadn't done, all the mistakes I'd made and who I probably shouldn't have let photograph me naked for a project that might not actually be a project. I didn't mention Fred.

I was listless without her, I had no one to keep me in check. I made no effort to socialise with nice people and would stay out late every night. I began to get pretentiously annoyed with the pretentiousness of art in general. I'd make my pieces as weird as possible on purpose, to see if the tutors could tell I was joking, which was mean of me. Once I fell asleep in life drawing, falling off a stool and cutting open my elbow on a wooden easel. The tutor took me aside and said I should 'consider' leaving.

When I told Hannah over Skype, she comforted me and then coached me, still serving as my loyal drill sergeant from an Internet café across the world. She didn't want me to drop out, said it was a waste of talent, but I couldn't face the thought of seeing him at art school, having to seem fine when I wasn't, so I quit. I couldn't face the sight of him with other women in the pub, so I quit that too.

Hannah came home and insisted I live with her until I got back 'on track'. I could tell she liked looking after me. She liked having me waiting for her at home when she got back from work. She even liked doing my laundry.

We got into a routine, something we'd never had as children. Slowly she helped me become OK again, less obsessive, more stable. A new boyfriend for her would come along every so often, and I would sleep with a random man occasionally, swearing to myself that I would never get attached to a man again. I never did because I had no need. We were a little island.

One day, a few months after I had dropped out and before it was light outside, she woke me up and said we were going away. She had packed a new suitcase, written our names on the label. 'HANNAH & RUTH'. She didn't tell me where we were going. Obediently I got dressed and let her lead the way. The Tube to the airport was empty. I did a dance around the pole in the centre of the carriage. When we went through a loud tunnel, she shouted, 'I LOVE YOU.' I shouted it back louder as the train emerged from the tunnel, as it became quiet and the sun shone through on to her face.

I hear the bell for last orders from across the street. People are leaving the pub and involuntarily I still scan the place for Fred. The father and daughter are getting ready to leave now, folding clothes and putting them in a Sainsbury's Bag for Life. I smile at the girl, then turn back to my book on death. I have half an hour left before my clothes are dry.

I could easily call her plumber. I could call a new plumber. But I like my washing machine being broken because I am broken too.

# 12

I ate four slices of toast this morning. I made one at a time, and the act of spreading while the next slice was toasting stopped me from thinking for just under six minutes. I have taken two antihistamines because they make me feel drowsy and they zone me out a bit. I chew and gaze out of my kitchen window.

Some days I look at the clouds and think I see her. I almost believe in otherworldly things. I look at the sky and I can acknowledge its beauty — it is clear blue, the clouds look puffy and edible. I begin to entertain thoughts of impossible things, feel the astounding endlessness of the universe. Despite this, I believe that there is nothing afterwards — it's final. You die and you're done.

I wish I could train myself to believe in something more; maybe I should become a born-again Christian, or see an expensive psychic.

I'm now standing in a circle and all I can do is look down at my shitty new black ballet pumps and everyone else's shoes. The circle involves Mum, Dad, Hannah's friend Leila and the celebrant, Marie. Mum is speaking to Marie, who she found on Instagram with Leila's help. I didn't want to be involved in anything to do with the organisation of this day, but I wish that the person who is about speak at my sister's funeral was not so obviously an unemployed drama school graduate who takes pleasure in the macabre. My mother likes her, I can tell.

Leila organised the flowers. Yellow roses are everywhere. It looks nice but I want to tell her that Hannah would be angry about the roses, she would have preferred the money spent on them to have gone to charity. I mumble quietly, bitterly –

Me: Hannah didn't like flowers.
Leila: Oh. She gave me yellow roses once, so I thought – she did like them.

I back away and watch people arriving. Most are not dressed in black. I want to tell them off, send them home. They should have worn black. This is not a celebration of her life, despite what the order of service might say. Hannah never wore black, she hated black and she would have hated everyone wearing black, which is appropriate – this day is for hating. The service is meant to start at 11.00 but the people are all inside now. I check my phone and it's only 10.55. Leila goes in, holding a single fucking yellow rose. My mum tries to usher me in as music begins to play.

Mum: Ruth, it's starting –
Me: But it's not eleven yet –
Mum: Come inside –
Me: It's only ten fifty-five –
Mum: Now –
Me: But there's still five minutes –
Mum: Everyone is here –
Me: But it's not time yet, I'm not ready.

I sit between my parents. We don't touch each other. Sometimes I feel my mother shift like she wants to touch me – or someone – but instead she just grips the seat. I can't believe that she is my mum – she was our mum – and she's lost her baby. I want to know what Hannah's birth was like; I've never asked her. This is definitely not the time to ask if she had a Caesarean or a water birth or if she remembers the midwife's name.

Leila, who's infuriatingly dressed in a pink-and-red striped dress, with red pointy heels, sits behind us, next to a man I don't recognise. There are rows and rows of Hannah's colleagues and 'friends', who I plan to ignore. I aim to get through this day by looking down, by getting back into bed as quickly as possible. I plan to sleep for days. Even though I don't like vodka, I have two large bottles ready at home, but no mixer yet. I have the films we loved when we were kids ready. *Space Jam*, *The Secret Garden*, *Home Alone*. I just need to remember to buy Fanta.

* * *

My mum is in a black gown with a shawl, stolen sunglasses and her signature dark red (almost black) lipstick. She looks glamorous. I try to see if there is a tag poking out from the shawl because it looks so new. I wonder if she got up early, if she woke up alone, if she had breakfast. Is her make-up running behind the dark sunglasses yet?

My dad sits very, very still. I don't dare look at him because we will both be embarrassed. Embarrassed for being here, that it has come to this. I wonder if he wants to shout, 'I'M SORRY,' like I do. I'm sorry I let her jump. I'm sorry I insisted. I'm sorry I didn't stop her. Is he sorry for not being around enough, is he sorry for never actively trying to get to know her as an adult?

This is the last time I will be in the same room as my sister. It's Hannah in there. Her body will have been put back together again. Would they have bothered to stitch her? Will her body have moved around in the coffin as she was flown home on her own, or as she was driven here and lifted up onto the tragic table? I visualise where her hand would be and rest my own on the coffin lid above it.

What food will be served at the wake? Eating is one of the few things I'm left capable of doing. I hate that Leila knows the menu before me. Has Leila lost or gained weight since it happened? Why do I care?

My dress keeps falling off my shoulders and I want to burn it as soon as I get home. I got it from Primark, it's black with small red flowers. I know Hannah wouldn't have wanted me to spend money on this outfit. She would have lent me something; she didn't approve of fast fashion. She wouldn't have let me near Primark, which is why I went in. To annoy her.

Would people laugh if my dress dropped to the ground right now in front of her coffin? Would I laugh?

I'm wearing a flesh-coloured bra. I don't remember buying it, but even in my daze it must have felt right to have something so unattractive and functional to wear on this day. I have no make-up on and my unwashed hair is tied up in a bun that's too loose and keeps flopping about.

Whenever I do manage to look up, I see that people are actively avoiding my eyes. It's just so fucking awkward. We're all here because my sister has died. She has actually died.

Everyone stares as he walks in. One of Hannah's

'favourite songs' is playing. He's dishevelled and late. People look and whisper, 'That's her boyfriend.'

It's Rowan.

I want to shout, 'That's not her favourite song, she didn't have a favourite song, who picked this fucking song?' as Mum gets up to kiss him on the cheek. I'm livid that he's late and has now become the centre of attention. She makes space for him on our pew and the service begins.

I don't cry.

★　★　★

When I went clubbing with Hannah for the first time I wore a bra like this with detachable straps. I was fourteen, she was eighteen. It was some shitty club called My Place in Earls Court and she'd let me borrow some chicken-fillet things to pad out my bra. They had what looked like gunge in. I liked playing with them and squeezing them like stress balls. She put them in for me and pushed up my cleavage.

Mum had been away for weeks in Stratford at this point and Hannah had been everything to me. She'd taught me about kissing, calories, Bacardi Breezers, the benefits of putting ice in wine, masturbation. Not that she'd cared particularly about any of those things – because she had just started up her charity and had been with her first boyfriend Luka for over a year. He was quite a bit older, twenty-five or so. She'd lost her virginity to him and had filled out enough to not need the chicken-gunge fillets any more.

I was dancing with her madly – so madly – and I felt moderately sexy for the first time. As I danced I saw a man looking at me so I danced harder until one of the fillets fell out. I froze. Hannah picked it up for me. I was mortified and ran to the toilets. She followed me.

Her: It's OK, Ruth, no one saw!
Me: I'm such a loser.
Her: No! It's funny. I promise, no one saw.

She put the fillet back in my bra, pushed my boobs up for me again and kissed me on the cheek.

Her: Come find me in a minute – I'm just calling Luka.

I checked myself in the mirror, and I remember thinking that I looked good, my boobs plausibly real. I left the toilets and a man came up to me in the dark corridor. I didn't see his face properly but he had a nice body, nice clothes. He smelt nice too. I thought it must be the man who had been staring at me as I danced to 'Love Don't Cost a Thing' – did he see the fillet fall out? I smiled nervously and he pushed me softly against the wall, his body weight pressing against me so I couldn't move. I didn't know if this was normal, if this was just what happens in clubs. He put one hand up my dress, and instinctually I clenched my thighs shut around his hand, trapping him. His breath was hot on my neck as the music boomed from the dance floor.

I tried to push him off me and as I did my thighs opened and he was able to put his hand up higher. I paused for a second, thinking maybe this would be good for me – for my first sexual experience to be with a stranger. So I let him, for a few seconds. But I didn't like it. I managed to run away. I couldn't find Hannah, so I just stood on my own on the dance floor in a trance until she came back and joined me for the *Baywatch* theme tune.

I saw the man at the bar later on, I recognised his clothes. I realised it wasn't the man who had been looking at me while I danced to J.Lo. This man was really handsome. I was confused. He caught my eye and I could tell he didn't recognise me, he did not know I was the girl he'd just fingered. I felt so stupid.

I didn't tell Hannah what happened as we sat on the night bus later. Her head was resting on my shoulder and she looked so happy, telling me what a nice time she had and how glad she was that I was grown up enough to go out with her now. I didn't want to ruin it.

Wearing this bra today, sitting here next to my poor sister, my poor poor sister who's in a fucking box, I'm glad I never told her.

* * *

I'm first out as another song I don't approve of plays. I don't follow her to the crematorium, I can't accompany her any more. I need air. I start walking.

I didn't expect my parents to organise horse-drawn carriages but I don't like seeing everyone get into Ubers like it's a normal day. They'll listen to the radio in the Uber, they'll make small talk in the Uber.

I keep walking. When I get to the pub for her wake, there is a buffet. I hate buffets, Hannah hated buffets too. Who organised the buffet? I hide in the toilets.

Even now, I don't cry.

Under the cubicle door I see red heels tottering in. Leila. I wait for her to go into a cubicle so I can escape,

65

but she seems to be waiting. I'm still and silent for as long as I can be.

Leila: Ruth? Are you in here?

I put my face into my hands and hold my breath. Leila must have organised the buffet.

Leila: Ruth? I saw you come in here. I just want to check you're –
Me: I'm fine, thanks.
Leila: Please, come out. You've been in there a long time.
Me: I want to be alone.

Surely she gets it. But the red heels stay put.

Me: Thanks? You can go.

I wait again, thirsty, hungry, exhausted and desperate. The heels turn and I think she's understood. Finally. I can leave and start my evening of forgetting. Instead she starts crying. Loudly. Impressively loudly. I'm forced to leave the cubicle. When I open the door I see her bent over the sink. A glass of chilled white wine sits on top of the metal hand dryer, lipstick print on the rim. I'm annoyed that she's got a glass of chilled fucking wine before I've had any.

I watch her crying in amazement. I'm the sister. I'm the sister. Eventually she straightens up and makes me hug her and I want to hit her. I stand still, arms hanging down by my sides, and I see my reflection in the mirror. I look so old. She lets go and takes my hands, even though

I haven't washed them. Her neon-green nails prick my palm.

Leila: Come with me.

I fake-smile, the best tactic. She leads me out of the toilets by the hand and waves at some people like it's a party. They come over and I realise one of them is Rowan. He doesn't smile at me but tries to hug me. I don't let him. He's wearing black Converse. The guy he's with looks a bit like him, but more dressed up, less scruffy. He starts saying all the things you would expect people to say at the wake of someone who's died young, by accident, the things you say if you don't really know the person, the things you say if you've googled what to say. He puts his arm around Leila and she turns in to him and starts crying into his armpit, which he doesn't mind.

I slip away without anyone noticing, past all the sad young people, the sad old people. As I leave the pub I look back and spy my dad by the bar. He's flirting with the barmaid, who's younger than me. Of course he is. Mum is nearby, smoking inside and talking dramatically about something that's not related to Hannah, anything but Hannah. Her sunglasses are on her head now and her make-up is not smudged yet. I don't want to see any of this.

I wait on the nearby street corner for my Toyota to arrive. Someone taps me on the shoulder and it's Rowan.

Him: Are you going?
Me: Yes.
Him: Do you have anyone – who can, I don't know
  – be with you?

Me: Yeah. A friend's at home waiting for me.
Him: Really?

He doesn't believe me. Why doesn't he believe me? I don't care. I don't want to see him ever again, or anyone who's been there today, listened to those songs, seen her coffin. I get into the white Toyota as Rowan watches. I stare down as the car drives away and focus on the task at hand.

Getting supplies. Getting home. I make it clear to the driver that I won't be talking.

Me: I'm on my way home from my sister's funeral.
    I need to stop at Tesco to get some mixer and
    paracetamol. Please don't ask me any questions.

But the driver has headphones in and doesn't hear me anyway. I get out my notebook to pass the time. I try to draw but I can't. So I start writing.

List of things she'll never do again:

She'll never have sex again
She'll never eat banana bread
She'll never get a parking ticket
She'll never boil a kettle
She'll never use keys
She'll never watch TV
She'll never brush her teeth
She'll never breathe fresh air
She'll never be early or late

But she'll never have sex again. This upsets me more than anything else. We didn't talk much about sex, other than if it was good or bad, or if the sizes or personalities involved were extreme.

I never thought of her as an overtly sexual person until I saw her eat a nectarine on the Tube. She didn't care about the juice, she just let it drip down her chin, and then she wiped it playfully with her hand. People watched; she didn't care. She was too busy enjoying the nectarine. It was mesmerising. From then on I would ask her more questions, want more advice. I was inspired to be more open, to be able to eat in front of a man, maybe one day even on a Tube carriage.

When I get into my flat, my head is already pounding from not drinking anything all day. I've bought two 2-litre bottles of Fanta Zero, and I pour half out of each down the drain. Then I pour in the vodka. I sit on the sofa, take two paracetamol and begin to drink. *Home Alone* is first.

The crying starts. It doesn't stop until it's light outside and I'm swaying, staring out the window, directly into the sun. I don't care if I'm hurting my eyes. I want to hurt something, hurt everything. I get into my bed and use her vibrator to help me get to sleep. She'd be so fucking angry if she knew I'd stolen it.

# 13

Hannah showed signs of being a businesswoman from a young age. She had the right mix of pure intentions and savage pragmatism. She stored her pocket money in her bedside drawer while I would spend mine on *Heat* magazine even though I was way too young for it.

I remember Hannah had a cupcake stall at one primary school fete. She had been looking forward to it for ages and made all of the cupcakes herself, painstakingly decorating them with her forehead frown-line going crazy. I wanted to be involved too, kept pestering her. So she allowed me to decorate half of them. I wasn't careful enough and they ended up looking like a toddler had decorated them. I cried all the way there because my cupcakes were ugly. She didn't want me to be discouraged, so she oversold her cupcakes for £3 and put a label on mine saying they were free. By the end of the fete, all of my cupcakes had been taken, remarkably, but there were still some of hers left. She lied and said it was because mine tasted better. We shared one on the walk home.

When we got back our parents were having a party. Hannah quickly took her tin of cupcakes on a tour of the living room and sold them all to the drunken adults, making £30. I watched her rush upstairs to put the cash in her bedside drawer, looking so happy.

She started up PaperbackKids, her scheme to provide kids with free books in inner-city London, as soon as she got to university. Her plan was to make books more accessible to all children, providing free childcare for working parents at the same time, involving and promoting small businesses and enterprises. She did pop-up events for a while and then, once she'd saved up enough after working in her City job for a couple of years, she bought a Portakabin on a back street in East London. It was a wreck at first, she had to paint it and deep-clean it. She did hours and hours of research about mould and how we could get rid of it ourselves, and coerced me into helping.

It was energising to see her making something out of nothing. Once it was up and running, 'PaperbackKids by Hannah' happened every Wednesday afternoon in Old Street. I helped her every week, making sure Wednesday was my day off. If I was feeling healthy, sometimes I would go swimming before at the pool nearby. The kids would arrive after school and hang around until 7.00. They'd get to look through boxes and boxes of second-hand books and sit and read on some second-hand beanbags, but it was more than that – she'd built a community. Hannah had to take the beanbags home to re-stitch them and add little patches of material every few weeks. She cared so much about tiny details, things that no one else would care about.

At the end they could take a book home for free, and were given vouchers for the small businesses involved that week. Hannah particularly loved looking after the younger kids and reading to them. I liked watching her because the voices she did were so bad. It was basically just one voice, one accent for every character – but she really tried. I would sometimes catch myself getting jealous of the attention she was giving to the kids, like I used to in the playground when she played with other children.

About a year ago, a boy called Jimi turned up early, completely on his own, even though he was only seven. He asked where Hannah was, with genuine fear in his eyes that she wasn't going to turn up. He adored Hannah and never let her go.

Me: She'll be here soon. We're just a bit early.

We sat silently next to each other outside the Portakabin, looking out for her. She was late that day, and turned up flustered. She gave Jimi a huge hug. Her hair was down for a change – usually at work she kept it up in a neat bun. Her gold eyeliner and mascara were smudged, and I could tell she'd been crying. I didn't ask her anything, I just tried to be as helpful as possible, which was exhausting.

Then Rowan arrived and it all clicked into focus. They'd had a fight, their first proper relationship fight – the big one, the one that sets up every other fight in the relationship's future. I couldn't really imagine Hannah being horrible to a man. I was sure that she saved her horrible side just for me. All of her exes were docile and unimaginative, so they never fought anyway.

Once we had a fight on the Tube and she shouted 'bitter evil hag' as she stormed down the Hammersmith and City line carriages. I followed her and called her so many things – but 'selfless cunt fraud' was my personal highlight. People thought we were doing some strange form of busking – one man even clapped. Hannah had this rawness in a fight that, at all other times, lay dormant. She became animalistic. For someone so gentle and warm, she could be a massive fucking bitch.

Now, with Rowan in front of me, I worried that she might just have let him see this mean side of her too, which meant they were now more bonded and cleansed than she had been with anyone but me. Or maybe he was mean to her, in which case I wanted to attack him.

His hair was messy and his eyes looked red too. What could have possibly gone on to make them both so distressed? He sat on the opposite side of the Portakabin and watched her as she read to Jimi on her lap, his chubby arm wrapped round her neck. I could tell that she knew he was watching her.

She wanted him to see her in earth-mother mode, but didn't want to acknowledge him, so she tried extra hard with her animal voices.

# 14

One white, one red. Today is her thirtieth birthday. I have mostly been quite disciplined about not drinking alone, at home, for fear that I will never stop, but tonight I've got the two little bottles.

She was awful at receiving presents, and got pissed off with gifts, saying that she didn't need anything. So to be safe I would get her novelty presents from petrol stations, more cheap earrings, or write 'I.O.U. AN EXPENSIVE GIFT' on a Post-it. I would always do a drawing for her, though. She liked them, I hope.

It's like she was constantly repenting for something she'd done in her past, and she felt guilty when people gave her things because she didn't think she deserved them. I struggled to think of anything bad she'd ever have done to make her feel like this, or any particular childhood memory to make her so averse to presents.

I have unplugged and pulled the broken washing machine into the living room and now I'm sitting next to it, so I can howl into it when I need to. I like hearing the echo. There's a fucking party going on in the flat opposite. The woman who lives there is really glum. I've never seen her smile, so I'm surprised she's able to have a party. She's put up some blue fairy lights, which make her flat look cold and unfriendly too. People are smoking out of her window, sitting precariously on her window-sill, tapping their ash into her already dead flowers. I turn my lights off so they can't see me.

We'd drink these small bottles of wine when we were going on a train. Like the time we went to see our mum in Nottingham – she was doing another mediocre play – and we left in the early afternoon. She bought snacks, I bought wine. We didn't talk about how we were both dreading seeing the play, or what our different strategies for caressing Mum's ego would be. We just sipped the wine and looked out of the window, occasionally commenting on the scenery – even though scenery talk wasn't something we were great at. Before it got dark, we played a game, 'How many sheep/cows/horses can you count as the train passes?' By this point we were quite tipsy.

When she was tipsy she'd get sentimental and bossy.

Her: You should drink red wine through a straw so you don't stain your teeth.
Me: OK, thanks for another Hannah's Top Tip.
Her: You have lovely teeth. Don't ruin them.
Me: Noted.
Her: I'm ordering you some steel straws. Right now.

Rowan kept texting her and she'd glow every time her phone vibrated. The glow that someone has when they're stuck doing something boring, but can bitch about how boring it is to someone far away which makes it all less boring. The boring becomes worth it for the text chat. She asked how things were going with Fred, pretending to forget his name, which was such a power play. She knew that my 'relationship' with Fred was still just sleeping with him every few weeks. I was trying to wean myself off him but hadn't yet been able to say goodbye.

Her: When are you going to actually end it?
Me: When I want to —
Her: It's not good for you. He'll get you sick —
Me: We use protection.
Her: No, you don't.
Me: How would you know that?
Her: You don't have the self-esteem to use condoms. He's fucking random girls, he might have something —
Me: I know he's fucking random girls, and I don't care, OK?
Her: He's not going to change.
Me: Go back to ordering me steel straws.

When we arrived at the Nottingham Playhouse we discussed the possibility of not actually watching the play, just going to Pizza Express and then arriving at the stage door at a precise time having pretended to see it. But Mum would sniff us out, and we were emotionally obliged. We found our seats, the ones Mum always made us pay for, after getting another wine. It was a sold-out crowd, which was a huge relief and surprise. We've been to so many plays where we've had to lie about how full the house was afterwards. A man sat next to us and started to make conversation with Hannah.

Him: You must be Meryl's daughter?
Hannah: Ummm, yes —
Him: I'm a friend of your mother's. She showed me a photo of you.

Hannah touched my thigh, instinctively thinking I would be upset that Mum only showed a picture of Hannah. But I was now quite drunk and didn't mind. Hannah kept up the conversation with the man, who I could tell was wearing a toupee. His face was younger than his style suggested though, probably mid-forties. From afar he would have looked like a businessman in his grey suit, but up close, in this theatre, the suit was shiny.

Her: Are you an actor?
Him: Yes, we met in rep in Stratford. We go to see each other's things every now and then.

Hannah turned back to me. We knew that this must be my mother's current fling. She had a thing for hapless younger men who were stupid enough to think she was wise and who didn't double-check her CV for inconsistencies.

The play was bad but Mum was good, as usual. She had a small part in the ensemble, a Noël Coward play that she'd done before, playing a different small part.

She got so drunk afterwards that we had to accompany her back to her digs early. It was embarrassing but at least she was happy, riding off her ego. Hannah and I got the last train home, with two more little bottles of wine, and she fell asleep on my shoulder. I tried to count the stars as she snored.

The party opposite is now spilling out into the street and seems to be getting louder. How can someone know this many people?

I look at my phone before leaving it in the kitchen for the night, as far away from me as possible. I haven't checked it in hours, in case there are any more sympathy messages for today. There was a time before all of this when I would get genuine kicks from my phone, unable to put it down. My battery would drain before the end of the day, every day. I would look at aspirational images on Instagram and feel inspired, or find things funny, or feel included. I was a true follower. I used to stare into the screen as if it could tell me secrets, save me. I used it to take naked selfies; I used it to take photos of my face filtered with a cute puppy nose and ears.

I still scroll, but I can't relate, and don't understand how I ever could have.

I have the early shift at Heathrow tomorrow. I long for this night to be over and to be sitting on the Piccadilly line on my way to work, starting a new day. I go to the bathroom and get ready for bed, using her moisturiser on my face, doing circular motions with my fingers the way she taught me.

I continue to watch the party in the dark until my eyelids get heavy, too scared to go to sleep. I dread the dreams tonight.

# 15

The Mediterranean

I have the phone ready to take another picture of her as she looks up, a bonus one she'll be happy with. The look of victory.

I shake water out of my ear while I wait for her to appear down below and wave to me. I notice the wind for the first time today – it's blowing softly, but blowing enough to move my hair. Another woman goes to the edge of the cliff, ready to jump in.

Me: Sorry, can you wait a second? My sister hasn't come up yet –

I scan the water down below, the waves are crashing into the rocks. They didn't seem to be crashing like that when I was down there. The woman says something to me in a language I don't understand, signalling that she is about to jump. I shout, with a voice that doesn't sound like mine suddenly –

No – stop – no.

And then I scream to the sea.

## HANNAH?

I'm running down to the bottom of the cliff, not allowing the thoughts to creep in – that this is wasting time, that she might need help. Maybe I didn't see her emerge from the water, she was too quick and must be walking back up to me. We'll cross paths and laugh and go and get food the way we planned. Everything is going to be all right. Like she said.

Then I get to the bottom and I can't see her anywhere. I shout her name again, not as loudly as I want to because I'm embarrassed, and I'm probably just overreacting. People start to notice me though. I dive into the water from where, just minutes ago, I climbed out onto the rocks after my jump, feeling nothing. I look up to see the woman who I just told not to jump, jumping off the cliff. She crashes into the water next to me. Immediately she comes up and begins shouting at me. She's angry with me. I start screaming my sister's name and then, reluctantly, unbelievably –

## HELP! SOMEBODY HELP?

The woman seems to understand 'help' and rushes out of the water. I dive under, wishing I had goggles, my eyes stinging. I go deeper and deeper until something grabs my foot. It must be Hannah, it must be Hannah playing a bad joke – though she's not great at joking, and she would never be this cruel. I turn around to see that this hand belongs to a male scuba diver who is signalling for me to come up. I swim up and the second my face is out of the water I see her.

She's being lifted onto the rocks by two other scuba divers. Her head is swinging to the side, and for a second it looks as though she's shrugging, just tilting her head knowingly towards me. But then I see that her neck is at an unnatural angle, like it's falling off. It is falling off, hanging by a bloody thread.

I rub the water out of my eyes. I must be imagining this.

My brain won't focus on anything until I'm out of the water and next to her. One of the scuba divers tries to hold me back from her, but I push myself forward. I kneel down, my knees hurting on the rocks. She looks like a cartoon character that's been through an explosion; she doesn't look real. Her face is smashed in, her neck is broken, I see bone and blood everywhere. Her legs are perfectly intact, though.

That must mean she's OK. She must be OK, she can be fixed.

Me: Hannah? Hannah?

I even say,

Wake up.

I hug her torso gently, afraid I will hurt her even more. I see that one of her ears is still OK too, the hoop earring untouched. I hear a siren.

Me: It's OK, we're getting help, we're OK –

But then I see her chest. Her chest is still, so still as the wind blows my hair more now. Another person jumps off the cliff, climbing out of the water near to where my sister now lies. I stand up and shout upwards –

81

## STOP JUMPING.

I wave my arms at them, because they probably can't hear me. But they do seem to stop, and instead of taking photos of their cliff jump, people are now taking photos of Hannah from afar. I think about nature programmes where animals run around with dead animals hanging out of their mouths, horror movies where killers saw off body parts. What's in front of me is more horrifying than anything I could ever have imagined.

Paramedics approach us carefully on the rocks; they have a stretcher waiting. The couple Hannah took a photo of come near to me, as well as the woman who dived in when I told her not to.

People start to gather around us, walking over from the beach to see what's going on, people on their holidays wanting to find out what's happened. Someone sees Hannah and screams, scared or disgusted. I acknowledge for a moment that she does look scary.

My sister looks scary. I use my arms to shroud her, because she'd be so embarrassed. I start mumbling.

Me: She was just talking about jellyfish, we're going
to get doughnuts, she put on factor 50 –

I stand still while they try to work out how to transport her, how many people they need, and I want to scream at them to hurry. But it becomes clear to me that they're not in a rush. They're not trying to save her. This is not a rescue.

Her phone starts vibrating in my hand – Rowan is calling.

I don't know what else to do so I answer.

82

Me: Hello?

Him: Hannah?

Me: No.

Him: Oh, Ruth — hey —

Me: Hannah can't speak.

Him: OK. I just want to say I've arrived at the airport and I'm about to get a taxi to the hotel. I should be about an hour — is that cool?

Me: You're early. She said you were arriving tonight —

Him: Did she? Oh —

I end the call and vomit onto the rocks.

Four people surround Hannah now, three of them in wetsuits, one in plain clothes. I don't know if they're all paramedics or lifeguards or if they were the scuba divers. They don't speak to me, but they gesture that they are now going to pick her up. I grip her hand. Her lilac-painted nails look so pretty. I have to let go as they walk slowly over the rocks towards the ambulance. A paramedic puts towels around her neck; I notice she's chewing gum.

Once we're by the ambulance, I look down and see that I am covered in blood, so much blood, and that I'm still clutching our phones and our little plastic bag.

They don't let me in the ambulance. Someone passes me a card as they drive away, slowly, no siren. The address of the hospital is on the card. I want to run after the ambulance, but I can't. I can't move.

Her phone vibrates again.

I look at her phone.

Rowan (text): Can't wait to see you. X

83

# 16

My whole world has smashed to pieces and I want to go where she's going. I run into the sea. I swim out and plunge myself under the water for as long as I can, but I can't keep myself under, I get too scared. I try again, and again. I retreat to the shore and sit. I huddle my knees into my chest, and let the waves crash into my calves.

The sun disappears and it's gone dark so quickly. Someone collects me from the shallow water, sometime later. I don't look at their face; they could be anyone. All I know is that it's not Hannah and that they have big hairy arms.

Voice: Ruth, Ruth.

It's the hotel concierge Hannah made small talk with when we arrived. He thinks I'm nice because my sister was nice. He pulls me up to my feet and wraps me with a hotel towel, checks my pulse. He starts rubbing my arms.

Him: You are blue –

The way he says blue makes me like him.

Me: We were going to go midnight swimming in the pool tonight. After dinner.

He keeps rubbing my arms.

Him: Your mother? Have you called your mother?

I shake my head. I hand him the card with the hospital address.

Me: Can you take me, please?

He nods and helps me walk to the hotel. I look back at the sea and the navy water is shimmering from the moon. How long have I been sitting? We get in the car and he's silent for the whole journey.

He parks outside a grey building. It's to the side of the hospital. I clutch onto his arm as we enter and he speaks to the people at Reception. I must be bleeding from somewhere, the towel he gave me is now stained. My hair is wet. The only word I understand him saying is 'sister'.

A man who looks like a doctor comes out, and he tells me to sit down. He hands me some papers. I don't look at them. I google translate 'Please can I have her swimming costume' and try to open my mouth but the concierge says it for me. I don't understand what's happening. The man shakes his head and says something. The concierge tells me gently that her swimsuit is destroyed, and that it's recommended I don't see her as it will be too traumatising.

Me: I've seen her already. I need to see her.

The doctor shakes his head. The concierge says something I don't understand, I think he is begging for me.

Me: It can't be destroyed – I saw her stomach –
her swimming costume was from Zara – it cost
£32 –

The man says something else, shaking his head. I make my plea, on my knees, on the cold hospital floor. I must see her, I must see her. Eventually the doctor agrees and leads me down a white corridor.

He opens the door and I see a bed. I walk up slowly to stand next to her, unsure why her head is covered by a sheet. I find the outline of her hand before uncovering her.

Then I see her face, her wrecked face, her broken neck. I put my cheek on her stomach. I am angry they took off her swimsuit, she's naked under this sheet – that's not OK, that's not OK. Why is she naked? Where is her swimming costume, did they cut it off? I hold her, even though she's broken. I pretend I'm holding her together again, until the doctor comes back in.

He hands me one of her hoop earrings in a little plastic bag. He looks me up and down and now I see I'm covered in her blood.

# 17

Costa, Heathrow Terminal 5

A woman with a protruding mole orders a large vanilla latte. Two hairs spring from the mole, and her hands are orange. I assume because of fake tan. Or too many carrots. Hannah went through a phase in her early twenties of eating a huge pack of carrot sticks and box of cherry tomatoes for lunch. Her hands and chin turned orange; it took years to fade.

I feel sorry for this woman, because the mole makes her seem older than her outfit and fake-tan habit suggest. She taps her card and waits for her coffee. She has no suitcase, just an ugly rectangular handbag, and she looks completely out of place in this airport, as if she's come here by accident. Maybe Heathrow is her nearest Costa, or her nearest Tube station.

I look at her knuckles. Hannah's knuckles stayed orange for the longest.

Once or twice a day I think of different scenarios. If she had jumped and not died. If she'd been left paralysed, unable to speak. Still alive but not really here. If I had the power to choose between keeping her in that state or having her be able to send texts to me from the ether

– what would I choose? I would choose her in text form. She was so good at texting. I decide I will keep texting her. Maybe that will help?

I eat some wine gums from my stash under the iPad and then study the mole again from a distance. I am obsessed with it, maybe because I know Hannah would be too. I know exactly what she'd say if she saw it today, what Mum would say too. They'd insist she get it removed, urgently, at whatever cost. They thought appearance could be fixed, improved, always be better.

But I quite like the mole. I text Hannah.

**Me (text): There must be a reason why this lady is keeping it.**

The airport is very quiet this morning; only five customers are in the seating area. I can hear the planes taking off more loudly than usual. I open the food cabinet and take out a brownie.

An employee, who's bored at the coffee machine, sees me doing this and winks. Her name is Sal. She's still the only one here I've spoken to more than once. She's worked in four different restaurants and shops within Heathrow in the last three years. I've learnt that she loves airports, '*to my detriment*' – and I've learnt that she loves phrases like that. She told me she has a phobia of flying so lives vicariously through all the passengers she meets. She chats to them, finds out where they're going, and tells them to come back and show her photos of their trips. I bet they rarely do.

As I put half of the brownie in my mouth, Sal sidles up right next to me – she's much too close.

Her: I like your thinking. I sneak at least one a day,
    to see if they notice.

I try to smile but I'm annoyed that she's interrupting
my enjoyment of the stolen snack, which was meant to
be a private moment.

Me: Yeah. I mean, they're just gonna be thrown
    away, right?
Her: Well, they should be. But sometimes they keep
    them out for a day or too longer than they should.

I stuff the rest of the brownie into my mouth. She
thinks I could be a new friend, she has no idea I'm
not equipped. I can't smile, I can't chat.

A man appears and asks for a macchiato, a drink I've
never understood. Sal goes back to the coffee machines
and I resume my job. The queue builds up again and I
feel mobbed by my own negativity. Unpleasant memories
keep popping up, making me feel bad. Why are they
coming now? Why can't all the memories of her be the
beautiful ones, the happy days, the perfect moments?

I don't want to be but I'm angry with Hannah, for
something that happened years ago.

She was twenty-three and I was nineteen, and she
insisted I come to Bristol with her for the weekend. She
had a business conference and didn't want to be alone
after her break-up from Brian, which was becoming
increasingly dramatic. The night before she'd sent him a
string of fifty-nine semi-abusive messages after finding out
he was seeing someone new. Brian had texted me to say
that he knew he had ended it out of the blue, but that
he'd have to go to the police if Hannah kept contacting

him. He didn't have the balls to apologise to her, so he went through me.

I forced Hannah to go cold turkey with the texting and we got the train to Bristol early one morning. I had no work all weekend so I was looking forward to staying in a Premier Inn for two nights with her, paid for by her company, watching films on her laptop and eating shit. She kept staring out of the train window and looking comically forlorn. She'd never been dumped before. I found it amusing, but tried to hide it.

We arrived in Bristol and she had to go straight to the conference, so I had the morning to myself. I checked us in and had a bath in the hotel room. I took some naked selfies, feeling fancy in the hotel, but felt pathetic because I had no one to send them to. But I reminded myself that I was here for Hannah, to counsel her through her first proper rejection. This was my area of expertise. I went to the harbour and watched the boats, wishing I liked boats and picturesque scenery as much as other people seemed to.

I went to a coffee shop and started drawing. There was a barista who was quite handsome, with curly ginger hair. He came to collect my empty cup and noticed my drawing. He then stated matter-of-factly that I was good. I giggled and thought for a second that maybe I am.

I stayed there happily for a couple of hours until Hannah texted me bluntly, with no emoticons, asking where I was. She had left the conference early and wanted to meet, which was unusual as she was normally so dedicated to work things. She met me in the coffee shop and found me chatting to the barista, who had come back to look at more of my drawings. He offered her a coffee and she said she'd like a macchiato, as if that was her coffee of choice, when I knew for a fact she'd never had a fucking macchiato. I realised she was trying to impress him, and she felt threatened because he was flirting with me. He left to make her coffee. She was jittery, clutching her phone.

Me: So. How many times have you texted Brian today?
Her: None. Zero.
Me: Let me check then —
Her: OK, five. But only about admin stuff — he left some things —
Me: Just throw them away —
Her: He left them on purpose to fuck with me —
Me: Or he just forgot them.
Her: Who's this guy?
Me: He's called Pete. He's nice —
Her: You know you're meant to be here to support me —
Me: I am!

Pete brought over her tiny coffee and Hannah took a tiny sip, clearly hating it. He smiled, said it was nice to meet us and went back to work. I let myself wonder if he liked me, if he actually fancied me. I'd rarely had a complete stranger pay me attention before. Hannah ripped a piece of paper out of my sketchbook, tearing one of my drawings, and wrote something messily.

Her: Come on, let's go.

As we left the coffee shop she hung back from me and slipped Pete the piece of paper over the counter. He smiled awkwardly, and Hannah strutted away in her silly work heels. Outside I shouted at her.

Me: What the fuck are you doing?
Her: Nothing.
Me: Stop being so desperate – what's happening to you?
Her: He liked me, I could tell.
Me: He was just being polite.
Her: He stared at my boobs –
Me: Probably because you were pushing them in his face?

She stormed off and I had to trail behind her all the way back to the hotel, not wanting to tell her I'd lost my room key and I couldn't have found my way without her. Once we were inside the room, she got into one of her skimpiest dresses and styled her hair. I shouted over the hairdryer.

Me: I didn't know we were going out? Like dressing up out? I didn't bring any –
Her: No. I'm going out.
Me: And what am I supposed to do?
Her: It's up to you, isn't it.

She threw the hairdryer down facetiously and left. I slumped onto the bed, powerless. I watched *EastEnders* for the first time. I waited. I paced up and down, had another bath. I tried to do some squats and some star-jumps. I waited. Eventually at midnight she stumbled in and plunged face down onto the bed, her make-up smudging the sheets. She started crying so loudly that I worried she was injured or had been attacked.

She kept crying 'sorry' over and over again. I asked her where she'd been and she slurred an explanation.

Her: I waited outside the coffee shop until it closed. When he came out, Pete – is his name Pete? Or is it Paul? Phil? Anyway we went to a pub and it was nice at first but then he kept asking where you were. So I left and then got drunk on my own by the boats. I hate house boats the most, Ruth. I don't see the point in living in a house – on a boat – what is it with people and fucking boats –

Me: I know, I know. It's OK, it's OK.

She put her head in my lap and fell asleep, snoring instantly. I stroked her hair, which was at that time dyed comic-book bright red. Her light brown roots were coming through, which she had never allowed to happen to this extent. I heard her phone buzz and it was a text from Brian. I deleted the text without reading it, followed by his number. Then I sent him a text from my phone.

Me (text): She won't be contacting you again.

# 18

I wake up to buzzing sounds on a Sunday. I find the vibrator under my sheets, still on. I've been in and out of sleep for most of the weekend. I can hear buses and cars and people outside, going places. I check my phone for the time. It's 3 p.m. and I have eleven messages from Fred. Fred who hasn't spoken to me in a long time, since before Hannah died. Or I haven't spoken to him maybe. I forget now.

Eight of the messages were from last night (eighteen hours ago).

Fred (text) 1: You around now?

(text) 2: Long time

(text) 3: Seriously tho how are you?

(text) 4: Hello

(text) 5: OK, sorry it's been so long I've been so busy, got new job

(text) 6: Earth to Ruth

(text) 7: I want to see you, plz

(text) 8: OK you're annoyed whatever

Three of the messages are from just now. He must have been drunk and now regrets them.

Fred (text) 9: Well fuck that was a lot of messages wasn't it?

(text) 10: Sorry about last night honestly, just want to see
   you

(text) 11: Miss your face

This kind of textual outpour would have made my heart race before. I would have agonised about my response and tried and failed to be cool and defiant. I reply effortlessly, without pretence.

Me (text): I was busy.

Three dots appear immediately.

Fred (text): How about the cinema one night?

Fred suggesting the cinema is as surprising as him telling me he's now an MP or an astrophysicist. We've never been on an actual date. The most romantic thing he's ever done for me was letting me have a chicken wing from his Deliveroo (which arrived as I was leaving).

Him (text): I just think it would be nice to do something
   together

Me (text): Why?

Him (text): I've missed u

Me (text): Are you serious?

Him (text): Meet me at 6 at Odeon LSQ?

I look up the films that are playing at the Odeon LSQ. None of them seem appealing, but I haven't been inside a cinema in so long.

Me (text): Sure.

I want to fall back asleep – this can't be real – but I drag myself to the shower. I use Hannah's eye cream to help me look less puffy. I wear one of her dresses I stole years ago. It was too small for her anyway, her boobs outgrew it. I never told her I had stolen it and she went crazy looking for it, which I enjoyed at the time but now feel bad about. I tie my hair back and attempt liquid eyeliner. One eye is lopsided but I don't correct it. I wear the black ballet pumps I wore to her funeral, the ones I've been wearing constantly ever since.

I get the Tube, enjoying the feeling of curiosity because it's rare for me to feel anything other than numb now. I count how many people I've slept with since him. Fewer than five, and none since Hannah died. I worry that he'll see it instantly, as though 'My sister died' is tattooed on my forehead. I take some deep breaths and remember that my mission is to have sex, to watch a film and to eat a shitload of popcorn.

He's outside the cinema when I arrive, though I'm surprised I manage to recognise him. His long hair is gone, he's wearing a white shirt and blue jeans with boots. He looks totally normal. Where is the paint on his clothes, why aren't his self-done tattoos on display? Why isn't he carrying an easel or a tripod in a bid to show and tell everyone that he's an artist?

He hugs me with one hand on my lower back, like he used to when he was being nice. He's wearing a strong cologne and I don't like it. I don't like his new look. I have to keep swallowing to stop myself from crying, as I realise he's meeting a new person too – Ruth without Hannah. I feel like I'm walking a tightrope – one step wrong and I'll tell him everything and then it's real again, the hell I'm in is real.

So I try to talk as little as possible as he buys the tickets and popcorn. I choose some pick-and-mix. Sweets will get me through this. One-word answers are safest.

Him: You look amazing.
Me: Thanks.
Him: Did you go away or something?
Me: No.

I'm being aloof. Something I've never been before with him, though I've tried.

We sit in the dark cinema. He eats popcorn too loudly, sips too loudly. He also laughs too loudly and looks at me when he's laughing to make sure that I'm laughing too. His white shirt is one size too small, and when he unbuttons it to give him more room to breathe I think of Hannah and her tight brown skirt on the plane.

The film could have been amazing or awful. All I can see on the screen is her.

The film ends and he puts his hand between my thighs. I let him. The lights come on and someone comes in to pick up rubbish. I look at her Odeon uniform while his hand moves higher and higher and I compare it with my Costa uniform. I wish it was navy, and that we had to wear a baseball cap too. Perhaps I should have applied to work here instead, it seems more anonymous with more time spent in the dark. He whispers in my ear, slightly too loudly.

Him: Let's fuck in the toilets?

I hear his words in all their blunt glory. There is no building this up. He's suggesting something and it's something that will of course be clumsy, dirty, unsatisfactory and quick – toilet sex is never a wonderful thing. However, I'm propelled by the fact that he wants me. He wants me again. I do my fake giggle and let him hold my hand and lead me to the disabled toilet to fuck.

The toilet is clean, at least.

He doesn't waste any time and turns me around, so my back is facing him and I'm pressing my forearms into the wall. The tiles make dents in my skin as he pushes himself into me, even though I can tell he's not really hard yet. He keeps trying, slight pain building up in my arms, and I keep thinking about how my knees hurt on the rocks by the cliff. As I knelt down to Hannah and her wrecked body.

He pulls out of me and tries to make himself hard vigorously with his hands, which makes a clapping sound. I turn around to help him but he stops me. I try to go on my knees but he stops me. He keeps wanking himself off harder and harder. I pretend to enjoy it, stroking my nipples over my dress and biting my lips like they do in films.

Eventually he gives up and the clapping sounds subside. He doesn't say anything, and neither do I. He just zips his jeans up and opens the door. I walk out and he begins to close the door on me.

Him: One sec, need a piss.

I feel nothing. I leave the cinema without telling him. I turn my phone off for the long walk home.

# 19

List of things our parents fought about:

Her vocal warm-ups in public
His nail clippings in the sink
Her way of saying, 'Hello, Mr Killjoy'
His way of saying, 'That's that then'
Her lack of care with money, other people's names
and the car
His lack of care with affection, food and us in
shopping malls

He used to be handsome. My dad.

Women would stop and stare at him when he was out with us, looking like an active parent to his two little girls, one geeky, one pretty, taking us out to buy ice cream or stickers. I began to recognise from a very young age that he would come to life in front of young women, and that around my mum he would retreat.

He wrote a sitcom in the late eighties that did quite well. My parents met when my mum auditioned for a supporting role in one episode. He liked her so much that he wrote her character into the second series as a regular. It didn't get a third series. He was somewhat crippled by the success of it, and its sudden ending. They both drank too much while they waited for something else to come along. We were never allowed to watch it, and years later whenever the theme song came on because a repeat was showing, my mum grabbed the control and turned the TV off.

The last family holiday we had was in France. I was nine and Hannah thirteen. The house had a swimming pool and my mother spent all day, every day, lounging next to it, in a swimsuit that she had starved herself for weeks to fit into. My father swam lengths in the morning and in the afternoon he made us do lengths too. Hannah was a good swimmer. For every three lengths she swam, I swam one. My dad called my breaststroke style 'unique', which I took as a compliment.

He took me aside one day in the kitchen to show me something. He had never taken me to the side on my own before so I was excited, and a little scared. He picked me up and put me on the kitchen counter. He had two bits of string laid out flat on the wooden table – one in a straight line, and one curved up and down to create lots of little bumps he called 'hills'.

Him: You are the hills.
Me: Huh?
Him: Which one of these lines do you think is the fastest route?

I traced both strings with my finger.

Me: Ummmmmmm . . . the straight one?
Him: Exactly. But when you swim, you go up and down, up and down – and it wastes time. Try

coming out of the water for a quick breath and getting back down as quickly as possible, without lifting your head out so much.

Me: Oh.

Him: You'll see the difference.

Me: It doesn't matter how fast I am, though, does it?

Him: You never know. What if a crocodile was chasing you?

Me: That would never happen, Daddy.

Him: You don't know that, Ruthie.

I knew he was joking but he said it so gravely.

Dad cycled in the early morning to the local village to get bread and pastries for breakfast while the rest of us slept. One day we decided we'd surprise him, and make our parents happy – so we got up early and set out on our walk. We knew roughly where the bakery was, following a path by a picturesque sunflower field. I got out of breath and made us pause by the sunflowers. Hannah was being quite strict with me, we were on a mission.

Her: Come on. Walk faster, Ruthie –

We ended up running all the way to the bakery, with her pulling me along on one of my 'rides'. The bell tinkled as we clambered through the doors. There was already a queue and the smell of *pains au chocolat* made my stomach rumble. We were next in line when my dad entered. He didn't see us, so we hid and watched him from behind the shelves of tinned olives. A pretty young woman was arranging some bread and Dad skipped the queue and greeted her with a kiss on both cheeks. She blushed. He had a conversation with her in French. I suddenly saw him from a stranger's point of view. He was handsome. He was charming.

This French girl must have been no older than eighteen or nineteen. Hannah got upset and stormed out of the bakery, slamming the door. My dad turned around and saw me standing there, looking confused. We walked alongside him on his bicycle all the way back to the house, silently. Mum staggered out as we arrived, sleepy and hungover, reaching for the bakery bag. She didn't kiss my dad hello or ask us why we were all coming back from the bakery together. She had finished her *pain au chocolat* by the time she reached her spot by the pool.

# 20

Costa, Heathrow Terminal 5

I yawn and feel my skin crack. My mouth is acidic from the steady flow of coffee I've been downing since 5 a.m. I'm on the early shift. As I take their orders, I avoid looking at people's faces. It's easier just to look at the iPad in front of me and ask for their names. So many people have boring names, which makes me feel better about my boring name.

An old man is next in the queue. I can tell he's old by his croaky voice, and I can smell smoke on his jacket.

Old man: Cappuccino.
Me: Small, medium, large or extra-large?
Old man: Large.
Me: Name?
Old man: Why?
Me: Just so we can call you when it's ready −
Old man: But I'm right here −
Me: I know but it's just −

I look up. His face is remarkably wrinkly, like a painting, and his camel corduroy jacket has pin badges all over it.

He looks like the perfect grandpa and I want him to be pleased with me. I wonder if he has children, grandchildren or great-grandchildren. I turn the iPad to face him, and his neon-orange Monzo card looks entirely out of place in his hands.

I never knew any of my grandparents. They were dead before we were born, from cancer and/or suicide. His payment goes through and I smile at him.

Old man: You're nice, aren't you?
Me: Your coffee will be ready at the end of the counter. I'll make sure you get it –
Old man: Sydney.
Me: OK, thank you.
Old man: That's my name.
Me: Listen for Sydney, then. OK?

He walks away and I see his wife waiting for him by the sugar kiosk. She has a walking stick in one hand and a white cane in the other, so I assume she's blind. She looks striking too, with her white hair and long red skirt. Her earrings are so heavy they're pulling down her earlobes.

He must have put them in for her. He must have to do so much for her, every day.

I look at the long queue of people waiting for their coffees. I haven't served a customer called Hannah yet, which is strange, but I'm bracing myself for it. I roll my neck from side to side, looking at the floor as I wait for the next order.

Barista: Sydney. Sydney. Cappuccino. Sydney.

I glance over to Sydney and he's chatting away to his wife, making her laugh. She's holding on to his forearm and her laugh is lovely, her face is kind. I quickly leave my station to deliver his coffee to him. He doesn't say thank you but smiles and puts his hand on top of mine. It's warm.

I get back to the iPad and continue to serve people, as impersonally as possible. Most people don't say hi, hello, please can I have – they just state what they want matter-of-factly. I'm used to this inhuman transaction now; I prefer it. I feel on top of things because I'm making good progress with the queue until someone says 'Hello' and nothing else and I'm forced to look up and see him.

It's Rowan.

He looks tired, he looks older, he looks completely shocked to see me. A pretty woman rushes towards him with a bag from WHSmith. She kisses him on the cheek and I feel sick.

Him: I didn't know you – I mean – How are you?
   I mean –

I look down again.

Me: What coffee would you like?
Him: How long have you worked here?
Me: What coffee would you like?
Him: Ruth –
Me: What coffee would you like, please –
Him: Um – two lattes? – Look –
Me: What size –
Him: Ruth, please –
Me: What size –

Him: Can we talk?

Me: Small, medium, large or extra-large?

Him: Please –

Me: I'll go with large.

I turn the iPad towards him, still looking down. He's standing still. The woman pays with her phone for them both. She touches his arm.

Me: Your coffees will be ready at the end of the counter. Listen for your name.

They move to the side as I serve the next customer. I avoid looking in their direction; my skin is on fire. His name is called and she takes the coffees to a table. He looks back at me and I look away. He follows her. The queue dies down quickly so I go and clean the coffee machine, to get a better look at Rowan and his new fucking girlfriend. He looks sad; she's comforting him with his head down.

I hate that this woman must know about my sister, that we're just a story to her. She's the polar opposite to Hannah: tiny, petite and dark-haired, tattoos all over. They look good together. I want to throw this coffee machine at them; I want to do awful things to her. I go into the back room. I pace up and down, I stamp on a coffee bag, I crouch down and hug my knees.

After a minute Sal comes back and finds me.

Sal: Someone is asking for you, Ruth. A man.

Me: Yeah, I know. I don't want to speak to him.

Sal: He seems nice! Shall I get his number for you?

Me: He's not chatting me up –

Sal: Oh God, your face is all red. Are you OK?
Me: I'm fine. Just – I want him to go.
Sal: OK, I'll sort it.

She comes over and squeezes my arm a bit too hard, and then leaves. I pace around for a bit, dizzy. She comes back two minutes later.

Sal: He says he's not leaving until he can see you.
Me: Tell him he'll miss his plane then.
Sal: OK, I'll sort it. I will actually sort it this time. Ha!

No, not fucking 'Ha', Sal.
I sit down on the coffee-bean bag I just stamped on, feeling sorry for myself. I knew everyone would move on, be happy again and leave me behind. I just didn't think I would have to watch them go on their way. I didn't think they would be this quick.
Sal reappears, thriving on the drama. I wonder when she last had sex.

Sal: He's not going and says he'll wait. He's quite a serious fellow, isn't he!

Enraged, I get up and push the doors open. He's standing by the muffins. I go right up to him, with his girlfriend in the background watching, the whole queue watching.

Me: Do you want my permission?
Him: I've tried calling you, texting you –
Me: So what? What do you want from me?
Him: It's been eight months, Ruth.

I do the maths quickly in my head. It can't be eight months. It can't be.

Him: I tried – I wanted to tell you –
Me: Just fuck off.

He's about to cry, he's about to cry. I don't want to see his pain, why would I want to see his pain? His shoulders hunch and he puts his hands over his face. His fingernails are dirty. He did try to text me. He did try to call me. I couldn't reply. I didn't even read them.

Him: I miss her. Don't think I don't –

I can't be human. I can't see it from his side, from anyone else's side.

Me: Well, you've got a new girlfriend.
Him: But that doesn't mean –
Me: I can't get a new sister.

I gesture to the pretty tattooed woman who's waiting for him.

Me: Have a nice trip!
Him: I won't go. I'll stay here and we can talk –
Me: No –
Him: I'll wait for you to finish work, I won't go –
    I'll do anything to make this better.

I don't believe him. He wouldn't stay. He's fucking with me.

Me: It can't ever be better. Just stay away from me.

I turn my back on him, return to the iPad. I start serving customers again. Sal comes up and squeezes my shoulders too tightly. I brush her away coldly.

Me: It's cool, I'm fine.
Sal: You're sure you don't want to leave early? I can
    tell them you're sick.

I shake my head. The thought of having to go home, or to Hannah's flat with no one to see and nothing to do but eat and watch TV and stare at walls in the dark makes me too sad. I put on a smile for Sal. I serve a Harry, Monica and Dave before the names get blurry again.

At the end of the shift I manage to escape without Sal giving me another fucking squeeze, or asking any more questions about the 'serious fellow'. As I walk through the airport towards the Tube, I glance at the departures board. I guess where they're going.

# 21

The Mediterranean

I am given an ice pack for the back of my head. Apparently I fainted. I also have no recollection of anyone putting a huge plaster on me, but there is one on my arm now.

When they forced me to leave her side, I tucked the sheet back over her and pretended she was just going to sleep. As we left, the concierge told me his name was Noè, and said a car from the hotel would be here to pick me up soon. He let me keep the hotel towel, which he draped over my shoulders. It's now covered in blood. I still have sand between my toes, my blister is festering. I'm in the mortuary corridor on a cold chair and I can't move. I will not move.

Rowan calls again. Eight times now. The vibration makes me jump each time. I guess it's been hours.

A policeman is sitting next to me writing notes, and I don't know what I've told him, I don't know if I've said anything. His breath smells of coffee and cigarettes and his skin is grey and crinkled. Maybe he'll die soon too. He says there might be an inquest in the UK. He says her body will be able to be transported back to the UK 'in a few days, hopefully'.

The way he said 'hopefully' hurt me. She's like an Amazon package now. My skin feels tight from the tears and the seawater and I'm extremely thirsty, but I won't drink if she can't.

Rowan calls again. Nine times now.

The hotel car arrives and the driver gives me a hug, like she knows me, like I asked for one. She must have been told. I don't want to get in the car, I can't leave my sister. But the driver opens the car door and suddenly, I am. I'm leaving her.

I need to sleep.

We get to the hotel and Rowan is standing outside the main doors. I look at his face and I know that he doesn't know yet. I walk towards him looking down, pulling the towel around my shoulders. It's dark and cold and I'm still in my swimsuit. His sunglasses are folded on his T-shirt, the same navy T-shirt he wore when I first met him in that City Pret.

I shake my head and collapse to my knees, I can't speak. The driver takes him aside and I hear the words. Cliff. Jump. Hit. Head.

Rowan doesn't say anything. His face doesn't really move but his whole body stiffens. She ushers him to sit down on the chairs outside the hotel. She comes back to me and strokes my back, while another person hands me some water and some paracetamol. I take them, without water. I ask for a sleeping pill. They go to find one for me as I lie down on the tarmac.

I wake up hours later in the hotel room, our hotel room, to the sound of banging. It's the middle of the night. I turn on the light and I do a double-take. Rowan is sleeping on the small sofa, his legs hanging off the side. I don't remember allowing him to stay in here.

111

Where would I have slept tonight, if Hannah had been here? I would have been alone, in another room she must have secretly got for me. How long ago did she plan for him to come? I feel betrayed.

I walk closer to him, unsteady on my feet. Tears streak his cheeks; his pillow is damp like mine. I realise the banging is coming from the people next door having sex. I thump on the shared wall. They don't stop. I thump again. They still don't stop.

I want him to wake up so we can talk about it, so we can go through it step by step to try to understand what happened, to clarify that it's my fault, because it must be my fault – but I realise the only person capable of walking me through it step by step would have been Hannah. I take more paracetamol and go back to bed.

I wake up in the morning and he's gone. A note on the hotel headed paper is next to me: 'I'll be downstairs.'

I'm still in my swimming costume, but I don't want to take it off. My feet look blue, still sandy. My scalp stings. I'm also still covered in blood, hers and mine.

I put on a hotel robe and leave the room, forgetting the key as usual. I head in the wrong direction, away from the lifts, so I go down the stairwell. It's strangely cold. I count eighty-seven steps. I push open the door to the hotel lobby and it's bustling and too hot. Happy people in hats and sunglasses, taking themselves out for the day to the beach, stuffed from breakfast.

I see Noè bent over by Reception, yawning. The receptionist brings him a cup of coffee. He looks up and sees me, smiles kindly but then stops himself. Smiling is inappropriate. I feel silly in this robe, I feel silly my sister isn't with me, so I walk straight past him following the smell of pastries.

Rowan is sitting alone on the veranda, looking out to sea. His hair is a mess and he's wearing a jumper even though it's so hot out here. He has a glass of water in front of him, nothing else. I sit down opposite him, having drifted in and ignored the request for my room number. I don't say anything and watch the waves. His phone vibrates. He lets it ring out, the vibration making the water in his glass tremble.

A waitress arrives and asks if I would like anything from the kitchen or if I would like to serve myself. He speaks for me.

Him: Just some water for now, thank you.

His phone vibrates again. He lights a cigarette but doesn't smoke it. Finally, he looks at me.

Him: Your parents. You need to tell them.

I shake my head and look inside to the piles and piles of pastries, the big bowls of fruit, the bacon and eggs, sausages and bread. I want to eat it all, but also – never to eat again.

Him: I'll tell them.

My glass of water arrives. Rowan looks at me again with his bloodshot eyes as he picks up his phone to make the call. The first call to make it fact.

I wonder what my parents are doing at this very moment.

# 22

Costa, Heathrow Terminal 5

A fire alarm has gone off and now we stand in the car park in our work groups. WHSmith, Costa, Boots. We don't integrate. Everyone is joking, chatting, some are taking selfies. Passengers are delayed from going inside, flustered that they might miss their flight. I try to spot the angriest people, any upset people. I find watching other people breaking down in public extremely cathartic.

Five minutes later we're allowed back in. No one says anything about what caused the alarm, if it was a real fire or only a drill. People are just grateful for the break from work. As we make our way inside, I walk behind the WHSmith couple I saw fucking in the back room. He squeezes her bum discreetly as they go through the rotating doors. Her ginger hair is scraped even more tightly into a ponytail than I've seen before and the top of one of her hair extensions is poking out. I want to know why she bothers with extensions – are they for him?

I watch them from my iPad position as they get back to work. She's stacking crisps, he's on the tills. At one point the shop is quiet so they meet up and have another chat. I find them fascinating. What could they possibly have to talk about? They spend all of their time together, work together, get the Tube together. Is that what real love is? Never running out of things to talk about? I won't ever have that.

On my lunch break, I am overcome with hopelessness. I open my notebook, and I see her, waving to me, on the blank page. I've eaten a panini that I toasted myself, and drank a hot chocolate that was made for someone else by accident so I took it. I draw the outline of her face from memory, wishing she was in front of me posing, like she would do from time to time on public transport. I draw her chin too pointy, lips curved too much upwards, so she looks pleased with herself. I hate it, it's not her. I rip the paper out and scrunch it up as Sal comes in and sits nearby.

I'm too self-conscious to draw in public so I stop and get out my phone.

Sal: Have you eaten?
Me: Yeah, I've eaten.
Sal: Nice?
Me: Yeah, it was nice.

It wasn't that nice, I couldn't taste it, and it wasn't quite hot enough – but this is the first real conversation I've had today. I google 'How to fake conversations when you're sad'. The results are too depressing so I go back to work before my break ends, leaving Sal alone.

The monotony of my job gives me some comfort. I know what I'm doing for the next four hours; I don't have to think about me.

On the Tube home, before it goes underground, I get

a text from Fred which is surprising after the recent toilet-sex failure.

Fred (text): Send me a picture

I stand where the train connects, with my back to the empty carriage. I pull one boob out from under my bra and take a photo. I slot the boob back into my bra and turn around. The photo is blurry but I send it anyway, glad to have some kind of Tube activity to stop my brain.

I see the three dots.

Fred (text): No, both of them.

I turn back around, haul the other boob out, take a photo. Then I put the boob back in and send the photo with the text:

Me (text): Put the photos together.

I wish I could see his reaction to my joke – I'm pleased with it. As I turn back around, there's a man in glasses sitting right there behind me, and quickly he looks down at his paper. He's seen the whole charade and looks worried I might flash him. I nearly do.

I get home and go straight to my bedroom to change into my Adidas tracksuit and order some food. I see that dust has settled on Hannah's urn but I don't have a duster. I made fun of her for owning a duster, said she was like a little old lady.

I gather up some empty plates and glasses to try to make the room less grimy. I've never been a particularly messy person but I guess I am now. I put the TV on and watch the ending credits roll for an episode of *The Simpsons* as I wait for my food to arrive, annoyed that I've missed the episode. I can't sit still and one eye keeps twitching; everything feels like it's twitching.

My phone vibrates.

Fred (text): No. Both together. In one photo. Now.

His demand depresses me and proves that he didn't find me funny. I forget about him quickly as my order is here and I rush downstairs. As I open the door I hold out my hands to retrieve the bag, hoping the Deliveroo man doesn't say, 'Enjoy your evening,' but he's already gone and the bag is on the doorstep. Then I hear my name being shouted from the street and see Leila rushing towards me. Fuck. I close my door.

Leila: Wait. Please –

She rings the buzzer as I hide in the corridor. I smell my food and suddenly don't want it. She buzzes again and again until I have to open the door. Her face looks pained; she's manipulating me.

Leila: I spoke to Rowan today – he says you're –
Me: I'm fine.
Leila: I know you might be upset about Rosa –
Me: Rosa?
Leila: Rowan's new – um –

Of course her name is a sexy and romantic and beautiful name like Rosa. Hannah would have hated her name being Rosa.

117

Me: He's a fucking dick –

Leila: I just wanted to check how you are –

Me: Leila, we're not friends. You don't need to check up on me –

Leila: Hannah would want me to make sure you're not doing anything stupid, that you're looking after yourself –

I hold up my Deliveroo bag.

Me: I'm eating, I'm breathing. Tell Rowan to go fuck himself.

Leila: He has to be allowed to move on, Ruth. We all do.

She's wearing a huge coat which makes her head look tiny.

Me: Stop posting photos of Hannah on Instagram.

I slam the door. I hear her standing still for a minute before walking away. Did she drive here? She was wearing flip-flops, as though she'd got dressed quickly for an emergency. I am the emergency.

I walk up my stairs, depleted. I sit down halfway up and rest my head against the cold wall, thinking of all the ways Leila tried to take ownership of Hannah during their friendship. Like by regularly buying her infuriating femi-nist-but-digestibly-feminist-slogan cards and notebooks. *'You go, girl!' 'Girl Boss!'*

They met at university and Hannah outgrew her intel-lectually but never stopped being her friend, because she was loyal to a fault. I know Hannah would have even been encouraging about Leila's new career as a 'Grief Insta-Guru'. She was encouraging and supportive of everyone.

I get back into my flat and lock the doors. I put *Hollyoaks* on mute and make up the actors' dialogue in my head, something Hannah and I used to enjoy doing because we got so bitchy. I open my food. I'm not hungry any more but I just need to keep chewing till I pass out. Later, I find a box of bread sticks in my kitchen. They're stale but I eat one after another, watching *The One Show*. I write a list in my notebook.

Things I wish I had said one minute ago:

Before I can start it, my phone vibrates.

Fred (text): Come over.

# 23

I wake up to find a hand clutching my left boob and a flashback of Fred lighting one of his new scented candles. My head is pounding.

His flat is familiar to me, but everything looks new and extremely neat. The damp smell has gone and his broken window is fixed. He has curtains now, rather than strung-up towels or newspaper. An old sofa, which I've only ever seen covered in clothes, now has a knitted blanket draped over it, and the scented candle sits on top of a crate I've seen on Etsy.

He squeezes my boob so I know he's awake.

Me: You got curtains.

I wait for the hint that he would like me to leave ASAP. I grew familiar with his hints, which was always one of these four:

1. Getting straight in the shower after sex, not speaking to me
2. Going to the toilet and shouting that he was going to 'be a while'

3. Playing PlayStation and making huffing sounds, not speaking to me
4. Putting my clothes on the bed and telling me he needed to have an 'important phone call'

But this time, I'm the one who wants to leave. I need paracetamol and my own bed. I sit up and aim to get dressed, but he pulls me on top of him and starts kissing me. I feel self-conscious, I feel disgusting and try to piece together what must have happened last night. I know I drank wine. I know I drank a lot of wine. He continues to kiss me slowly and play with my hair. I don't like it, it feels like a head massage and I don't trust it – he must know about Hannah, he must follow Leila online or have found out somehow. He's just being extra nice because he feels sorry for me.

I close my eyes and I see Hannah. She's blowing me a kiss, before she jumps. I want to zone out. So I get on top of him and start fucking him. I look around his room. His Mick Jagger poster is in a frame now; he has a shoe rack. I still see Hannah, I can't stop seeing Hannah. She'd be so annoyed I am here, that I've let him in again.

Afterwards he falls back onto the bed and checks his phone. I go to the bathroom. It's been so long since I've had sex that I forgot how messy it is, and how many secret toilet trips are involved. He didn't ask if I was on the pill, I didn't make him use a condom. Maybe he'll give me cash for the morning-after pill like he once did before asking me to leave.

I don't have a full-length mirror at home, so I make the most of the chance to analyse my figure in his. I have got bigger since the last time I was here. I'm fuller in the face. Softer. More like Hannah.

Baffled by his new clean bathroom, I check under the cupboard to see if my make-up bag is still there, hidden away because I was too timid to ask if I could leave my toothbrush. It's still there. I open it and find my toothbrush and a 'shimmer' cheek highlighter which I sometimes applied just before we fucked, thinking that would help things along. I tie my hair up and wash my face with his exfoliator, use his moisturiser which is specifically for male skin but I don't care.

I walk back out of the bathroom naked, feeling the new aspects of my body, my new jiggle. I don't care if he finds my make-up bag, I don't care what he thinks about my body. I feel nothing except the slight pain in my vagina, which is shell-shocked. It feels nice to have something physical to focus on.

Before I can stop him, he takes a photo of me as I walk towards him. Sound on, flash on. I think of Hannah mid-jump.

Me: Don't –
Him: You got a new body.

He gestures for me to lie down with him. I obey because it's easier, putting my hand on his chest so I can feel his heart beating. This heart will stop one day.

I imagine his funeral. Would I go? He starts to drift back to sleep, with a half-smile. I pretend I'm drifting too.

I look back as I leave, unsure of the new Fred, unsure of myself.

# 24

I walk home along the canal, like I used to. A nursery group crosses my path. Tiny children in pairs holding hands in neon overalls with something that looks like a rope tying them all together. They stop to feed the ducks. The nursery workers, about my age, are having an animated conversation about their upcoming night out which seems inappropriate around children. I listen and judge.

Pigeons start flocking over to get fed as I catch a glimpse of my slouching reflection in the water.

I stop by a new coffee place halfway back to my flat. The type of cool place that has no name and eighteen different types of coffee bean. The kind of place I used to like before I worked at Costa and realised the quality of the coffee beans doesn't matter if somebody you love dies suddenly.

I order a flat white and the barista tells me they only have oat milk, is that OK? And I want to say, 'No it's not fucking OK, it will never be OK,' but I don't. These baristas wear aprons made out of coffee-bean bags. I can see the huge turnstiles at the back, and a woman pouring beans into a funnel.

I am handed my coffee and take a sip. It tastes amazing.

I finish it in three sips and I run all the way home and go straight to my bathroom and of course I have a UTI already. I have a new rule of only allowing myself to check Instagram when I'm on the toilet. So I get out my phone to kill some time while I try to wee, ignoring the pain.

My fingers and thumbs move without my control. I search for Rowan's account and immediately she comes up on his feed, in the last photo he posted a few weeks ago. It's a picture of Rosa drinking a cup of coffee, her tattooed fingers and chipped maroon nail varnish cradling the handle, a rainbow tattoo on her wrist. It's the only one of her I can find, and his first post in a long time. I scroll down to see photos of Hannah. Beautiful happy Hannah. There is no post to say that she died; to the Instagram world he just got a new girlfriend. Hannah has quickly become something you have to scroll back to find.

I click on his coffee-cup photo of her to see if she's tagged. She is, which upsets me. Tagging someone feels intimate. They're serious. I go to her profile and scroll through every photo this woman has posted going all the way back to 2012. She's had multiple personalities since then. She's clearly self-aware, she looks really good but not annoyingly posey in any of her pictures. She's going for that laid-back, naturally beautiful 'I just get along better with men' vibe.

She hasn't instagrammed Rowan yet apart from an artful photo of him from behind, walking in the dark. The street lamps are lighting up his hair slightly. He's holding a cigarette and is walking through the cloud of smoke.

Hannah never instagrammed Rowan. She was scared of jinxing their relationship. Her Instagram still exists. I make sure it's still there every few days. I can't bring myself to look at her posts but I need to know she still follows me, and that I can still follow her. Her followers went up after she died. Fucking creeps. The post I made about her death – I know all of her passwords – got 3,315 likes. It was a photo of her I took on the morning of her twenty-eighth birthday, clutching a pink fleece blanket I got for her from a service station.

*For those of you who don't know, Hannah died tragically in an accident last Wednesday. Details of her memorial are below.*

I didn't want to write 'passed away' because that made it sound nicer than it was. Passed away is for old people who die in their sleep. Passed away sounds calm.
My phone vibrates.

Fred (text): You left without saying goodbye. <sad emoticon>
    See you soon? X

He's never used emoticons before. Not with me, anyway. I don't want to lose the option of someone familiar, so I text him:

Me (text): Yeah, see you soon x

He knows nothing about me, knows nothing of Hannah, and I feel ashamed. I don't even know what star sign he is, though Hannah diagnosed him as a Gemini early on.
I get off my phone and the toilet, unsuccessful. I line some pants with a sanitary towel and cover myself in

125

Sudocrem, a trick a girl who had lots of sex taught me in sixth form. I have two slices of toast with butter and Marmite; then another. I open my kitchen window to let some air in. I look up at the sky – a beautiful spring day with pretty clouds.

I don't like how nice the weather is.

# 25

2008

I helped her pack. At least I thought I was helping her. Then I realised she was taking everything I had placed into the suitcase back to our shared wardrobe. Half of the suitcase was full of her make-up and cheap high heels; she was barely taking any clothes.

Me: You're gonna form a new identity up there with a new wardrobe, aren't you?
Her: Maybe. But the bonus is you get to keep my clothes.

She was leaving for Manchester University. I was fourteen, hated school, hated my friends and now Hannah was abandoning me and I hated my life. I lay on her bed, pounding my fists to get her full attention. She came over and sat next to me, pushing my shoes off the bed.

Her: You can come up and visit literally every weekend.
Me: How? I can't drive.

Her: Get the train –
Me: With what money?
Her: Get a job!

She started plaiting my hair and I got tingly; I felt at once so loved and so scared of the impending change. She took the hair tie out of her plait and used it for mine.

Me: You really wouldn't mind me coming up every
   weekend?
Her: I'd love that.

I believed her. She pushed me back onto the bed and continued to pack.

Me: What if you get a boyfriend, though?
Her: I'll still want you to visit.
Me: What if he doesn't want me to?
Her: Then I'll dump him.

I pulled my new plait to make it slightly looser. She always did them too tight.

Me: What if I get a boyfriend and he doesn't want
   me to visit you?
Her: Then I'll kill him.

I laughed. But she didn't; her expression was suddenly quite severe.

Mum said I couldn't go with Hannah to Manchester to drop her off because I had school the next day. Dad said he could never focus on driving with both of us in the car anyway. Hannah waved out of the window until

I couldn't see her hand any more. I stood outside crying until Mum told me to come in. We watched *The West Wing* and had a Chinese takeaway that night. The only thing I could eat was my fortune cookie.

*A Golden Egg of Opportunity falls into your lap this month.*

Mum wanted to switch fortunes because she wasn't happy with hers.

After three episodes Mum fell asleep on the sofa, so I snuck out and went to the park. I saw that a group of teenagers had broken into the bowling green, and were sitting in the middle drinking and riding their bikes, ruining the carefully tended grass. I sat on a bench and texted Hannah. She texted back within twenty seconds.

Hannah (text): I miss you too.

Soon after, I got my first Saturday job and began saving up for train tickets to Manchester.

# 26

Costa, Heathrow Terminal 5

My dad is waiting for me to finish my shift, sitting with the coffee I served him. It's in the massive mug which Costa is famous for, with a handle on each side. You could probably fit four servings of coffee inside, it's basically a bowl. Last week a Japanese family asked me to take a photo of them all holding one. I said no.

When Dad came over to greet me he didn't lean in for a hug, he just started rambling. All I took in was:

Dad: We need to sell Hannah's flat.

I told him to sit down and wait for my shift to finish, and I got back to concentrating on the queue, not letting myself take in the significance of what he just said.

Me: You can tap here and your drink will be ready
      at the end of the counter. Listen out for your name.

These words are now ingrained into me. I serve a Zackary, a Priya and a Sarah. None of them look at my face. Sarah orders a frappé with extra caramel sauce, but we've run out and I can't summon the energy to tell her. I think about running to the back room or hiding in the toilets until my dad goes away. Would he just leave?

I tap the button for chocolate sauce, and wait for Sarah to get shitty with me, but she doesn't even notice the substitution. How could someone miss that? It makes me smile just as my dad turns around to look at me. He looks reassured in that moment, that his daughter is still able to smile. He doesn't need to know that the smile was because of fucking chocolate sauce.

I find it strange that he's here, that he insisted on coming all the way to Heathrow. I last saw him at the funeral and we've avoided each other since. He looks like he's been up for days and hasn't taken a sip from the giant mug yet. He's staring vacantly ahead, occasionally jotting something down in his black Moleskine notebook of 'ideas'. He's always used a black Moleskine with blue ink. As a girl I found one he'd left on the sofa, and out of curiosity I looked inside. A couple of the pages were dense with tiny illegible handwriting, but most pages were bare, with just scattered words and sentences like:

Umbrella stand – make more of
The tiger analogy
Ponds, check

I was confused, because he carried it everywhere, and always seemed to be writing, but I couldn't ever seem to find the evidence. I decided that he must write in invisible ink so people couldn't steal his magical ideas.

I think he's still writing his novel, the same one he's been working on for ten years.

'Dream big' is what he used to say to us. He usually

131

said this kind of thing when he was drunk and had been awake for more than thirty-six hours. We'd be having our cereal, and he'd stand in front of the cartoons and tell us how lucky we were because we could do anything we wanted to do. There was never any pressure on us at school, or to get into university, get a 'real' job. He fetishised the artistic life, which, in turn, put Hannah off, and as a result she worked harder than anyone at school.

I see my dad looking as I turn the iPad towards the next customer to pay. I know he's not proud of me, but he wasn't particularly proud of Hannah either, despite her achievements. He doesn't have the faculty to care about anyone else; he's so consumed with his own failure.

On my break, I walk towards him. I see over his shoulder that the page is still empty. He's clutching his pen, the skin by his nails is cracking. He looks up and tries to shield the notebook from me but we both know that I've already seen. He looks angry. I sit down opposite him.

Dad: We have to do this, Ruthie. Let's just get it over with.

I don't look at him; I bow my head.

Me: It's only just happened.
Dad: It might feel that way –
Me: Please, let me sort it out. Give me some time.

He stands up, pushing his chair back, which makes a noise.

Dad: I can get people to do it for us. You don't have to do anything –

Me: But I want to do it. It's her stuff, her things. I'll do it.

He takes a sip from the giant mug and it looks ridiculous. I almost laugh.

Dad: OK. Fine.

Did he prefer Hannah too? Does he hate me?

Dad: Your mother will help, she's aware.

I say what I need to for him to leave.

Me: I'll sort it, OK, don't worry.

He picks up his notebook and puts it in his pocket, so it's folded in half.

Dad: Your mother will oversee everything.

It still feels odd to me when he calls her my mother, it's so formal. They were in love once. Do they both blame me?

Me: It won't all be gone, obviously. I'm going to keep some of her things, Dad.

He leaves as quickly as possible, without touching me or attempting to touch me. I watch him go and then get out my notebook.

Things I want to keep:

Everything.

On the Tube home I chew gum so hard my jaw begins to hurt. To stop thinking about Hannah's things and all the ways I'm being forced to let her go, I focus on what I'll eat when I get to her flat; if I'll order food or have the last of the vegan chicken nuggets she kept in the freezer, which Hannah bought for me in another desperate attempt to get me to go vegan.

She once dragged me to a place she wanted to try which specialised in serving meat that wasn't meat but looked exactly like it. I was reluctant because it was so early on a Sunday morning and I wanted to sleep and I thought we had endless time. I've never understood the point of getting up to go somewhere to eat breakfast when you have breakfast at home.

We sat at a table which had a cow-print vinyl table cover. I didn't like it – I said it felt 'slimy' and was generally horrible about the restaurant decor. We were about to get into a big fight but luckily the coffee and food arrived which made it all OK. She took a photo of me eating the fake bacon. I took one of her eating the fake sausage, which she told me to delete because it looked obscene and then her face froze and she went pale.

Brian had just walked in with an extremely pretty woman, not dissimilar in appearance to a youthful Hannah. Hannah stood up instinctively and I yanked her back down, like a game of whack-a-mole, and reminded her to breathe. The couple were seated at a table on the other side of the restaurant. Their vinyl tablecloth was a pig print, and we watched them as intensely and subtly as possible for the remainder of our meal.

Her: I could go and pour coffee on him? Shall I pour coffee on him?

Me: You'll get arrested if you go anywhere near –

Her: She's twelve. He should get arrested –

Me: He looks so gross. Forget about him.

Her: He doesn't look gross, that's a lie –

Me: Fine –

Her: He's clearly been at the gym, look at his arms –

Me: Stop looking –

Her: I got a fucking coil for him.

I started laughing.

Me: Would it make you feel better if I told you this fake bacon tastes exactly like bacon and that I'm grateful we came here?

Her: Yes.

Me: Good.

I lied, it didn't taste exactly like bacon, but she seemed to relax after that. He saw me on the way out and I mouthed, 'FUCK YOU,' at him, and it felt amazing.

# 27

I find Mum sitting outside Hannah's door. We don't hug.

Me: You're here?
Mum: Your father summoned me.

I swallow; my chest tightens. She's being fake jolly and I hate it.

Mum: You look tired, darling. What have you been doing?
Me: I've been working.

I think she thinks I still work at Wahaca and I can't be bothered to tell her otherwise. I open the door to Hannah's flat and I panic that I've left too many windows open since I was last here; my heart palpitations start.

Me: I don't understand the sudden rush –
Mum: Your father needs the money. His book –

She shakes her head and does a quiet laugh, which is mean of her. She doesn't seem sad. Why doesn't she seem sad?

Me: How are you?
Mum: I'm fine, darling. In fact I had an exciting audition today –

I try to look interested.

I haven't seen her since the inquest, after which she fled the country to be in self-imposed 'hiding'. The tabloid papers enjoyed splaying open and amplifying our family tragedy by calling Hannah 'reckless' for jumping off the cliff. Some papers suggested that she committed suicide, ignoring the fact that hundreds of cliff jumpers visited that spot every day, that it was a popular tourist destination. My parents' faded nineties fame meant that the story was picked up and we were 'papped' arriving at the inquest. There was a photographer hiding behind a bench as we walked towards the court, pulling his camera out like a gun.

Images from that day still haunt me: the flash of that camera finding my face, the long grey walk from the station to the coroner's court on which I saw one magpie and one dead worm, and the face of the frazzled coroner's assistant who I noticed wore heels in the morning and muddy running trainers in the afternoon. Mum wore her sunglasses in the courtroom, and Dad didn't say a word except to ask for a cup of tea when everyone else was having water. He yawned at one point and I worried the journalists would see. My parents held hands as the cause of death was ruled.

'Death by misadventure.'

My mum gets up from the floor now, holding her

shoes. I notice she is barefoot, with chipped black nail
varnish on her toes. The heels of her feet are cracked
like mine. Her hair is freshly dyed dark red with a new
blunt fringe – it almost looks like a wig. She sees me
looking.

Mum: The character I was auditioning for had a
fringe. Do you like it? I suit it, no?

I nod, rather than lie.

Me: Where are you staying?
Mum: Here, tonight, at least. I've been in Norfolk
with a friend.
Me: A friend?

She ignores me, instead of explaining, and we go in.
She looks around the flat and I wonder when she last saw
Hannah. Did they ever meet without me?

Her: We have a lot of work to do.

I hate this 'we', I hate her calling it 'work'. There's the
sound of keys turning in the door and then Leila appears,
wearing her huge coat.
Mum and Leila hug. I want to pounce.

Me: You've got a key?
Leila: Oh, yeah. I've had it for ages.
Mum: Leila's going to help us.
Me: I don't need help. I want to sort it –
Leila: I don't mind –
Me: I want to sort it myself.

I need to get them out of here. This is not their space. Mum hasn't been inside Hannah's flat in years, always preferring to meet us at theatres or fancy restaurants, places she could people-watch and pretend people were watching her. I see her clock the piano and I move protectively towards it.

Mum: I had one like that once. How odd.

Hannah and I found it at a second-hand music shop. We had our initials engraved into it. We varnished it and painted it baby pink. She said she would keep the paint for when she had a little girl and I told her off for being so gender-specific. The first song she chose to learn was 'Maybe This Time' from *Cabaret*.

Leila: Ah, we loved coming back here and singing after nights out.
Me: What?
Leila: God, her voice was amazing, wasn't it?
Mum: I got her singing lessons at secondary school.

My face feels very hot. Bullshit – there was no way Hannah brought people back to her flat and had sing-alongs. She would have told me if she'd sung with anyone else. But then why would Leila lie? And why is my mum lying about singing lessons? I want to look in my books on death and see if it's normal for people to start making shit up when someone dies.

Me: I'm having a shower.
Leila: OK, we could start labelling stuff? I bought some labels.

139

Of course she bought fucking labels, from her favourite shop Paperchase no doubt, with unicorns on. Mum comes up behind me and squeezes my shoulder.

Mum: Your father has stopped the water apparently, and the electricity will go soon.
Me: What the fuck –
Mum: You look bigger, darling. Have you been stress eating –
Me: Yeah, I have. Have you?

Her cheeks flush, I forget how easy she is to rile. Weight and Career. Two subjects I can use to floor her.

Me: You don't have to be here. Please let me handle everything. Please –

I make myself cry, to get what I want. Mum backs away from me, Leila comes over to hug me but I turn my back on her. I cry louder and say again –

Me: I need to do this on my own.
Mum: Stop screwing up your face. Crying isn't good for your skin –
Me: Hannah would want me to do it –

She knows I'm right. She never tried to get in between Hannah and me. Our relationship made her role somewhat obsolete and she didn't fight it. Now, she wants an escape and I'm giving it to her. I go to the bathroom, lock the door and sit on the floor with my back against it. I hear them talking outside, Mum suggesting they go and get a drink, Leila saying she'd still like to help. Eventually they leave.

I turn the shower on, I don't care if it's cold. I have been expecting my dad to do that for weeks. I get undressed. The freezing water hurts but I want it to. I close my eyes and cry, properly this time. When I get out, I grab my phone from the floor. Dripping and naked, I text Rowan. It's time to include him.

Me (text): I have to clear her flat out. Is anything yours?

I get dressed in Hannah's clothes, still shivering, and leave the flat in search of some non-vegan food.

# 28

Maybe he won't reply.

I sit at a bus stop near her flat and wait, eating a bag of stale crisps. I check the expiry date on the packet and see that they went off last year. Before she died. A bus drives by, completely full. A mother with a buggy sits next to me and she makes a little grunt as the bus passes but doesn't look that bothered. Her baby won't stop smiling at me and the mother notices and smiles too. I don't deserve smiles. I want to know where they've been, why they're out so late. My phone buzzes.

> Rowan (text): Yes – but I'm not sure what yet – can I come round please?

> Me (text): OK. Be there in one hour.

My wet hair is soaking through my clothes and my black bra is showing through Hannah's white T-shirt. Were the mother and baby smiling because of that? I head back towards Hannah's flat. On the way I go into the newsagent's where I got the stale crisps and put the half-eaten bag back on the shelf. I check the expiry date on a Mars Bar and steal it.

I eat it sitting on her bed.

I haven't changed her sheets since. I've watched her TV but always put the control back in its place. Things haven't really been moved, everything is almost just as she left it, barely touched. Her hands were just here. She still has five Fairy Liquid tabs and half a bottle of orange squash left.

My hair is still wet so I find the hairdryer. One of her strands hangs from it. I take it off and put it in my pocket to add to my collection. I keep them under my pillow like, I imagine, a serial murderer would of his victims. I don't care if it's weird. I dry my hair and use some of her products, scrunching them into the ends like she did so mine is curly too. I look in the mirror and see her in the reflection – she's twirling her hair.

Me: You don't even have curly hair, you just scrunch
    it –
Her: Don't be jealous of my natural curls –

She disappears and the hair-product smell remains; it makes me want to cry. I go through her chest of drawers and try to find a top she wore all the time, a top she got when she was fifteen, with pink hearts. I find it and hold it tight. Then I go into her kitchen and get a plastic bag. I put the heart top in there and wrap it tight, to keep the smell of her contained.

The door buzzes. I see him on the video monitor. He looks tired, but not as tired as me. I leave the door open for him and wait on her little pink sofa, the spot where I've spent so many hours, falling asleep, eating, crying. He walks in and his clothes are cool, as usual. A vintage-looking sweatshirt with a tiger on it and tight grey jeans, emphasising his skinny legs. Where has he just been? She told me he was a musician, but I was so uptight about their relationship, I didn't ask many questions about his career, or lack of it. I hope now that my stubborn lack of interest didn't actually hurt her.

Where he's from, where he lives, how old he is, if he prefers tea or coffee. I know so little. He's a stranger, effectively. A stranger who's seen me wailing, covered in my sister's blood. A stranger who I walked with once by the river, ate granola with.

Other than Brian, who was a doctor, Hannah had always gone out with lawyers or accountants – plain men with stable jobs and money to spare. She met Rowan in Dublin when she was there doing some research and visiting a school for PaperbackKids. He was teaching some small children the piano and she got lost in the school. She told me that story and I felt sick. It was too cute.

Her style changed as soon as she met him; she started to wear tighter, arguably uglier, dresses. She seemed more youthful; she would laugh more, she did less vigorous exercise. She texted me more gifs, more emoticons, was less quick to shout at me. Now he's here. The man who made her truly happy is wandering around her flat but she's not here. This is the place where they fucked and cooked food and watched Netflix and probably made plans for the next weekend, for the future.

I wait for him to ask to keep her piano.

He paces around in silence. I wonder where Rosa is, if she's waiting for him outside or in bed? I don't say anything. I just move from one place to another, watching him. He hasn't been back here since she died. He texted me once a few months ago to ask if he could go round. I never replied. That was cruel of me.

He goes to the kitchen and comes back with a mug. He doesn't need to tell me that it's his. It's brown and chipped and has a guitar on it. He sits on the sofa.

Me: Do you want a cup of tea?
Him: Are you sure?
Me: Yeah. I mean, I'm really bad at tea but I'll try.
Him: I can make it.
Me: There's no milk –
Him: It's OK.

I hover in the kitchen as he makes us tea, knowing where the spoons are, feeling extremely weird. He uses his mug and hands me one I never liked. One of the feminist slogan mugs that Leila got for her. We take it back to the sofa and sit quietly, neither of us drinking the tea, neither of us mentioning the lack of milk. I'm afraid I'll cry but I feel compelled to talk to him.

Me: My parents want me to start getting rid of her stuff. I don't want to.

He doesn't say anything for too long. I watch his forehead crease, lines moving up and down. This must be his thinking face. It's nice.

Him: I can help you.
Me: How?
Him: I know a place.

I yawn and begin to feel the sugar crash from the Mars Bar. I see my Costa uniform on the floor in the bathroom and go and put it all in her washing machine, a washing machine I was jealous of because it's a better one than mine.

She's down to four liquid tabs now.

Him: Let me help you? Please?

I don't feel I can answer him right now. I go towards the bedroom.

Me: I need to sleep now.

I don't close Hannah's bedroom door. I get into her bed, on my side, and fall asleep quicker than I have in months.

In the morning, I wake up to find my clean Costa uniform on the foot of the bed. I get dressed and find him asleep on the sofa. The window is open, his cigarettes and lighter on a chair. He's used his mug for ash. I close the window and think about putting a blanket over him, but don't. I close the door quietly, taking one last look at him, and make my way to work.

On the Tube I write a list of her things which need to be moved. Somewhere, somehow.

List of her things:

Her bed
Her sofa
Her cactus, her plants
Her carpet

Her piano
Her clothes, her shoes
Her pillows, her sheets
Her notebooks, her files
Her books, her records
Her plates, her cups
Her lamp, her mirror
Her pictures in frames
Fuck. Fuck. Fuck.

I almost fall asleep at work, which is weird as I slept for so long last night.

I watch as one employee – I think his name is Marcus even though he doesn't look like a Marcus – is given a plaster by another employee from the elusive first-aid kit. The tiny plastic box looks like a child's toy. Marcus cut his hand while slicing a fucking panini and apparently there's blood all over the chopping board behind me. Everyone crowds around Marcus to check he's OK, but I don't look back. I don't want to see blood this morning because I don't want to think of her blood, her blood on the rocks by the sea, her blood washing off me in the shower.

On my break, I walk to the Starbucks on the other side of the terminal and have a large vanilla Frappuccino with an extra shot, which makes me jittery. I pass by a group of sporty-looking teenagers, presumably off on some kind of school trip abroad. Their teacher stops them so he can take a group photo. He gets them to shout, 'WINNING,' instead of cheese.

I have to clear plates and cups for two hours because the airport is so busy. Everyone has decided today is the day to flee. I hear snippets of conversations at the tables, nothing out the ordinary: who's been left in charge of feeding the cat, watering the plants; sightseeing plans, medication, sun cream. I think about Rowan and how he was curled up like a child on her sofa this morning. What's he doing right now? Is he having morning coffee with Rosa?

On my way home, impulsively I stop at a Snappy Snaps.

I get just one photo printed. When it slides out, hot from the printer, the Snappy Snaps lady picks it up and looks in awe at the photo of Hannah jumping off the cliff. I snatch it back off her.

Snappy Snaps lady: Wow, you look amazing.
Me: It's not me.

I eat popcorn chicken from KFC on the walk to Hannah's, with the photo safely tucked inside my note-book. When I get there, the door is double-locked. I open it and find that there are flat-pack boxes laid out by the sofa with a Post-it on top: 'I got these boxes for you. Let me know how I can help. R'

So he must have had a key too, if he could get back in. Why didn't he use it before now? I check to see if he's taken anything, but everything seems the same. His guitar cup he used for ash sits on her coffee table.

I take my shoes and socks off and sit on the sofa, finishing the popcorn chicken, feeling the carpet I never really liked between my toes. Hannah would have hated me eating KFC on her sofa.

After a while, I text him.

Me (text): I would like your help.

I head straight for her bed and am startled to see that he's made the bed, he's even arranged her pillows. I fall asleep with the photo in my hands. When I wake up disturbed in the middle of the night, I have a text from him.

Rowan (text): Anything x

# 29

I like how he's taking control, even if it's just his way of absolving guilt.

My Uber drops me off outside a huge building which I've never noticed before, even though it's exactly halfway between my flat and Hannah's. A sign, which looks like it was meant to be temporary but has stayed put for years, hangs above the main doors: 'STORAGE ETC.' I see Rowan standing in the car park by his battered old car, which is full of Hannah's things. He holds the door open for me and I try to hide my face from him, swallowing back tears already.

No one is behind Reception. I hear a radio and banging coming from somewhere in the back. I ring the bell on the front desk and eventually a man comes out. He doesn't seem friendly; but that's maybe because he has a large scar across his right cheek and a cigarette hanging out of his mouth. He hands us a form without saying anything and Rowan takes the lead, again, signing the form for me as I look around. There's a dirty sofa behind us, so huge I don't see how it could have got in here or fit in any house. A piece of A4 paper with shaky handwriting is stuck to it: 'TAKE ME'.

A young man appears, barefoot and in a dirty white

T-shirt and shorts, from the room behind Reception. He's sweating and has boxing gloves on. He goes straight up to the scarred man and takes a packet of cigarettes from his back pocket. He must be the son, they look so alike. It hits me that never again will anyone remark upon how similar Hannah and I look when we're out together.

I pay the first month's fee and a deposit and take the key. Rowan tells me to carry on ahead, as he goes back to his car to get the first load of stuff.

I get into a large creaky lift with the dad, whose scar makes him look like a gangster. For a second, as he pushes the button firmly, I prepare myself for something bad to happen, for him to murder me, stab me, shoot me – right here, right now. But he looks at me and his eyes are kind and I wish I could stop being so paranoid every single second of the day.

The lift doors slide open and I follow him down a corridor. There is a delay for a few seconds before the lights flicker on, and I feel calmer in the darkness; it feels appropriate. He leaves me at the door of my unit, and makes his way back towards the lift. I stand still, too scared to open the door. He looks back at me as he waits.

Him: All right?

Instead of saying 'no' I shake the keys at him and attempt a smile. Should I have tipped him? He gets into the creaky lift as Rowan gets out, rolling our suitcase and holding her cactus. I close my eyes as I unlock the door and push it open, thinking of Hannah opening the door to our hotel room and falling on to the bed in delight. I open my eyes to see the small bare room. It's basically a concrete box with a puny ventilation unit. Harsh strip lights, one

151

of which is broken. The air is musky, no windows. My blood pumps faster round my body and I'm glad that she doesn't have to go through this.

The young man from downstairs silently rolls in a trolley, transporting her chest of drawers and her mirror, which I never liked because it was unflattering. He's no longer barefoot. Rowan gives him a five-pound note. The boy thanks him with a big smile, showing a gold tooth.

I go up to the chest of drawers and untie the string around it, which was keeping the drawers in place. I put my hand on top and start inspecting, checking it's not been scratched or damaged at all. Her clothes are still inside, apart from the heart top that I stole. I sit, defeated, on a box. I've labelled this one 'HER CUPS' with a green Sharpie. I cover my face with my hands. He comes close to me, so close that I can hear his breathing, and puts his hand on my back. His hands are cold, like mine.

Him: What about the piano?
Me: What about it?
Him: Would you like that to come here too?
Me: Yes. Everything.

He checks his phone and looks perplexed as he texts. I like the thought that Rosa might be annoyed that he's with me.

# 30

2003

The bell went to signify the end of break time as I got a text from Hannah.

Her (text): Meet me outside the locker room, now.
  OK?

I ran there even though running in corridors was banned, excited that she needed me during a school day. Before she even turned around to see me, I could tell she was chewing bubblegum from the wobble of her ponytail. The bubble popped as I called her name. She looked like she'd been crying; mascara had stained her cheeks.

Me: Jesus, are you OK?
Her: Yeah. You didn't have a lesson, did you?
Me: No.

I lied – I was skipping maths, which was becoming a habit – but I wanted to please her. She pushed open the doors to the locker room, which was on the basement floor of the school. It seemed empty, but she checked every aisle just to make sure. She stopped by a locker that was neither hers nor mine. It had a shitty heart drawn on the front in a permanent marker, even though doodles on lockers were banned.

Her: She thinks she's so special, that she's better than me, better than everyone.
Me: Who?
Her: Gina – fucking Gina –
Me: What's she done?
Her: Parading her new denim designer jacket around –
Me: Hannah, tell me what she's done to you –
Her: That jacket is disgusting anyway –

She opened the unlocked locker door and inside I saw the disgusting denim jacket. It didn't look expensive, but it had a fancy label in so I accepted that it must be. Hannah took the jacket out and put it on. It was slightly too small for her, especially over the shoulders, so she struggled a bit. She took the bubblegum out of her mouth and handed it to me with an unfamiliar glint in her eyes. Then she turned her back to me so I could no longer see her face.

Her: Pound the bubblegum into the jacket.
Me: What?
Her: Stretch the bubblegum out –
Me: Why?
Her: And push it into the jacket. Come on –

Me: I don't understand –
Her: Just do it. Do you love me?
Me: Yes, but –
Her: Then do it.

I stretched the bubblegum out so it was like a thin pancake, and laid it on her back as she bent over.

Her: Right, that's it. Now punch it in with your fist –
Me: That'll hurt you –
Her: I don't care. Just punch the gum in. So it sticks.

She held her ponytail up so it didn't get in the way. I did as I was told. Once the gum was successfully stuck to the jacket, irreparably ruined, I helped Hannah to take it off. She stuffed it back in the locker, grabbed my hand and we ran. She let go of my hand once we were in the clear and kept running. I shouted after her.

Me: Hannah?

But she didn't turn back.

Me: See you after school?

She disappeared down a corridor, as if nothing had happened. I was stunned. I went back into the locker room. I had Post-its in my bag, so I wrote 'SORRY' on one and stuck it on the jacket. Before closing Gina's locker, I saw an Impulse 'Hint of Musk' body spray I'd been wanting to get from Boots. I stole it. Then I ran out again and hid in the nearest toilets. I had fifteen minutes to kill until geography. I sat on the toilet, feeling used, spraying the sickly-sweet aerosol into the air above me and letting it float down over my shoulders.

# 31

I hear the piano as I walk down the corridor towards the unit. I'm scared to go in, that he'll be self-conscious that I've heard him. So I knock first, as if it's his flat. He gets up, nervously opens the door, and I see that the room has been transformed. He's arranged everything already. The bed is where her bed was in her bedroom, near the chest of drawers. The sofa is facing the same direction it was in her sitting room, on top of the carpet. The piano is in the corner. Her lamp is on the bedside table. He sits back down at the keys, anxious.

Him: I hope it's OK –
Me: No, no. I mean, yes. Just weird.
Him: You don't mind?

I don't mind. I like that it feels as though we're in her space, or at least a weird and sad alternate-universe version of it. He relaxes and I sit down, taking in everything. The cactus on the coffee table. The plants near the bed. The TV propped up against the wall. The blanket on the arm of the sofa. He starts singing very quietly, his voice deep and beautiful. My body stiffens in the way that it does when music comes on at a party and everyone starts dancing around freely. I could only ever dance around Hannah.

I try to imagine him serenading her, but I can't. She'd find it embarrassing.

He goes on singing for ages and I find it funny, but I like it. I begin to potter about, checking what possessions are here and what still needs to be brought.

I start stripping the bed and pillows. I put on the clean sheets I've brought from my flat, but I get the corners mixed up like an idiot. He stops playing and comes over to help me, flying the duvet up in the air and down again. He picks up a pillow and hugs it. I don't know what to do, if he wants to hug the pillow for longer or if he wants me to say something meaningful – so I hand him a pillowcase and we begin putting on the pillowcases I bought from Home Bargains when I was starting university. Hannah didn't approve of my Home Bargains purchases. For my next birthday she gave me a silk pillowcase, said it was good for my hair and skin; that it would stop me from waking up with a huge crease in my cheek.

Him: Is it OK if I have a key for this place too? So
    I can sit with her. Talk to her, sing to her.

I like how direct he's being, but I still feel wary. I wait for a bit before responding.

Me: I don't know if I can get on board with the
    'talking with your loved one once they're gone'
    stuff.

His feet start to tap.

Me: But yeah – OK –

He looks grateful and goes back to quietly playing the piano. I need information.

Me: Did she laugh?
Him: When?
Me: When you sang to her.
Him: Yes. At first anyway.

He looks beyond me, like he's remembering a nice moment, and I want so badly to see it too. I want to know everything. I am desperate to know everything.

Me: Did she sing back?
Him: Yes, later on.
Me: Hannah wouldn't sing in front of me too much because she knew I'd get upset because she had a much nicer voice.

He laughs a little and it feels nice.

Him: I was teaching her to play, you know?

I didn't know.

Him: She said you had a nice voice.
Me: Did she?
Him: Yes.

My face feels like it's smashing into a million different pieces as I start to cry, uncontrollably loudly. He comes over to me and sits on the bed. I fling myself back on the bed. He lies down next to me and holds my hand. I don't know how long I cry for.

When I wake up, he's still next to me and it must be morning. We both have our legs hanging off the bed and I'm still in my Costa uniform. I sit up quickly, worried I'm late. He stirs.

Me: I fell asleep. I didn't mean to –
Him: Me neither. Sorry –
Me: I need to go to work.

I go over to Hannah's chest of drawers and find some black leggings. I make sure Rowan isn't looking as I find some of her knickers too.

Him: I'll come with you –
Me: What?
Him: Let me travel with you to work. I have nothing else to do.
Me: Really? It's a long way out –
Him: I know –

We stare at each other and acknowledge that, of course, he knows where Heathrow is. He gets off the bed and needlessly straightens the sheets. I didn't think he would be a tidy person. While his back is turned I duck behind the chest of drawers and get changed. He looks a bit awkward as he accidentally catches what I'm doing.

Him: I'll be outside.
Me: OK.

I see him stroke the piano as he leaves.

As I lock the door I whisper to her, even though it feels stupid.

Me: Bye, Hannah.

# 32

On the Tube there is only one free seat, which he encourages me to sit in. He stands in front of me, like he's my guard. I haven't been on the Tube with someone other than Hannah in a long time, and I don't know whether we're meant to talk. His jeans are so tight and I'm face to face with his lower body and suddenly it's impossible to not think about his dick, and remember what Hannah told me about it. She said it was beautiful.

Me: How can a dick be beautiful?
Her: It needs to be attached to a beautiful person.
Me: You're deluded, you know. You've gone crazy.
Her: Rowan, I've gone crazy with Rowan.

He eventually gets a seat next to me and stares at his phone. I catch a glimpse of his iPhone background and I'm shocked to see that it's a photo of Hannah. He knows I'm looking but doesn't stop.

Me: Doesn't Rosa mind?

He looks awkward, as we both become aware that we are having an intimate conversation in front of strangers.

Me: They all have headphones in, don't worry –

He smiles softly.

Him: I can't change it.
Me: And does she mind?
Him: She just – understands.
Me: She seems very understanding.

I can't help myself. He puts his phone in his pocket.

Me: I stalked her on Instagram. She's very pretty.

He seems unfazed and looks down at my lap.

Him: You have Hannah's hands.

I look at my hands too. I could cry.

Me: I know. We were hand twins. She had better
    nails, though. I bite mine.
Him: Me too.

It's nice to realise that I can still look at my hands and
it's like I'm seeing hers. But now I'm thinking of how I
held her hand on the stretcher, how cold it was, how the
seawater had made her skin shrivel but in a different way
to how it shrivelled in the bath. I'm thinking of her lilac-
painted fingernails.

He puts his hand over mine, sensing my shift in mood.
I watch his foot tapping, as I feel the stares of strangers
watching us, like we're on one of the reality TV shows
I used to love: The Grieving Couple with Tears in their

Eyes having an Intense Chat on the Tube. He grips my hand a bit harder and I like it but don't grip back.

Him: Can I teach you piano?
Me: Why?
Him: I just think Hannah would have wanted me to continue teaching.
Me: I'm sure there are loads of people who want piano lessons –
Him: I want to teach you, though.
Me: So you can pretend my hands are Hannah's?

Before he can answer, his phone vibrates and I see he's got a text from Rosa <pink heart emoticon>. We arrive at Heathrow and are swept up amongst people rushing. Suddenly he's agitated. Maybe it's the crowds and the fact that we have to stand on the escalators because everyone has a massive suitcase. Maybe he wants to get back to her.

Me: Do you think Rosa will mind if you teach me piano?
Him: What? Why would she mind?

I don't answer and walk fast towards work, in front of him on his phone, texting, though I can't stop looking to check he's following.

At Costa, Sal and some other employees see me arriving with him and wave. I wave back. At least they might think I'm normal now because I have someone with me. He waits by the counter as I get Sal to make him a latte, remembering that's what he ordered when he came here last time.

He looks around at the busy airport and I assume he's

thinking about when he was here with Rosa too. How could he not be? Did they have a nice trip? Or is he thinking about the time before, when he was travelling to meet us in the Mediterranean, not knowing Hannah was already dead? Would he still have come if he'd known before he boarded the plane?

I see a woman take a photo of her panini and I begin to get angry. What kind of person takes a photo of their panini and wants to share it publicly? I can't stop looking at her. I find people who post pictures of their food absolutely baffling. The phenomenal confidence that strangers want to see what another basic stranger is putting into their body? Who wants to see your plates, your cutlery, your taste? But Hannah was one of these people. I would text her the second she posted a picture of food, which was usually some kind of variation of avocados on toast:

Me (text): No one wants to see that.
Her (text): The pictures aren't for them, they're for me.

Now I think of the avocados on toast that she ate, which went into her body – a body which was working – when she was here, alive and with me. I don't mind those pictures any more. I don't mind them at all.

I give Rowan his latte and he stifles a yawn which pisses me off.

Him: Rosa wouldn't mind. She knows I've been helping you.
Me: OK. Whatever. I'm extremely grateful.
Him: What?
Me: Nothing, I've just got to go.
Him: OK. Have a good day.

Me: Thanks.

Him: If you need anything just text me. Also – I'd
   really like that key too.

Me: I know. Sure.

I watch him walk away and I think about how easy it
would be to hurt him. Not give him a key. I've got what
I needed from him, all of her stuff is taken care of now.
I could just cull contact right now and make my life
simple. Alone. But he touched my hand on the Tube, so
easily, without fear that I'd bat him away. But it felt nice
waking up and knowing there was another person in the
bed with me.

⋆  ⋆  ⋆

The day passes in a blur of annoying happy people. I
hide in the back room for my lunch break and watch
old YouTube videos of *You've Been Framed*, which are
so funny they make me forget about everything for a
spilt second. I like watching people hurt themselves so
ridiculously but being OK afterwards, I like watching
surprises. I like seeing the dates in the corners on the
old video recordings, dates when she was alive. I write
a list of my favourite clips to remind me to watch them
when I'm feeling the worst.

Top 4 of my favourite clips:

Bride and groom falling into the river as they get
   married on a boat
Bouncy castle deflating as soon as parents get on to
   bounce

Cat in sunglasses on a lilo in a swimming pool having
   the time of its life
Little girl trying to run away from her shadow

Another Costa employee comes over and sits near me,
so I have to stop watching. She's on a video call with her
headphones in and speaks with a heavy accent, I can't
work out where she's from. Her hair is purple and lips
dark red, the same shade my mum uses. Her name tag
says Paloma and I'm jealous. She gets up to undo the top
button of her trousers before sitting down again, like
Hannah used to do. Before she can make eye contact with
me, I go back to work.

★   ★   ★

On the Tube home, I look at the photo and go into a
trance, retracing the steps of that day, our last steps
together. If I'd woken up earlier, so she wasn't alone on
the beach, she wouldn't have got a chance to stare at
people jumping off the cliff and get excited. I could have
distracted her, I could have got into a fight with her – I
could have done something to stop it from happening.
I could have done something.
   A young girl sits opposite me, maybe late teens. She
has dark circles round her eyes and is definitely drunk,
wearing barely any clothes. She has cuts on her stomach
and her legs are goose-pimpled and bruised. People scowl
at her, tut. She is chewing her lower lip and clutching a
charm bracelet. One of the charms is a shell. She puts
her head between her knees, and people move away, even
though the Tube is moving, afraid they'll be vomited on.
The girl doesn't vomit though. She sits back up and looks

like she's just beginning to fall asleep. I go and sit next to her.

Me: What stop are you getting off at?

She doesn't register that it's me who's speaking, and her eyes are now closed, but she answers.

Her: Turn-pike – La-aaa-ne.

Her slurring is bad and I consider staying on the Tube with her, making sure she gets home safely. But I'm also angry with her. I'm angry that she's been careless with her safety tonight, angry that she'll probably be fine. Still, I can't just leave her like this when no one else seems to give a shit. I write on a Post-it:
'PLEASE MAKE ME GET OFF AT TURNPIKE LANE'
I prop it up on her lap. As I reach my stop I make her wake up and listen to me.

Me: You have five more stops. Five. Say 'five stops'
    to me.
Her: F-ive s-tops.

I get home late, have a shower, and order food from a place I can walk to in under five minutes, a place that does above-average spring rolls which I can eat ten of before blinking. I go down to collect it from the front door in just a towel, something I've become lazily accustomed to doing. I eat too much and fall asleep on the sofa, and wake up in the middle of the night with the towel on the floor, naked. Waking up in the night is a

168

curse, because then it's impossible to stop the fucking flashbacks.

At the beginning I would shut the images away like I was swatting a fly – I would distract myself with any other thought, any other image – Kim Kardashian's lips, icing sugar, a neon-pink flamingo, almonds – anything. I would shout out loud 'ALMOND ALMOND ALMOND' or 'FLAMINGO FLAMINGO FLAMINGO' and force my brain to picture an almond or a fucking flamingo. That's stopped working, so I need a new plan.

Ocean sounds, train sounds, bird sounds, white-noise sounds, water-dripping sounds.

I get into my bed and turn on my sound machine. I ordered it late one night, early on after it happened, along with lots of other stuff I don't particularly need, want or use, with money I shouldn't be spending. I lie there thinking madly until I hear the first bird – I turn off my sound machine so I know it's an actual bird. I get dressed in the dark.

I walk to the storage unit.

# 33

I arrive at the storage unit and the boy behind Reception doesn't look up, so I don't say anything to him as I call for the lift. It's 5 a.m.

I notice he's got a bandage around his arm and cuts on his face and that he's reading the *Daily Mail*. I think of Hannah's graduation picture they used in one of the shitty articles about her death. I know she would have hated that photo being shared – she wasn't looking her best that day. It was before she worked out what was actually too much lip liner, and that chestnut lowlights were not in fact 'her thing'.

Even though she posted a lot on Instagram, which usually suggests a mental health imbalance, she had a good, sane relationship with social media. I on the other hand never really posted, but would creep. She used to tell me how much time I wasted stalking strangers. I said that it was just for 'fun' but she knew I ostensibly just used it to track Fred.

The only time she ever lowered herself to my social media level was when she first started seeing Rowan. She wanted to know if he had an account, but didn't want to look herself, so she asked me. His social media presence at that time was quite small. She liked that. Her first mysterious man.

She had one boyfriend who took beautiful pictures of her all the time, and I got so jealous. His name was Francis. She didn't like him much, but he was a rich boy and she thought he could help her with PaperbackKids. He did turn out to give her quite a lot of money for the first few batches of books, and he was completely infatuated with her. He used nice filters and would take photos of her without her realising, never looking at the camera. He posted them all on Instagram. She only found out about the photos because of my stalking. She dumped him soon after, feeling violated. I think she was glad she had a valid excuse to end it.

I took a screenshot of every photo he had taken of her and saved them in a folder on my phone. I felt I had to because she looked so amazing in all of them, and this guy was actually quite a good photographer. She said she was appalled that they even existed, but sheepishly asked me to send them all to her. When I went through Francis's Instagram I scrolled back and back and back to see that he had a habit of photographing women without them knowing, so Hannah wasn't the first. I counted five girlfriends in his Instagram lifetime. None of them were named or tagged, just anonymous pretty creatures. Things to be liked.

I checked up on him the other day and he's now a beard influencer/enthusiast, proudly posting a picture of his 'designer' beard daily. Hannah would have found that funny.

The lift is taking for ever to arrive, and making its scary sounds. I look over at the boy at Reception and wonder if he has a girlfriend. I'm not sure why I like knowing strangers' relationship statuses. He has what Mum would call a 'weak' jawline, and mild acne, but I like his black eye and his face. He could be in a cartoon. He catches me looking at him and smiles, once more revealing his gold canine.

Him: You're here early –
Me: Is there a stairwell?
Him: You don't want to go in there.
Me: Why?
Him: Wait for the lift.
Me: But it sounds like it's broken.
Him: It is. Still works, though.

He keeps smiling at me. I don't know what to do other than smile back.

Him: I'm Mickey.
Me: Ruth.

I want a new name, I should have a new name, for the new sister-less me. I could change it. I told my mum when I was thirteen that I was changing it to Destiny as soon as it was legal and she said that she didn't mind. I kept saying names, trying to find one she'd be annoyed about, but she liked them all, or couldn't be bothered to dislike them, so I never went through with it.

Me: You shouldn't read that paper.
Him: Why?
Me: It's all lies.
Him: I know.
Me: So why are you reading it?
Him: Because my phone's on charge.

The lift arrives.

Him: Your boyfriend's up there already.
Me: Oh. No, he's not. He's – my sister's.

I get into the lift. He waves as the door shuts and the lift seems to go up faster than usual. This time I hear the piano before the lights come on. I stand still, face to face with the door, before realising that Reception guy is probably watching me on CCTV. I find the camera and wave to it. Jesus, am I flirting?

I push open the door. Rowan stands up shiftily.

Him: Hi –
Me: Hi.
Him: The boy downstairs let me in.
Me: His name's Mickey.

I don't know why I told him that. He closes the piano lid and sits on the floor, cross-legged on the carpet. He looks hopeless.

Me: I'll get you a key today.

I almost say sorry. I think about taking off my coat, but I've forgotten what I'm wearing underneath. All I know is that I'm definitely not wearing a bra.

Him: How are you?
Me: Fine. Just cold. You're here early.
Him: So are you.

I keep the coat on and sit opposite him. I cross my legs too like we're in primary school, sitting on our assigned spots on the carpet. His eyes look wired, ten-coffees awake.

Him: I couldn't settle and – I have a gig in Brighton
  tonight and wanted to clear my mind –
Me: A gig?
Him: I don't really do them any more. I guess I just
  – I don't know why, really. I just needed to play
  again. I haven't since –
Me: Cool.

I don't want to know about what he did before, or
what he's going to do. I look at his arms, bare. He's in a
grey T-shirt which has holes in. I try to work out if it is
truly old or if it's one of those 'distressed' T-shirts that
costs £50. I can't imagine him spending money on clothes,
or at least I hope he doesn't. Maybe Rosa bought it for
him. I notice his tattoo, a childlike drawing of a boat. He
begins to rub the tattoo softly with his hand.

Him: I got it for Hannah.
Me: A boat?
Him: A kid from PaperbackKids did this drawing for
  her and she loved it so much.

Now I feel guilty I haven't got a tattoo. I go over to
the bed and fall face down. As I land I smell her, even
though she's not here and the sheets have been washed,
even though it's been so long.

Me: Can you still smell her?
Him: Yes.

I curl up on the bed.

Him: You OK?

I'm a bad sister for not getting a tattoo.

Me: I just want to sleep. To be able to sleep well.
Him: I don't think anyone really sleeps 'well'. Do you?

I sit up.

Me: What?
Him: I just think we all have trouble in the night,
    even if we don't realise.
Me: You mean bad dreams?
Him: Yeah. Our subconscious fucks with us.
Me: Maybe.
Him: I've always had bad dreams. I get maybe a
    couple of hours but I spend the night just thinking.
    Safer than dreaming.

He stands and paces around. Things about him begin
to add up, like his tapping, his thin-ness. He's always doing
something.

Me: When you sleep, do you dream of her?
Him: Yes.

He sits on the bed next to me, the bed they were
together in. This is where they made love, this is where
they fucked.
    Almond, almond, almond, flamingo, flamingo, flamingo,
flamingo.
    He lies down. I notice the bump in his trousers; the
material has bunched up to make it look like an erection.
Or maybe he does have an erection. I panic. My heart
thumps so strongly he must hear it too.

He moves his legs onto the bed and folds into a foetal position. His chest rises and falls. I can't work out if I want to jump on him, hit him, have him hit me, or if it's that I want him to fuck me. He could be anyone, we could just have sex and pretend he's not him and I'm not me.

I imagine what his mother looks like; his parents must be beautiful to have made him.

I get up and begin sorting, even though I don't want to, even though I've been putting it off. I go through a box of Hannah's paperwork, piles and piles of A4 paper, all of which can be thrown away. Why did she keep pointless admin stuff from years ago? Then, luckily, I see a doodle she did in the border of one random page. It's a sketch of a palm tree with a girl sitting underneath as a coconut falls. It's different to her usual style of drawing, must have been done years ago.

Rowan sits up again.

Him: Do you want to come to this gig with me
    later?
Me: In Brighton?
Him: Yeah –
Me: I don't know –

I watch his feet tapping again. My anxiety builds.

Him: It might be good for us.

Us? I fold her doodle and put it in my pocket. It feels as though I'm stealing something.

# 34

We are now in his car on the motorway. I need a wee and we've been driving in borderline awkward silence for half an hour. He can't listen to music when he drives, because it distracts him. Hannah told me that, and I found it off-putting knowing this detail about a man I barely knew but she was getting to know so well. It turns out he's quite a cautious person.

His car is old and has a bit of rubbish on the floor but it's not dirty. I notice a lip balm in the car console and know it's not Hannah's. She only ever wore one type of lip balm because she was allergic to so many things. As a teenager she would buy a lip gloss and then ten minutes later have a huge bump on her lip – almost like a boil. She would get so upset but keep buying new lip glosses and balms and testing them out. The only one that didn't make her react was Carmex. The lip balm in front of me is a cherry Nivea. I look out of the window, counting the red cars, then the blue cars, then grey. Dad didn't like noise when he was driving either. I wonder if Hannah clocked that similarity.

We pull into a service station. We have to wait ages to get a parking spot, and he turns the radio on loudly while we wait. It feels weird that he's still not talking. Once parked, he gets out of the car to smoke as quickly as he can. I walk away without saying anything. In the service station toilets I see the vending machine for chewable toothbrushes. It reminds me I didn't bring anything with me, no toothbrush, hairbrush, pants, nothing.

I look at myself in the mirror and see Hannah. I am wearing a top of hers, from the storage unit. I opened the drawer as quickly as possible and grabbed whatever I could without looking. A white top, low-cut for even Hannah. I never saw her wear this, I don't know why I chose it.

I look tired from being up so early. I get out my dirty make-up bag and apply some turquoise eyeliner. Hannah said it suited me and I trusted her. My hair is more coppery-coloured after using her reddening conditioner for months. My bra is too small now and digs into my sides, but it pushes my boobs up, and as I walk around, the power of having larger breasts is clear. I like it. Old men stare, young men stare. Women stare. But then I walk past a woman wearing a baggy tracksuit, similar to my grey one, and she doesn't stare. There's a coffee stain near her right breast. She has a stressed, wincing expression on her face. I feel sorry for her. I wonder if I have a new radar for a particular kind of pain, a radar for people going through something that can't be explained.

I buy us two packets of crisps, assuming he likes salt-and-vinegar – everyone likes salt-and-vinegar and if he didn't Hannah would have told me. It feels nice buying something for two again. I arrive back at the car and Rowan is smoking another cigarette. He bites the nails on his one free hand and looks off into the distance towards the motorway, cars shooting in and out of view.

I've never seen a grown man biting his nails. I want to hug him – he looks so stressed – but the idea of my new boobs stops me, the idea of them pressing into him makes me feel weird. We get back into the car without speaking and he turns on the radio again. He turns it off once we reach the motorway.

I look out of the window and avoid looking at the clouds. When we were girls we would lie on the grass in the park looking up at them to see a rabbit, a dinosaur, candyfloss. Once she saw a gun. I couldn't see it. When we got a bit older and would do it, I'd joke 'penis!' or 'vagina!' and she would laugh but then tell me off for being crude. She didn't like crude jokes; she didn't talk to me about sex stuff as teenagers, even though I could tell when she started having it because she started wearing a perfumed moisturiser which I'd later steal.

She brought a boy back when she must have been about fifteen. She told me not to come into the bedroom for 'half an hour'. I asked why. She said she was just having a 'half-an-hour-long private conversation'. I looked at the clock and started counting down the minutes. Our parents were out, as usual, and I wanted so badly to know what Hannah was doing. So I put some crisps in a bowl, because I thought it was more 'grown up' to have crisps in a bowl, and went upstairs, spilling only one or two on the way.

I opened the door without knocking and caught a glimpse of this boy with his trousers down. Hannah's school shirt was open so I could see her bra. They were both standing in front of each other, studying each other like aliens. Quickly, she took me to Mum and Dad's maroon bedroom and sat me down. She wasn't angry. She sat with me, ate some crisps. The boy came in after a while, now fully clothed, and said he had to go. Hannah waved him goodbye and she was mine again.

It's 5.45 p.m.

Me: What time are you onstage?
Him: Umm. I dunno yet.
Me: How long till we're there?
Him: Soon. Look – can you see the sea?

I can. I haven't seen the sea since I went into it alone the night she died, wanting to die, ready to die. I feel stupid for not thinking about how I would feel, seeing the sea again. I just thought of the car ride, the getting there. We drive on in silence with my head down; I look at his legs to distract myself. His jeans are fading around the knees. He is wearing his old black Converse that he's probably had for longer than he knew Hannah; they've probably seen him through multiple girlfriends.

He wore them to her funeral.

He parks in an NCP car park which is almost empty, but he drives round and round to get to the open-air top floor. He goes to the boot to get out his guitar while I gather the energy to undo my seat belt. Then I hear a thud. I look in the front mirror and see him bent over on the boot, shaking. Big howling cries. I leave him for a few minutes until they subside.

I don't stroke his back or say anything – I'm unsure what to do and I don't want to be pushed away. Would he push me away? He straightens up and wipes his face with his T-shirt and we stand opposite each other. In this intimate silence I fear I'm about to say something inappropriate, like addressing how loud his crying was, or telling him how tragic he looked bent over his battered car. But before I can hurt him we begin walking down and down and down towards the exit of the car park.

On one of the levels down below, a photo shoot is under way. A model is standing in a floaty white dress, whilst an assistant holds a fan at her feet to make the dress float in the air. A photographer keeps telling her to 'keep doing what you're doing'. They don't notice us passing by. We reach the street level and push open the dirty steel door; the sun bleaches his face.

Him: Can we go for a walk first?

He's heading for the sea before I say yes. When we get to the beach, I don't stop looking at the pebbles and I'm glad it's not sand. My feet begin to hurt in my flimsy ballet pumps. He's got his guitar case slung across his back, but with each step it's making hollow sounds like there's no guitar in there.

We walk and walk, further and further away from where I think the gig is happening. He's faster than me, he has long legs. Hannah must have felt so tiny next to him. He stops and takes a sip from his water bottle. Lips wet, he offers me some. I take a sip and don't worry about how often he cleans his water bottle. Does he have a special bottle cleaner like Hannah? She ordered one for me too from Amazon after she saw me topping up day-old water with fresh water. She then spent fucking ages telling me fun facts about bacteria. We sit down on the pebbles.

I pretend I'm checking the time and look at my phone for as long as possible before I have to look up again. When I do I see the waves crashing, a ship in the distance, seagulls squawking and circling and I want to squawk too, wish I could fly away. He looks out at the sea.

Him: It's weird, isn't it.
Me: Yeah.

Will our conversations ever last longer than a few sentences at a time? He looks in pain and my heart aches for him. For me. For the sea. For everything. I don't like seeing him like this. The word 'Recovery' keeps coming up in my books on death. Is spending time with him delaying my 'recovery', delaying his? Or is even the idea of 'recovery' stupid? How inappropriate would it be to get out my book on death right now and read to him about what we should be doing, how we should be coping and behaving?

Me: Don't you have to go to your gig?
Him: I guess.

He makes no effort to move, eyes still on the waves. The waves that day looked so calm just before she jumped, and so rough when I dived in to find her. Do I tell him that? Have I told him anything about that that day? Maybe I should. Maybe that's what he needs right now.

Me: It was her idea, you know. To jump, I mean.

He doesn't respond, nothing moves on his face. Does anyone believe me? I can't sit on the pebbles any longer – my bottom half is numb – so I get up. He stays sitting and silent. Part of me wants to run away, run to the train station, run home. But I can't leave him.

Me: Rowan? It's cold and I –

He wipes his nose and starts rubbing his face with his hands, as though he's trying to wake himself up.

Him: I can't do the gig. I don't know what I was
    thinking – I'm sorry I brought you here – I –
Me: It's OK –

He hangs his head and starts crying again, quietly. I kneel back down on the pebbles and hug him from behind, which forces me to stare out at the sea. It's overwhelmingly beautiful. The sun is starting to set and I feel the warmth from his back. He takes my hands, both of them, and puts them over his heart. I feel how thin he is, paper thin, no fat at all. I can feel his bones. Hannah wouldn't have liked that, she would have tried to feed him up. She would have looked after him. As I think of all the meals she would have cooked for him, he pulls me round in front of him and holds my face.

My knees hurt, and a sharp pebble digs into me as he kisses me softly. I can't bring myself to pull away, even though I know I should. I close my eyes when I see that he's closed his.

I sit on him and immediately I feel that he's hard, which scares me. I jump up. He stands up quickly too. We stare into each other's eyes as he shakes his head from side to side, which I don't know how to interpret. He starts walking away, still shaking it. After a second he turns around and signals for me to follow. Now he's kind of smiling, which makes me kind of smile too. What the fuck is happening?

Before walking on, I take a photo of the sea with the sun setting behind it. I want to confront this sunset, to remember it. I wipe my wet face with Hannah's top and follow him. We go up a road with shops and bars and the sounds are jarring to hear after the calming waves. People are drunk, people are happy. I want to trade places with one of them, to stop feeling so heavy, to have a Big Friday Night Out with the Girls, even though I never had a Big Friday Night Out with the Girls. I have no Girls.

We get to the venue and his face changes – he's terrified.

Me: You don't have to do this, you know – it's just
  a gig –
Him: I'll let people down though –
Me: Fuck it. Fuck people.

He seems to appreciate me saying that.

He goes up to the young girl behind the ticket desk. I don't hear what he says but I see her nipples poking out beneath her top, as though she's Rachel from *Friends*. She's a redhead, like Hannah, and I guess like me now too. She's wearing red lipstick and I dislike her instantly. She's touching his arm, trying to get him to change his mind, probably telling him how 'talented' he is despite never having heard him play.

If I wasn't here, he would be going home with her. But he comes back to me. He smiles for the first time all day.

Does he know it's me? It could just be a big fucking mistake; maybe he's just forgotten everything, forgotten that I'm not Hannah. Do I remind him that she's dead, right now, and that I'm Ruth? I'm Ruth, and we've just kissed. We walk towards the chip shop opposite as if that was the plan all along.

# 35

I wake up when the car stops. I don't know where we are. It's dark and I look at the clock: 1.12 a.m.

Him: I didn't know where you live so –

He gets out of the car and walks around to my side to open the door for me. I'm a little scared until I see the Storage Etc. lettering. The lights aren't on in Reception. I assess the situation, sleepily. I should be asking him to drive me home because that would be the right thing to do, but I'm unsure if I've ever cared about the right thing to do. I get out.

He walks ahead of me as he locks the car. The 'beep' makes me jump but he doesn't notice. I open the doors with my keys, feeling bad that I haven't given him any to this place yet, that Hannah isn't here to give him a secret set.

In the lift he presses the button with one finger. Before the stupid old lift creaks upwards, he turns to me and rubs my cheek with the same finger, which Hannah would have flipped out about. She'd have shouted, 'How many people do you think have touched these buttons?' I don't understand what he's doing.

Him: Turquoise cheeks.

Me: What?

Him: Your make-up, from the crying.

Me: When was I crying?

Him: In the car. On the beach. You've cried everywhere, haven't you?

Yes, I've cried everywhere. On the Tube, bus, plane. In the car. On the sofa, in the bed, on Hannah's bed, in the storage room, at work, sitting on the toilet. In Tesco's, Sainsbury's, Aldi, Boots, Snappy Snaps, Pret. I wasn't a crier before. I wish I was still living in the before.

Me: You cried too.

Him: Oh, I know.

He seems relaxed.

The lift doors open and we walk in the darkness until the garish lights make a horrible sound, like they're angry to have been woken. A moth flies about, circling dizzily. I stop to watch it.

Hannah and I had a moth that lived in our bedroom. It was white, with black dots, and we used to say that it reminded us of a snowy owl. This moth was beautiful and would occasionally land on a wall or a book nearby and we would both just stare at it, silently. It felt as though the moth was our resident for years and years but I realise now that it can't have been. Once we were at the cinema and, during the adverts, something reminded us of our Snowy Owl moth, which prompted Hannah to look up facts about how long different types of moths can live.

He's already opening the door to the unit. Hannah's room? What do I call it? Our room? I follow him in and go straight towards the bed. I click the switch on the bedside lamp, even though there are no plug sockets in here. It's like being on the set of a play that's yet to open.

The shift in energy, now that it's late at night, is evident. I feel odd. He goes to the piano and starts playing, singing quietly. He mumbles a few words. I can't make out what he's saying but I think he sang 'Han'.

I lie down on the bed and google 'white moth with black dots', wanting to know the proper name, scrolling through the Google images until I find our former resident. A Macro Moth, apparently. I save the image on my camera roll. She'll never see a moth again. I stare at the photo I took on the beach today until I need to close my eyes. I listen to him play.

When I open my eyes he's lying down next to me, both of us fully clothed and above the duvet. I hear him breathe, which reminds me to breathe. I turn away from him onto my side, clenching my fists, screwing up my face. Something could happen. Something can't happen. Do I want something to happen?

Within a minute, our bodies are extremely close and we're hugging. I hate the term 'spooning', it gives me the ick, but that's what we're fucking doing, both unable to look at each other. His forearm is riding against my nipples and I'm embarrassed because they're getting harder by the second. I feel him behind me too. I keep my eyes closed as he starts rocking.

Then I turn around to face him.

# 36

I wake up relieved. We just fell asleep. The ventilation unit is making a weird sound and the air is stuffy.

He's still sleeping on his side facing into me. His skin appears darker on the white sheets, and he looks older with his face squashed against the pillow. Did Hannah watch him sleep?

We both must have undressed in the night, because it's so hot in here. His jeans are still on, his top off. I sit up crossed-legged and stare down at my body, which feels unfamiliar to me. I'm still in Hannah's white top, but I'm only in my pants, my pubic hair poking out of the sides. I hope he hasn't noticed.

I tried waxing once, at a proper salon. Hannah went to this place every two months, and she encouraged me to go with her, but I was too proud and pretended that I didn't care about my pubic hair. The reality was that I didn't have regular enough sex so there seemed to be no need. She said she didn't do it for the men, but for herself, which I told her was absolute bullshit.

Once, though, I did go with her, thinking it might change my luck, that maybe men could sense the women who attended to their vaginas. The lady led me to a room and said to get undressed, then handed me a towel. When she came back in I was ready, with the towel covering me. She came over and arranged the towel in a different position and shielded her eyes when she saw that I was fully naked.

Waxer: I meant just the towel on the bottom half.
Me: Oh God – sorry, you said to get undressed.
Waxer: You don't need to take the top half off for
   a wax –

She started laughing at me. My cheeks went red and I tried to reach for my bra and T-shirt. She handed them to me and left the room. I got dressed again. When she came back in, after recovering from the laughter and mumbling a quick apology for her lack of professionalism, she put the hot wax on my skin for the first time and I felt like I was being burnt alive. I screamed for Hannah, and bit my arm until it was over.

Hannah told me later that she could hear me from the reception area.

Me: Why didn't you rescue me?
Her: Because I thought it would be good for you.
   It's more painful the first time. Then it gets easier.
Me: Liar.

She paid for my wax and couldn't stop laughing all the way home as I hobbled alongside her. I had a new-found respect for her and her pain threshold that day.

Now I'm sitting here restless and I want to know if he's dreaming about her.

I walk to her chest of drawers and take a deep breath, preparing myself to see all of her folded things, to smell her. I find some leggings and a big T-shirt which I think were our mum's. I write on a Post-it 'Gone to work'. I want to add a little doodle but I know Hannah would have done that. So I don't.

I get out of the lift on the ground floor and see that Mickey is gone. His dad is outside, smoking and sticking up a 'TAKE ME' sign on an abandoned wardrobe. He nods at me as I leave.

I pace up and down the industrial road, waiting for my Uber. I'm not wearing any knickers or socks. I'm starving, even after the huge plate of chips last night. I finished Rowan's too. He watched me eat and it felt nice to be sharing food with someone, in public, rather than robotically shovelling it down my throat, alone in my flat.

An Uber-looking car approaches and I hope that the driver doesn't speak to me. It's 7 a.m., and I'm already desperate for the toilet. I get in.

Driver: You all right, love?

The driver is female, and she doesn't know it but I really like being called 'love' – it gives me a tingly feeling. It's done so ever since I was little and one of my parents' slightly famous friends who looked like a grizzly bear called me 'love' and swooped me up in his arms whenever he arrived, kissing both of my cheeks. I realise now he probably just couldn't remember my name.

I don't want to be rude so I muster up the energy for some casual conversation.

Me: Fine, thanks. You?
Her: Yeah, just started, can't complain. Yet!

I do that fake laugh where you just breathe out audibly through your nose. I'm bursting now, so I keep looking out of the window for places that are open.

The car smells of cocoa butter, one of my favourite smells. I never remember to buy it for myself, but Hannah did so I'd use it at hers. She'd spread it all over her body, rigorously and daily. Sometimes I watched her do it and filmed her, because she looked so insane, and then she'd make me delete it. I wish I hadn't, that I could watch those deleted videos now.

I breathe in and close my eyes. I try not to think about Rowan sleeping, and how I don't trust him. I don't think I've ever trusted a man. I would never admit it out loud because it sounds childish, but I'm just more comfortable in female company. Obviously I should go to therapy, I should have been in constant therapy, but I quite like knowing I have a problem a therapist is being denied from devouring.

I notice that the driver has a photo of a little girl wearing an Elsa costume on the dashboard. She looks at me in her mirror and smiles.

Driver: She's six on Saturday so I'm working all hours this week so I can take the weekend off. We're having a *Frozen* cake, obviously.
Me: That's nice.
Driver: Siri, open Spotify. Play 'Let It Go' from *Frozen*.

The song starts playing, too quickly and too loudly, and immediately I'm transported back to being in a lukewarm bath with Hannah leaning over the sides to chat to me, sitting cross-legged on the bathroom floor. We were midway through watching *Frozen* on one of our hungover mornings. It was between Christmas and New Year and

191

we'd had a horrible festive period. She'd just dumped her first boyfriend post-Brian and was needy, whilst I was dealing with a prolonged bout of cystitis after a week of fucking a random guy who thought my name was Amy.

Throughout the film I had to take long pauses to go to the bathroom. I was having a bath on Hannah's orders; she said it would hurt less if I weed underwater. It did hurt less, she was right. How did she know these things? We didn't finish the film but said we would one day. 'We'll watch it when we have kids,' she said. I ignored her.

I get out my phone and think about texting my mum, which is rare. The last text I received from her was two weeks ago, a screenshot of a tweet by a 'fan' of hers, saying how wonderful she was in an episode of *Call the Midwife*. She was in the first series as a minor character. She played the mother of a young nun. When the episode aired, she thought this would be the role that changed her career. It didn't, obviously. I should text her.

Me (text): Hey, Mum. How are you?

Then I delete it. Shouldn't she be asking how I am?

The driver lady is now singing along, quite skilfully, carefree and happy. By the time the song ends I have tears rolling down my cheeks. She glances at me in the mirror but doesn't really notice and I'm glad.

Her: Sorry. Quite loud for this early.
Me: You have a nice voice.
Her: Ah, thanks, love.

I stifle a smile but want to get out – I need some air. I look through the window and see a coffee shop.

Me: I can just get out here if that's OK, at the
    traffic lights.
Her: Sure thing.
Me: Thank you, have a nice day.
Her: You too, love.
Me: Happy birthday to your daughter.

I close the door and walk as fast as I can towards the
coffee shop, proud of myself for enduring a casual chat and
for not wetting myself. As soon as I'm in, I order a flat
white and ask where the toilet is. The stern barista gives
me a four-number code, which of course I forget, so I
have to go back and ask him for it again, with my bladder
about to burst.

Afterwards, I sit on the high seats looking out of the
window. My coffee arrives and I drink it quickly. Someone
taps me on the shoulder. I turn around to find Leila.

Her: Ruth? Wow –
Me: Hey –
Her: I genuinely thought you were Hannah.

My heart begins its thudding.

Me: Yeah . . . my hair –
Her: Sorry. I shouldn't have said that, should I?
Me: It's fine.

Her braids are different, woven with purple and pink,
and I can't help but notice that she's also pregnant. Really
pregnant. Her big silver hoop earrings press into my cheeks
as she hugs me tightly. I stare at the bump.

Me: You're –

Her: I didn't know when to tell you – but I guess
    I can't hide it any more.

I try to work out the timing. When did I last see her?
One of her braids is tangled up in her necklaces, specifically attaching itself to the crucifix. She sees me looking
and takes hold of it, protectively.

Her: I've been going back to church. I don't know
    why but it feels good, I feel better. Like there's a
    reason for things.

Quickly I remember why she annoys me so much.
Instead of telling her that there is no reason, there's no
fucking reason at all for things, I glare at another of her
necklaces. It has a letter H dangling, gleaming.

Her: H for Hannah.
Me: Yeah, I got that.
Her: I wanted to have her with me each day, you
    know? Something to remind me.

I try to smile, be polite, even though the fact that she
needs reminding and is feeling 'better' is supremely offensive to me.

Her: You should come over for dinner one day?
    With Danny and me.
Me: Danny?
Her: What?
Me: I don't know a Danny, do I?
Her: Ummmm, I think you do! Rowan's brother.

Me: I didn't know he – Hannah never mentioned
    he had a brother.
Her: She must have. Hannah loved him. Rowan will
    come for dinner too, he's always over anyway.

I can't think of anything worse, an evening spent
reminding me how little I knew about my sister, how
little I know about Rowan. I look around the coffee shop,
head spinning, heart hurting, newly hungry.

Me: Sorry, I need to eat something –

I aim for the counter, pointing at a *pain au chocolat*.
Leila sips from her coffee and watches me take the first
bite, which feels bitchy of her. I look at her bump again
and, of course, it's a perfect bump, so perfect it looks like
a fucking scoop of ice cream. A huge scoop.

Me: How far along are you? Is that what you say?
    Or how long left?
Her: Not long left now. Little girl. She was a bit of
    a surprise. We'd only been dating a few weeks
    when I found out. She's a blessing though.

I don't believe in blessings. And I want to know if
Hannah knew she was pregnant before she died. Would
she have been the first to know and put in charge of one
of those gross baby showers I see on Instagram sometimes?
I'm amazed Leila hasn't broadcasted every single step of
this pregnancy so far with daily vlogs.

Me: That's nice.

I don't think it's nice, but what else can I say? I take another bite, annoyed by how delicious the *pain au chocolat* is and about how I'm having to eat it with an audience. I feel the H necklace watching me too. I get up.

Me: I should get going –
Her: Please, come for dinner at ours. It would be good to see you. You'd like Danny –

I resent her, her new relationship, her new future. I should say 'congratulations' but I can't.

Leila: I hope you're taking care of yourself.

Danny. I begin to remember meeting a Danny. At the funeral. I hone in on Leila's big, darting, annoyingly pretty eyes.

Leila: If you need anything please just call –
Me: I don't like phone calls.

The only person I could ever 'call' was Hannah. I leave the coffee shop without saying anything, taking the second half of the *pain au chocolat* with me.

# 37

Her electric toothbrush and charger; her hair products and shampoos. These were the first things I took from her flat, just days after she died. I took them back to mine and didn't use them for a few weeks, but then I knew she would want me to.

I get into my shower and wash my hair with her shampoo and conditioner. Afterwards, I blast the cold water onto my back. My mum swore by cold showers; she tried to make us have them from a young age to wake us up, and today, I need to be woken.

Last night at the unit feels unreal.

I think of his bare chest, his snore, how he is probably still asleep. Does he know I'm gone yet? I think of Leila's H necklace and her pretty bump. New life is inside her, growing every minute, while I'm disintegrating.

I go into the bedroom and avoid looking in the direction of her ashes.

When they first arrived, I tried to find a place to put them that wouldn't upset me so much every time I see them, but that was stupid. I'm always upset anyway. I sit down next to the silver urn, in my towel, and put both my hands around it. I wish I could speak out loud to her, tell her how I'm feeling, but I'm so far away from being able to do that. I don't even know how I feel. I get some fairy lights, ones which fell from my wall a while ago, and wrap them around the urn. It feels a bit like decorating a withering Christmas tree, but it's better than covering her with a tea towel.

Black leggings, black socks, my maroon Costa T-shirt. My uniform. I tie my hair up without drying it. Hannah's hair dryer is at the storage unit. I need to bring that back here. I only ever dried my hair when I stayed at hers. She said her hairdryer was special and didn't damage hair because of its 'ion technology'. Whenever I wanted to annoy her from then on I would mimic how geekily she said 'ion technology'.

I've left the window in the kitchen wide open and I wonder if any birds came in last night. It feels like something has been in here. I put two slices of bread in the toaster and enjoy the remainder of the *pain au chocolat* whilst I spy on the garden of the flat below. They have a little girl, white-haired, angelic. She must be under two, still unsteady on her feet but always pottering about trying to help the mum water the plants. I hear her having nightmares sometimes.

The neighbours in the next-door garden have a toddler too. I've never seen the families talk to each other. Sometimes, in the warmer months, I've watched from above as both toddlers played by themselves in their gardens, no clue that there was a potential tiny friend just metres away, hidden by the broken fence, which is caving in more than it was last week because of the rain. I wonder which family the fence bothers more, or if it's only me from my high vantage point who's noticed.

The toast pops. Marmite and butter. Toast helps, Hannah said. I start a list in my notebook:

## List of Hannah's good advice:

Toast helps
Never put your bag on your bed. GERMS!
Always wear a night-bra
Don't worry about VPLs
Don't shave your vagina
Avoid the news at bedtime
Clean your wallet once a week
Clean your iPhone once a day
Clean your doorknobs once a month
Never go to bed on a fight
Save so you can spend

She used to say that last one when I worried about how much money she spent on our holidays, treating me, never letting me pay for a thing. She loved being the Big Sister.

I worry my list doesn't do justice to her, that it makes her sound basic. I worry someone will find the list and laugh at it, laugh at her. I try to remember other stuff – all the wise things she said too – but suddenly I've eaten all the toast and my mind is blank and I'm terrified this is the beginning of forgetting.

# 38

The first period I've had since Hannah died starts on the Tube, as I wrestle with people's armpits. I wasn't worried when I stopped having them; it made complete sense to me for my body to cease all normal function when she died.

I'm annoyed that it's chosen today to come back, though, because I wanted to start swimming again. I see someone rushing from the platform to make the train, ignoring the fact that the carriage is full, just managing to get inside. Her bag gets trapped in the doors. The train stands still until she dislodges it, and the driver makes a droll announcement.

> Announcement: If anyone else wants to be as selfish as the person who just ran for the doors and delayed us, be my guest. It's not my problem if you're late, mate.

Some people stifle a laugh, but I go further. I laugh uncontrollably in this woman's face. She doesn't flinch, she's got headphones in, she's looking down already at her phone.

I get off at Terminal 5 and go straight to Boots. I

recognise two of the workers, having been in here a few times to buy kids' chewy vitamins that I eat like sweets. Mostly I come in here to buy paracetamol. Sometimes I just take it when I'm feeling extremely sad. Of course it does nothing, but the act of swallowing pills has always been comforting to me, maybe because Mum did it so much. Paracetamol and supplements and whatever else multiple times a day, for everything and nothing. Her handbag was a rattle.

One of the workers is a man with a shaved head; he has a tattoo behind his ear of a bomb. I'm surprised that kind of tattoo is acceptable for someone working at an airport. He's over-friendly and talks too much. When he asks if I've got a Boots card, he seems so unbearably sincere. I have Hannah's Boots card; I'm collecting points on her behalf even though I don't know how to redeem them, or if they ever can be. I like the thought of some of her accounts still being active.

The other worker here is a plump lady, and although it's not necessarily polite to describe someone as 'plump', it seems as if the word was created for her. She looks like she's in a constant state of bliss, arranging the shelves, never at the tills, happily doing her thing with a serene expression. She reminds me of the fairy godmother in Cinderella. She smiles softly at me as she stacks some stuff near the condoms and lubricant. I wonder if she's ever been fucked really hard, kind of hating it and kind of liking it, if she's ever spoken dirty. I can't imagine her being naked or screaming at anyone on the street or eating a burger with meat juice dripping down her chin. She doesn't belong here, in Heathrow, near condoms – she belongs in a Disney bubble with a wand and talking birds sitting on her shoulder.

I smile at her as I cramp. The fairy godmother turns to look at me and I wonder if she can smell the blood. At the tills, I try my hardest to avoid getting into an extended chat about the consistently shitty weather with the bomb-tattoo man. On closer inspection, he's young. Just a silly boy. I almost snap, almost tell him that I like our shitty weather, the shitty weather feels appropriate to me, so please – please – stop talking about the fucking shitty weather. But I don't. I just smile and leave with my pack of giant pads. Ones that are primarily for incontinence or women who've just given birth – I find them the most comfortable.

In the queue for the toilets, I squeeze my thighs together to control the blood. A cubicle becomes free. I observe the damage. My pants are ruined, and my black leggings are soaked through the crotch area. I blame Rowan. He did this, he made my hormones do this.

I have to take my shoes off so I can remove the leggings and throw away the pants in the sanitary disposal. I don't want anyone to see under the toilet door – I always look at people's feet when they're in the cubicles and I can't be the only one – so I quickly close the toilet lid and stand on top. I have a quick glance into the next cubicle. I catch a glimpse of the top of a blonde bun and some shiny black heels, a woman doing a shit whilst scrolling through Twitter, and I feel glad I did that. It feels naughty and for a second I forget that I'm in such a mess, and that this mess is my life.

I line a massive pad in the leggings and put them back on and leave the toilets without washing my hands, afraid that I'll see someone I know who will note how long I've taken in the toilet. Why do I care about things like this, why have I always worried too much about the wrong things?

I walk aimlessly for a bit before reaching for my anti-bacterial gel. I squeeze some onto my hands and I see there is blood, dried blood, all over them. I rub my hands together and the gel doesn't make the blood completely vanish, instead it turns my hands a pale purple colour. I rub them onto my leggings, thankful that they're black. The blood is gone, my hands feel sticky, and I keep walking and walking. It's still too early for my shift, so I aim for Starbucks.

I look at my reflection in the glassy Heathrow walls, and see that I'm scowling without even realising. Hannah would tell me whenever I creased my forehead that I'd get wrinkles, and put her hand over my forehead to stop me. The thought pains me, and I begin to pinch my face like I've seen in some of those '*Vogue* Beauty Secrets' YouTube videos with famous people. We loved watching videos like those in bed, one after the other. She unashamedly sucked up celebrity tips, and would seek out the products or jade rollers they used. In her favourite one, the actress Jessica Alba slaps herself in the morning, hard and repeatedly, to wake up her skin. Sometimes when I slept over I'd wake up to the sound of slapping.

I could be late if I wanted to be. No one checks.

With only fifteen minutes before my shift is meant to start, I arrive at Starbucks. I order a Frappuccino from the unfriendly woman with feline black eye flicks and thick silver hoops behind the till. She doesn't speak to me, she just turns the iPad towards me to pay after I say the familiar words which she's heard me say many times before: 'Venti Mocha Frappuccino.' She doesn't look at me for longer than she needs to, and busies herself straight away once payment has gone through. She has an extremely long and ragged brunette ponytail. Hair that should have been cut a while ago because I can see, even from where I'm standing, how split the ends are. Did her mother always have long hair too?

The combination of syrup and ice is delicious and I drink it too quickly which gives me brain freeze. I feel weird walking around with no pants on, the pad is rubbing against my skin and is almost soaked through already. I stop and sit at the end of a row of seats and hold the Frappuccino against my forehead to cool me down, to calm me down. I must look insane. I watch a plane take off. Then another. Then I'm late.

I touch my hair, loose around my shoulders, and feel how soft it is. Hannah's conditioner has really helped. If Hannah was with me right now, she'd tell me off for bitching about that lady's split ends, but then offend the woman herself by recommending a hair oil without a prompt. She was usually so kind to strangers, even if it was with unwanted advice. Although sometimes she would throw me and say something meaner or nastier than even I could have dreamt up.

Like once we were walking down a street and two joggers didn't move out of the way for us. Hannah screamed, 'FUCKING LOSER JOGGING CUNTS!' at them in a voice and accent I'd never heard her use. I loved those moments so much.

I mutter, 'Fucking loser jogging cunts,' over and over again as I make my way to work to make me feel better.

# 39

2009

Hannah stood outside the bathroom door, coaching me. I was now fifteen, so I already felt inadequate that I was having my first period so late. Everyone at school had been having them for years. The sudden arrival and its implications of maturity freaked me out, so I kept it hidden it at first, thinking that Mum wouldn't notice the bloody knickers in the bin. My plan failed. She called Hannah, who rushed home from uni to congratulate me, so weirdly happy about it. She even started crying, which proved she had been as worried as me about my delayed development.

Her: You need to crouch down –
Me: I am crouching.
Her: Then you very carefully push it in –
Me: I am pushing –
Her: Once it's in –
Me: It won't go in –
Her: That's because you're scared –
Me: I'm not scared. It just won't work. Maybe they don't work on some people –

Her: It's a tampon, Ruth. Relax.

Me: Don't tell me to relax in your unrelaxed voice –

Her: Sorry –

Me: Let's look it up – maybe some vaginas aren't compatible with –

Her: Try lying down and lifting your bum in the air –

Me: No!

She pushed open the door and got a tampon from the box. She put out a towel on the bathroom floor and lay down. She pulled her knickers down and then made me lie next to her.

Me: This is too weird –

Her: It's fine, I can't see anything. Just listen to what I'm saying and copy me –

She lifted up her bum in the air and then instructed me step by step how to insert the tampon. I tried to copy her, but it still wouldn't go in. Once hers was in, she sat up. Eventually I gave up and we sat together, back to back on the towel.

Her: It might take you a bit of time, but that's OK.

Me: I don't like them. How can everyone act like they aren't a massive deal?

Her: Everyone has different scales –

Me: I'm never trying that again. Seriously.

Her: You can't just give up –

Me: I can.

She pushed my back with hers and held my hand, and then we began laughing because she now had a tampon in for no reason.

# 40

The last bit of Frappuccino goes in the bin as I arrive at work. I get into the back room and hang up my tote bag, which contains nothing valuable apart from my notebook, gum and phone. I think of the holes we dug in the sand, our little plastic bags from airport security. Then I go through the doors to my station. The iPad and the queue are ready and waiting, and as the previous worker leaves silently he looks at me after his night shift with an expression that translates as, 'Fuck this shit,' which I appreciate.

Two people are making the coffees. I only know one of their names, because it's such a good one: Paloma.

Paloma has constantly changing hair; today it's almost silver. On my first shift here, I saw two sisters sitting together, taking selfies in their new sun hats. I went into the back room and began hyperventilating. Paloma saw me. She went on loading stuff onto a trolley. She didn't come over, she just left me to it. I respected that – there's something nice about someone knowing that they can offer you nothing.

I've gathered little bits of information about my fellow Costa employees over the months, but nothing has sparked my interest. Lots of people are doing this job and another job at the same time, or a degree. No one works here for longer than six months before moving elsewhere, moving on, away from the airport and its strange atmosphere of timelessness.

The day passes. I turn off my brain and do my job. Then I find myself sitting on the Piccadilly line opposite Paloma. She gets out a Hello Kitty Tupperware box and starts eating little sandwiches, cut up into childlike quarters.

Her: You going home now?
Me: Yeah.
Her: You tired?
Me: Yeah.

I'm surprised she's making the effort to chat with me as she attacks her sandwiches, uninhibited to eat and talk in public, chewing with her mouth open. She moves on to a bag of grapes and a Weight Watchers protein bar. I try to seem more friendly.

Me: Are you going home?
Her: No. My other job. I work there only a few nights a week for extra cash.

Her accent is heavy, I'm guessing Russian. I'm afraid to ask, in case it's offensive. Her skin is olive, kind of pale right now but I can imagine how golden it must become. I'm amazed she has the energy to do a night job, as I sit here ready to be swallowed up by this Tube seat, followed by my sofa, my bed and darkness.

Me: What's your other job?
Her: Strip club. Not the stripping though, obviously.

She picks up a roll of stomach fat and shakes it at me. I can see joy in her eyes. I can see that she likes life. I feel extremely jealous of her, almost carnal in my desire to grab something from her Hello Kitty lunchbox – stuff it into my face and swallow, in the hope that a sliver of her joy can be shared.

She says she's getting off at Hammersmith, and she puts the Hello Kitty box back into her bag as she gets up and says goodbye. The train starts to slow into the station. She doesn't look back as she steps off. The prospect of going back to my flat or Hannah's empty one, watching Netflix, ordering food I can't taste – sleeping but not really sleeping – I just can't. So I go after her, managing to slip through the doors just before they close. I hang back, and wait for her to walk up the stairs.

She walks fast. Luckily her hair makes her easy to spot. She stops off at the bagel stand in Hammersmith station and eats one as she walks. I am impressed by her appetite, a real appetite, not a fake one like mine, activated by grief. She stops at the traffic lights, takes her hair out of her tight ponytail and runs her fingers through it, shaking her head about as she waits for the green man. Once she's crossed the road she puts some lipstick on in the reflection of a darkened shop window. She takes some high – very high – heels out of her bag and switches shoes.

She arrives outside Secrets strip club. I've heard of it, walked past it many times; it's well known in West London and has been here for decades. I've never walked past it at night though, when it's alive. She greets the bouncer with a kiss on the cheek, and she gives him a bagel. He eats it while chatting to her, like this is routine and has happened many nights before. I want to know what they're laughing about. She goes inside.

I cross over the road and the bouncer doesn't chat to me, doesn't ask for ID and I'm inside before I'm ready to be. I pray that Paloma doesn't see me as I go through to the bar. It's very dark and quite busy already. The music is loud, the blue lights otherworldly. I immediately spot her at the other side of the bar, now with just a black strappy top on, her boobs spilling over the top. I'm glad she's far away. I order a drink quickly from another woman, who's wearing a sequinned silver bra and skirt and speaking to a salivating man next to me. I manage to get the drink and move to a seat near the corner. Women are on the platform, dancing slowly. All in thongs. If they are in a bra it comes off pretty fast. They seem happy. Happier than me and happier than the men in here. I sit very still watching them for quite some time. Maybe an hour.

I watch one dancer in particular, with long dyed black hair, severely straightened. Her next-to-naked body is oily, and her hair keeps rubbing back and forth in front of her boobs, getting greasier and greasier. I wonder if she has to wash it every night. Her thong reminds me of tooth floss, and I remember that I need to change my pad. I finish my drink and go to the toilets as quickly as possible, checking Paloma is not in view.

I take a photo of the cubicle door, 'TEXT AMY or CALL MICHELLE for "FUN"', I don't know why. The toilets are empty; they smell of lemon bleach, and are so clean it implies sex happens in here. I think of Fred at the cinema and how he would never fuck me on my period. I line my leggings with a new pad, which compared to the dancer's thong is a nappy.

My eyes twitch and I feel faint with hunger. I need to go home. Do the dancers eat before dancing? What kind of snacks do they have in their dressing room? I look in

Paloma's direction as I leave. She doesn't see me, she's chatting to a man who's only chatting to her breasts, which she's pushing together for him.

Suddenly I'm driven with the idea of food, eating all the food.

* ★ *

I get home and raid my cupboards like a beast. The last of some old cereal, a few crackers, two custard creams and one slice of bread. That's all I have, and I eat it all as I look out my kitchen window at the stars, listening to foxes fighting and/or fucking in the darkness below.

I leave again, on a mission, and walk to the twenty-four-hour Tesco Metro down the street. I buy:

- One big bag of Kettle Chips
- A KitKat Chunky
- Salted cashews
- A two-litre bottle of Diet Coke
- A mint Magnum
- Fizzy Haribo
- Banana chips

I don't know where I'm going as I eat the crisps. With each step and each crunch I fall into a trance. I eat the Haribo next, one after the other, saving the gummy rings for my fingers. Salted cashews washed down with Diet Coke. By the time I've finished the Magnum and the KitKat I know my destination and I feel giddy with the sugar and salt. I finish with the banana chips. They were Hannah's favourite. I try to hold on to the high feeling until my body forces me stop. I throw up so violently behind a tree that it makes my eyes water. I catch my breath, wipe my face and keep walking.

I go to unlock the door of the unit but it's already open.

I push open the door and see him. His bare back is facing away from the door, he's in the bed asleep. I want to run to him but anger stops me. Anger that he left the door unlocked, anger that he kissed me. My stomach clenches and I need to throw up again.

I run down the corridor, which seems to be endless, in search of the toilets which I've been too scared to use before now. When I find them, the smell makes me want to throw up even more. It all comes out, until I have nothing left in me. I sit on the dirty toilet seat, catching my breath. I stare at the cubicle door, no stickers or numbers or names of girls in this toilet, but stickers and numbers for three variations of 'MAN WITH A VAN'. I wash my hands with a trickle of brownish water, and look in the mirror that's so dirty that I can barely see my own reflection, just a blurry outline, in which I could be Hannah.

A moth flies down from the flickering lights and lands on the wall near me. I almost say, 'Don't look at me.' I go back towards the unit.

He's still asleep. His T-shirt, at the foot of the bed, is different to yesterday's, so he's left this room. The piano lid is closed. What has he been doing in here? I start loudly going through her stuff, desperate to achieve something tonight – to move forward in the mess and the vomit, to wake him up. I can't keep her things like this for ever, amongst the filth and the moths and the fact that I have betrayed her.

I miss the way that Hannah and I would argue. She'd

become shrill, nasal, which was funny as she had for a while maintained a low and rather husky voice, from her years of smoking as a student. She was very strict about me not smoking, showing me the lines around her mouth which she claimed were there because of smoking – vanity derived from Mum. After she quit smoking she got into Bikram yoga and veganism and facial oils and meditation and all the fancy health-fad things. Once I went with her to a Bikram yoga class in Old Street and we got chucked out because the teacher heard me saying, 'This is bullshit,' in the downward dog position; it was 'disrupting the flow of the room'. I thought Hannah would be annoyed with me in the changing rooms but she said she was glad that we got to leave early because we had the showers and free moisturiser to ourselves.

I sit on Hannah's carpet and go through another box – her vinyl records and cookbooks. I don't want any of them, and that saddens me. I watch him breathe, in and out. I'm afraid of what I'll say to him in this mood. Afraid I'll leap into his arms, even if he's indifferent. Afraid he'll be able to see inside me and the 5,000 calories I've just eaten and thrown up. His eyes start to open.

# 41

Him: How long have you been here?
Me: A while. When did you arrive?
Him: About two hours ago.

I want to tell him that I liked the kissing.

Him: I'm sorry.
Me: What for?
Him: I just – I didn't call you today –

I am glad he didn't.

Me: You didn't need to. I mean, why would you –

I turn away from him and drink some Diet Coke, to
try to change the taste in my mouth.

Him: You OK?
Me: Just tired –
Him: I did nothing today. I felt too . . . I dunno. I
    felt weird.

I want to tell him I've just followed a woman to a strip club, about the Haribo and the crisps and the vomiting. But I can't speak. I just want to feel better, immediately. I take another sip of Diet Coke and walk towards him. I know what I'm doing.

He sits to face me, I stay standing. His jeans are crumpled on the dusty floor. His boxers have a hole in, which I like, and his breathing makes my shirt go in and out very slightly. After a while of resting his head against my stomach, he puts his hands under my shirt and touches my boobs over my bra. As he tries to pull off my top my hair gets caught. I have to wriggle out of it as he unclips my bra. Once I'm detangled, I notice how long his eyelashes are. With his eyes half-closed he sucks my nipple. I have never liked that until now, I get too embarrassed.

I unbuckle his belt and kneel down.

He puts his hands on the sides of my head, his fingers massage my scalp, but he doesn't push me in any direction which I'm used to and expect. I pretend I'm not me and close my eyes. His hands move to my nipples and time seems to stop. Everything goes the good kind of blurry. I like the soft sounds that he's making as I move in and out. After he comes, he guides me up and begins to pull my leggings down. I remember my period. I push his hand away and make him lie down. I lie down next to him and make an extreme effort not to succumb, not to let him near my giant fucking pad. We breathe in and out in silence until I'm dizzy. He closes his eyes and he runs his finger up and down the middle of my chest, and draws a circle over my heart.

The last thing I see before I fall asleep is his boat tattoo.

★  ★  ★

I wake up to the sound of piano, with my hands covering my breasts. Before I fully open my eyes I lie there and listen; try to recognise the song. I think it's 'Tiny Dancer'. I sit up and fully acknowledge that I'm half-naked. He sees me forage for my bra and T-shirt as he keeps playing. I see that he's finished my Diet Coke – the empty bottle sits on top of the piano, the lid right next to the edge, ready to fall off.

Him: Sorry, I'll get you another one. I can go to the shop now.
Me: It's fine.

He's still in his boxers. My head pounds from what I put my body through last night, from my period – and I look around Hannah's weird room and feel so deeply confused.

Me: What time is it?
Him: It's only eight.
Me: I need to go home. Before my shift.

I get dressed. The second my bra and Costa shirt are back on, he gets dressed too so we're equal. We do this in silence. I want to make a joke about how we've treated this storage room so far like a sleazy motel, but joking feels wrong right now. He doesn't seem to be looking at me. Did I make him – let me – give him a blow job? Can that be a thing? Either way, I want to get out of here. I want to get out of this room.

Me: I think I need to re-think this place. Have you seen the moths? The toilet? It's so dirty. I need to

217

start going through her things and actually – you know – maybe –

He comes over to me and hugs me. I'm relieved.

Him: Don't think about that right now.

He smells of sleep and me.

Me: Sorry, I just feel slightly strange after –
Him: I'll come with you again. To work.

Rather than tell him there's no need, I rest my cheek on his biceps and kiss it – gratefully. If I had to say goodbye to him right now, I would spend the day going insane. I need to know I didn't invent the tension, the sexual tension – which is something I have been prone to do in the past.

Me: OK. We need to rush.

He gets his shoes on and as I bend down to put on mine, I feel blood pour out of me. He strokes the piano as he makes his way to the door, accidentally pushing the Diet Coke top off the lid. I see the cliff, I see Hannah jumping, I see her flying. He opens the door.

Me: I'll just be one minute.

I open Hannah's drawers and rummage for some leggings, anything. I find some grey trousers, ones she wore for work. I open her knicker drawer and pick some nice ones. I see a box of tampons. I take one, even though

I won't use it. I rush to my bag, get out another huge pad.

I pick up the Diet Coke lid as I leave.

I lock the door and see him waiting by the lift, his head against the dirty wall. A moth flies about and we both stare at it as the lights flicker.

\* \* \*

He goes into the newsagent's to buy some cigarettes. He comes out with a Diet Coke for me. He smokes and I drink on the walk to the station. We pass a primary school and see a mother in a bicycle helmet parking her bike. She leaves a toddler sitting in the back seat of the bike while she rushes her son into school, late. The toddler looks fine for a moment until he realises he's been left behind and begins to scream. We stand close by until the mother comes back and kisses the toddler, instantly calming him with a babyish voice.

> Mother: You thought I wasn't coming back, didn't
> you?

They cycle off and we keep walking. I choke on some of the cigarette smoke and have to stop again to cough. He puts his hand on my back.

> Him: Sorry.
> Me: Did Hannah mind you smoking?

He doesn't answer, just shrugs. I get annoyed.

We manage to get seats on the Tube. His foot begins its tapping and his thigh presses into mine. I don't know if he means for it to. His stubble has grown longer, he looks as dishevelled as I must do.

There's something about being with him on a train that catalyses my need for clarity and information.

Me: Who do you live with?

He pretends he can't hear me. So I speak louder, not caring if people look.

Me: Who do you live with?
Him: My brother.
Me: Danny?
Him: Yeah. You've met Danny?
Me: Kind of –
Him: I can't really hear you –

The train is loud and screeching but I know that he can hear me. I smell his breath, I don't mind it. Women stare at him, he's beautiful, his breath right now would be forgiven by most people. As I sit here in my sister's corporate trousers and my coffee-stained Costa shirt, I am sure people think I'm not with him, that he couldn't be mine. But then he touches my knee.

Him: Are these Hannah's trousers?

I nod. He squeezes my knee but stops when his phone vibrates. Rosa. I think of Rosa for the first time in a different way. I have betrayed her too.

The older couple sitting opposite us are definitely going to Heathrow too. They're holding hands, the man is wearing a trilby, and the silver-haired woman is already in a kaftan. Their suitcase between his knees, stickers plastered all over it. I study the stickers. My favourite is the one which says simply 'I'VE BEEN TO HAWAII'. The suitcase has an elastic strap round it, padlocked. They have a conversation in whispers, looking quite mischievous. Maybe they're planning a robbery, or maybe they're just talking about who printed off the boarding passes.

I am bored by my own curiosity. Rowan's other foot starts tapping and he stares at the stickers too. At Heathrow, he keeps up with my pace as I power through the station into the terminal. When we get nearer Costa I turn to him. He's out of breath and is clutching a cigarette already.

Me: You live with your brother, Danny.
Him: Um, yeah. Why?
Me: I bumped into Leila.
Him: Right. Yeah. That's been quite – mad.
Me: She's fucking pregnant. Why didn't you tell me?

He's not fazed, still seems calm, which riles me even further. I want an explanation. I want to know why he came with me again this morning; does he feel as guilty as I do? We should talk about last night, we should talk about us, we should talk about Hannah.

Him: Why are you angry?
Me: I'm not angry.
Him: You are.

The books say I'm allowed to be angry. Let me be angry. I'm angry with his rootlessness, I'm angry with his passivity, I'm angry with the people stampeding past us with their wheelie suitcases, I'm angry with myself.

Me: This is fucked up – it's so fucked up.

I start pounding his chest and he lets me. People don't stop and stare; no one cares, they're on their way to somewhere better.

Me: What about your new girlfriend – you got a
  new girlfriend –
Him: It just happened.
Me: So things just happen and you take no
  responsibility?

I pull away from him. He rubs his eyes. He regrets coming with me, regrets everything.

Him: I don't know what to say.
Me: Neither do I.
Him: I didn't think and it was all too fast, I just
  needed someone.
Me: So now you need me?
Him: I need something, I need to be close to her.
Me: Hannah's not here any more. I'm not Hannah.
Him: I know.

# 42

I put my bag in the back room, sit on a chair that's been removed from the café area. A customer spilt coffee on it, and it's yet to be washed and saved. I don't know if it can be. As I sit down into it I smell sugary coffee. Sal comes in, wearing her blue Crocs like we work in a hospital. She's pear-shaped with a round bottom. I've noticed that she eats every hour and here she is eating a banana in two bites.

Sal: Ready for another day?
Me: Sure.
Sal: Let me make you a coffee, you look like you
   need one.

She winks at me, and I worry that she's just seen my outburst with Rowan. Why does she wink? Her cheeks are rosy, naturally rosy, like she works on a farm. I hate that I think that she would look better in make-up. So much better. I hate that I want to punch her, with her cheeks full of banana.

Me: Is it OK if I quickly go to Boots? I need some
   tampons.

Sal: Of course, hon. I'll take your spot until you get back.

It's easier to say something believable like, 'I need some tampons,' rather than, 'I need to wash my entire body because I've not been home and I just gave my dead sister's boyfriend a blow job.'

As I walk to Boots, I see people being dropped off in the car park and waving goodbye. Hugging goodbye. Shaking hands goodbye. I watch each one of these goodbyes with new fascination. Are they aware that this might be the last time they see each other?

Three of the best airport
goodbyes I've witnessed:

1. A man kisses his girlfriend as she heads up to Security. On the escalator he shouts up to her urgently, 'You forgot your phone.' She panics and walks down the escalator, annoying everyone on their way up. She almost falls. Once she successfully gets to the bottom, it's clear she did not forget her phone. She smacks him and they kiss again, for longer this time.

2. A lady waits for her incredibly skinny teenage son to check in. He seems embarrassed to say goodbye in public, so she hangs back and watches him go. But when he puts his suitcase on to be weighed, he looks round and sees her crying. He runs towards her, leaving his suitcase, leaving the queue, and stands in front of his mother. He puts his forehead on her shoulder. She pats his back and wipes her tears, sends him on his way

again. He looks back once more and waves, sweetly, like a little boy.

3. A woman waits outside the terminal, peering in to watch her friend checking in. She's smoking so can't come inside. She holds one hand up to the glass to get a better view, but can't see her anywhere. The friend sneaks up to the glass from the inside and jumps in front of the woman, scaring her and making her laugh so hard she drops the cigarette and starts having a coughing attack. The friend rushes outside to say sorry. They hug and sway, rocking with laughter. When the friend goes back in, she looks back to see the woman giving her the finger from outside.

The bomb-tattoo man sells me a toothbrush, a Tangle Teezer, some Simple moisturiser, and some giant pads. As I tap my card and Hannah's Boots card, I catch him looking at my lips, which makes me bite them, want to hide them.

Him: You look nice today.
Me: What?
Him: You look nice today.

Staggered, I walk fast out of Boots and to the toilets further away from Costa. I go into the cubicle at the end which has a sink. I brush my hair harshly, pulling some strands out and tying it back in a bun. I wash my hands and then my face and put some moisturiser on which stings. I sit on the closed toilet seat and check my phone, needing some basic shit to stare at on Instagram, maybe an inspirational quote. But it's dead, no battery.

I walk back to work and a pop song comes on in which makes my whole body seize up. Dua Lipa's 'New Rules'. Hannah loved this song, she would recite the 'rules' to me as if they were biblical, lip-sync to it in Ubers and send me videos of her re-enacting the music video in her office with her blinds closed, as business meetings were happening all around her. I stand deadly still and listen to the lyrics. I want to cry, but I don't, the moisturiser has just settled into my skin and she'd tell me it was a waste.

I am ready to start in my iPad position. Sal delivers me an iced mocha. I take a sip in front of her to please her, then she tells me she's 'popping off' to the loo. I think of the Haribo from last night, how I threw up one of the snakes, a whole snake, in fact, in my vomit. I watch her walk off in a different direction to where the staff toilets are, unable to imagine her existing outside of Heathrow.

I spot the couple from the Tube here, sitting on high stools with their coffees. The man still has his trilby on; the woman, who must be in her seventies and has her back to me, has a severe VPL, which makes me smile. It would have made Hannah smile, too. He puts one hand on her back as he dives down for another bite of pastry. The pastry crumbs go all over his lap. She brushes them off for him and looks around the airport, wide-eyed. They check the time on his watch and stand up, ready to go. She kisses him fully on the mouth and he grabs her bum. He passes her the suitcase and she walks away, leaving him sitting in Costa with the remainder of his pastry.

She's going away on her own.

Six out of ten of my next customers order the new special – a Salted Caramel Latte. At the end of my shift, as I gather the energy to get the Tube home at rush hour, I sit on the ruined chair in the back room again and stare at my photo, which I've not protected adequately enough in my tote bag. It upsets me that the corner has been bent over, creating a little crease where the sun meets the sea. I stroke Hannah in the photo with my thumb.

As I leave Costa, I see him, waiting for me.

Me: What are you doing?
Him: I just wanted to tell you. I'm going to break up with Rosa.

I don't say anything. I keep walking and he follows. We don't confirm where we're going but what's about to happen feels inevitable. I look into his eyes a few times on the Tube. I wish he'd seen what I'd seen. I wish someone else had seen her dead too.

# 43

We go straight to the bed without speaking. We avoid each other's faces and I put mine down into the bed, scrunch the sheets in my hands. My trousers come off easily, they were too big for me, and at one point he stops and rests his face on my back for a bit. It's so tender that I almost laugh. But then he goes hard and fast and it's over quickly. He comes inside me, I guess because it's pretty obvious I'm on my period. There's blood all over the sheets like we're in a true crime scene. He lies on the bed as I stay on all fours on my elbows, recovering. I'm glad that he's not touching me, I don't like being held after sex anyway. He bounds naked towards the piano.

I walk equally naked, clumsily, to a box marked 'FLANNELS AND TOWELS' with the green Sharpie. I cover up the bloodstain on the bed with a small white towel. I listen to him play sweetly, covering my breasts with my hands and crossing my legs. After a while I find something to wear in her chest of drawers. I recognise a T-shirt — one that she couldn't throw away. It's Brian's. Does Brian know that she's dead? I duck behind the bed and put a new pad on my pants. Something stabs my foot, a splinter, and when I try to get it out, I see that the soles of my feet are black with dirt.

He stops playing and looks at me, as I stand up, repulsed by the floor.

Him: Are you hungry?
Me: Um, I guess, yeah, kind of.

He gets dressed and leaves, smiling as he closes the door. Fifteen minutes later he comes into the unit with a large cheap pizza and a large bottle of Diet Coke. I think of the last pizza I had before she died, walking up the hill to the hotel, so full. Hannah never ate pizza when we were abroad, she ate the fancy things. Even back home she was a pizza snob and never ate one like this with me. But maybe she ate the shitty, plasticky pizza with him?

We sit on the bed and he takes out his laptop, which looks extremely old, and puts Netflix on. He has two users – his, with a dog avatar, and Hannah's, with a little princess one. I pretend I don't notice and open the pizza box as he scrolls through the billions of random shows I don't want to watch. Hannah wouldn't let me eat in the bed. But I would sneak in toast sometimes, and she'd lay out a tea towel for the crumbs. I worry that the grease from the pizza box will soak through to the sheets, so I put it on top of the towel, on top of my bloodstain.

Eventually, we settle on *The Thick of It* and speed-eat the pizza. I wish he'd got two, but I'm flattered that he didn't think I'd be able to eat a whole one on my own. I think I actually laugh at points, despite having seen every episode five times, either with Hannah or by myself. He falls asleep first. I put the pizza box and Diet Coke bottle on the floor and pull the duvet over him carefully.

I wake up in the middle of the night and he's hugging me from behind, stroking my skin, and I smile. I close

229

my eyes and drift back to a half-sleep. I can smell pizza and I hear the sea.

★ ★ ★

When I wake up he's gone. He's taken the pizza box and closed the piano lid. I pick up the Diet Coke from the floor, take a sip and wait, assuming he's just gone to the toilet.

I open a box full of her plates and bowls and take out the only one I used at her flat. It has a world map on. I stand still, holding my favourite plate, looking at the door, until I realise I've been waiting an hour and fourteen minutes. I get dressed and leave, taking the rubbish and her plate.

On my way home, I try not to think the worst, but I can't help it. He must have died, been murdered. He's got hit by a truck or stabbed in the street. Or he's killed himself and left a note telling everyone what we've done to Hannah, our betrayal. I walk fast, in an emergency state. No one is in Reception as I leave.

I see children on their way to school, eating their breakfast on the go; I see the same toddler waiting for his mum in the bicycle seat outside the school gates, crying. I see people on their way to work, walking the way you walk when you're so very close to running late but don't want to start running yet, and I'm jealous because I have nothing to do and nowhere to go. The empty day ahead without work is terrifying.

I can't face the Tube, so I walk and walk, and in a way I'm glad my phone is dead so that I don't listen to the same Disney playlist. As I walk up my pathway I see the white-haired toddler from next door coming towards me.

She smiles, and I smile back. I feel bad that this innocent small thing is seeing me like this – the morning after – in a baggy T-shirt with a pizza stain, dirty feet with no socks and Hannah's grey work trousers. Compared to this John Lewis mother who's avoiding looking in my direction, I am a wreck.

The toddler ambles ahead and her name is called. Maya.

I remember when I found a list of Hannah's baby names. I knew she was staying the night with her boyfriend at the time, so I let myself into her flat and pretended it was mine. This was a regular weekend pastime. I ordered food, watched her Netflix, used her face creams and oils, tried on her clothes. She'd get back the next day knowing I'd be there, ready to be fake-angry about how I'd messed everything up. In fact she enjoyed cleaning up after me. One weekend, I got into her bed and opened the bedside drawer, looking for her vibrator, but instead found a folded-up piece of corporate headed letter paper. Inside was her list.

Hannah's Baby Names:

Mary
Hattie
Isadora
Mateo
Johnny
Hayden

It terrified me, I wasn't ready for her to have a baby. I ripped up the list and threw it away. I wish I hadn't now.

I open my front door and all of my windows are already open, so I do my usual check for pigeons. I look at the fence, check that it's still caving in. The other toddler from next door is in her garden, sitting on a bright play mat, toys all around. The mother is lying back on the mat with her eyes closed, resting, until the toddler crawls onto her stomach. The mother picks her up, arms stretched, suspended in the air. The toddler giggles and squeaks and they both look so happy. As they come back down to earth the mother catches me looking. Quickly I close my window.

I run a bath and sit on my bathroom floor; I close my eyes and listen to the sound of the running water. But the floor – it feels so sticky. I open my eyes and scan it. I see blobs of moisturiser, bits of chewed-off nail, and my hairs are everywhere. I stand up, wash my feet in the sink with soap. Then I get some flannels and dip them in the bathwater. I spray the whole floor with antibacterial spray, then clean it with each foot on a wet flannel, shuffling back and forth. When those flannels are dirty I get new ones, dipping them in the bath and spraying and cleaning, spraying and scrubbing. On my knees, with my feet or my hands.

Once I'm finished, I move on to cleaning the sink and the door handles, then the living-room floor, the kitchen floor. I hoover everything, even kitchen surfaces. I don't stop till it's spotless, by which time I'm red in the face, sweating and out of breath. The flat looks like someone else's. It's always felt as though it's meant to be someone else's, as though I'm just squatting. It's only a matter of time until my parents take it off me and decide it's theirs again, though it's so run-down it would never sell. It's strange to think that Hannah will not know any future postcodes that I may have.

As I drain the dirty bathwater, I have a shower and

clean my teeth more thoroughly and vigorously than I have in months. I use the last of Hannah's tooth floss and let myself cry. I dry my face, put on some moisturiser and I'm ready to start the day again, fresh.

My phone buzzes and I run to it, naked, pathetic with hope that it's him, telling me where he went and why he left without saying goodbye. But it's from my dad.

Dad (text): I'm in town tonight – dinner?

And I slump down on to the clean floor.

I know I should see him; what if I don't reply and then he dies tonight and I live for the rest of my life knowing I didn't go for dinner with my dad, when I could have? I have no plans, I have no one.

Me (text): Sure, text me where and when.

I look out of the kitchen window and see that the mother and toddler have gone back inside.

# 44

We meet at a cool new chicken restaurant in Piccadilly.
I feel a surprising sense of comfort seeing him as I walk
in. My stomach churns with excitement as I pass a waitress delivering a whole roasted chicken to the table next
to us. My dad smiles at me, salivating.

    Me: Hannah wouldn't have let us meet here. It's not
      very vegan.

His smile fades instantly, and he tries to get the waitress's
attention. I take this as my cue to not talk about Hannah.
He says he's already ordered us a bottle of red wine, a
whole chicken and some chips. The waitress clears away
the two bottles of beer he's already drunk.

    Me: How's writing?
    Him: Really good. Best I've done in a while.
    Me: That's good. Do you know when you might be
      finished?
    Him: You know it's never 'finished' –
    Me: Yeah, no, obviously, but do you have a deadline
      from your publisher or agent or whatever –

I see the little vein in the side of his forehead get a bit bigger and I know I've accidentally pushed him too hard, too soon. Or maybe I meant to. He ignores me. The red wine arrives and he drinks it as soon as the glasses are poured. I take a small sip.

Him: So we need to discuss some things.
Me: Really? Like what?
Him: Is the flat empty yet?

I want to hear him say her name.

Me: Hannah's flat, you mean.
Him: Yes.

The waitress arrives with the posh thick-cut chips. I don't like thick chips. I am intent on pushing him now.

Me: Well, yes. Hannah's flat is now almost empty.
Him: That's good.
Me: It's not good, is it?

He bristles and I notice his beard is now fully grey. He's lucky his hair is still thick at his age. I wonder if I would have fancied Fred if he'd had no hair when I first met him, and if not, would I have done better, so far, in my life? What was it I found attractive about him, initially, other than his indifference?

Him: I know you don't want me to put the flat on
    the market –
Me: Hannah's flat –

Him: Your mother needs the money, and so do I,
    frankly. Until this book is out, at least –

We both know it's never going to be out. He likes
being in a constant state of creative purgatory. The
chicken arrives, and as it glistens and steams I feel sorry
for it, because it was alive once. I feel sorry for myself
too. I'm sitting opposite a man who makes up half of
me, yet barely knows anything about me. He cuts into
the chicken and I want to stop him but I don't. He puts
a breast on my plate, as he casually watches a waitress's
bum walking by. I stare at the chicken while he goes to
the bathroom. I can't eat.

He chats to the waitress on his way back. His smile
looks fake, he seems kind of desperate and it's embarrassing.
He sits back down, smelling of handwash. He eats only
a little of the chicken, no posh chips, but he finishes the
bottle of wine and my glass too.

He needs to think I'm OK so that he can leave. So I
tell him I'm enjoying my job, that I like the people-
watching. I don't tell him that I haven't thrown away
anything of Hannah's, that I'm still waiting for her to
come back, that all her stuff is safe in a dirty storage unit
with moths and bloodstains.

I tell him I might look into doing a sculpting course.
I know this should pique his interest because his father
was a sculptor and he idolised him, probably because he
died when he was very young. I have no interest in
sculpture, but I like pleasing him. He brings the conversation back to his writing, because of the wine.

Him: The idea came out of nowhere.
Me: What's it about?

Him: That's a big question.
Me: It's a simple question –
Him: Ruth –

He's angry and stops me talking with another fake smile, different from the one he used for the waitress. Even though there's only a drop of wine left, he drinks it. I wait for him to say more about his fucking book, but he doesn't; he's ready to go and spend time with someone who doesn't love him. I want him to know me but I don't know who I am without her, so why would he? He gestures to the waitress with the gliding bum for the bill.

Him: So?
Me: So? What?
Him: How are you?
Me: Now that's a big question.

I shake my head as tears start to form and he looks away; I think I catch a glimpse of pain but I can't be sure. He doesn't prod me any further. He over-tips. We leave the restaurant and stand outside as he lights a cigarette and I think of Rowan. I want him, I want him. I look back and see the waitress with my full plate of chips, eating one after the other.

My dad takes two drags and then chucks it on the ground. I stamp on the remains as we walk away, like I did to all his discarded cigarettes as a child, just in case they started a fire and our house burnt down.

He's got his shabby suitcase with him as he always does. I wonder where he's staying tonight, why he's never asked to stay with me. A black taxi with its light on comes down the little Soho street and he waves it down. I worry he won't hug me goodbye, but he does. Not an emotional or long hug, but nevertheless a hug.

Him: So, I'll see you soon.
Me: OK.
Him: Take care of yourself.
Me: I'm trying –
Him: I know.
Me: Good luck with . . . the book –
Him: Thanks.

He gets in. I stay smiling in case he looks back, but he doesn't. All I know is I heard him say 'Notting Hill'. At least he has somewhere, or someone, to go to, someone to pretend everything is going great to.

I walk through Soho past neon-lit tattoo parlours, a late-night frozen-yoghurt Tinder meeting point, and through the old sex alley towards Berwick Street. A crinkled woman in a short leather skirt and fishnet tights, who could be in her twenties or her fifties, smiles at me as she blows her vape smoke in my face. I look in the window of the comic-book shop. I used to go in there regularly before I got too threatened because all my art school peers' work was now on display, being celebrated. I cross over Oxford Street, still hungry and still tired. I think about getting an Uber but decide against it; I don't want to speak to anyone or wait for ages because of my low star rating. So I go into a Sainsbury's Local, in search of something sweet. I see the cereal aisle and bound towards it. That's what I need, that's what I want – but then I see her.

Her tattooed fingers give her away. Rosa. Headphones around her neck. She's browsing the herbal teas, predictably. She doesn't notice me even though I'm staring; she chooses her tea (detox fennel mix) and puts it into her basket, which also includes white bread, cheese, milk and chocolate. The contents of the basket confuse me. She takes out her phone. Is it a text from him?

She walks right past me, staring straight ahead. I see a woman in silly but fun pink dungarees and frizzy hair waiting for her at the checkouts. She helps Rosa load the stuff into an eco-string bag, and I notice they have a synchronicity about them which suggests they have been friends for years. They even complement each other aesthetically. I'm sad for a second that I no longer have friends, but then I was never a good friend anyway.

I watch her pay for both of them at the self-service checkouts. They look relaxed as they disappear from my view into the night. I know he hasn't told her yet by the way she walks. I buy some Crunchy Nut corn flakes, Coco Pops and whole milk, and hear my mum's voice in my head, who only allowed skimmed milk in our house: 'Why waste calories on milk?'

I walk in what I think is the direction of home.

# 45

I wake up on the sofa the next morning with a cereal hangover, if that's possible. The empty Coco Pops box, Crunchy Nut corn flakes box, bowl and spoon are on the coffee table. The curtains are wide open, the TV is on mute and I have less than an hour to get to work.

I have a shower in my new clean bathroom. My period has almost ended, and even though I forgot how fucking annoying they are, already I kind of miss it. I get dressed in my uniform, which is dirty and reminds me that I need to go to the launderette, and put on the first podcast that pops up for the walk to the station. I play it louder than is comfortable, anything to drown out my thoughts.

I miss her. It's too early in the day to be this sad. I think about Rowan and then pinch the skin on my arm to stop myself.

On my break I go to Boots and buy some paracetamol and a Ribena from the fairy godmother. I take a fast walk around the airport and I think I can see him from a distance countless times. The man in a navy T-shirt in WHSmith looking at car magazines, or the man with good forearms ordering an Americano. The man with a guitar case carefully putting his toothpaste into a plastic bag at Security. Then it's simply the way someone's shoulders are sloped, or anyone with hands in their pockets. It's everyone wearing black Converse, then it's anyone in black shoes.

Sitting on the toilet, scrolling through Instagram, emboldened by how proudly strangers display their lack of self-awareness online, I say out loud, 'I could text him?' I want the woman pissing in the cubical next to me to shout back, 'Text him, yes, text him,' but she doesn't and I don't. I can't text him.

I go to the windows to watch the planes. It's always busy by the windows; people like to watch big things shooting off into the sky. I sit there for a while; three planes take off. I used to be scared of flying until Hannah told me some statistics about how rare it is to die in a plane crash – stats I'd undoubtedly heard before, but coming from her they meant something. She'd pick up all the free magazines and papers on the walk to the departure gate and read them one by one on the plane, and then take them with her for additional holiday reading in case she finished her books. I must have the magazines from our last holiday in the unit. If I find them, I'll keep them.

I miss her, I miss her texts.

There wouldn't be an hour in the day without us texting random shit to each other. When we first got mobile phones we would text each other from within our house. She'd be sitting upstairs on her bed, books splayed every-where, geekily texting me 'cool' facts she was learning from her geography or history coursework. I would send her a running commentary of *The Simpsons* from the sitting room. We both liked Marge the best and would create Marge Simpson fan fiction: I would draw her and then Hannah would help me create little comics and storylines. When Marge had a fourth baby with a famous scientist so the baby was born extremely clever and immediately went to university. When Marge became a stand-up comedian. When Marge stole a litter of puppies and went to jail.

I feel heavy as I walk towards work, and with each step, it's almost as though Hannah's sitting on my shoulders and she knows everything. I deserve to feel this way, to be punished by her, to explain myself. I glance at my reflection as I have another harrowing thought, and I look fine. I look like I'm completely fine.

Sal is at the tills and she smiles at me. I see the back of Paloma's newly pink head bobbing from side to side as she froths milk. She sees me and smiles too. They like me. Why?

Maybe I should stay close to them, the people who like me, and work a double shift. I'm scared of another evening on my own. For so many months I needed to be solitary, to cut people off. Now, after this short burst of him, I don't know how I could have spent even an hour alone.

He's gone back to Rosa. He must have.

I get behind the iPad and take an order from a tall man holding hands with an equally tall, super-skinny lady – two cappuccinos. They're smartly dressed and look like they enjoy posh sports and posh things. I see dandruff on his jacket and he says 'cappuccino' in an attempted Italian accent and it makes me laugh. He looks at me like I'm a piece of shit. So I add 'two extra shots plus extra caramel on both' on the order note for Paloma. I go up to her to reiterate the order, discreetly. She knows I'm fucking with them and gets on board. For the first time since I've been here, I feel like I'm part of a team.

I go back on autopilot mode, to get through the day, but by the end of my shift, my arm is bleeding because I've been pinching myself. Pinching helps.

I know he can't save me. But I feel like I'm on a bridge, between two cliffs. It's dangerous and rickety and could collapse at any second. I was put on this bridge the day Hannah died and I either make it to the other side – or I just give up and fucking die too. He's put himself on this bridge with me and he's struggling like I am. But whatever he's doing, even if it's just being nearby, it's helping me.

I don't care if he's fucking other people, I don't care if he's texting Rosa, apologising to Rosa, making plans with Rosa – I just want him to stay on the bridge with me until I know where I'm going.

I don't text him on the Tube, I don't text him on my walk back from the station, I don't text him when I get home. I turn off my phone and put it in the kitchen, so I can't check it at ten-minute intervals throughout the night. I watch *The Thick of It* until I fall asleep.

# 46

A single magpie sits on a street lamp outside my window, looking straight at me, as though it's toying with me. I watch the world waking up, cocky cyclists without helmets, people not looking as they cross the road. The glum woman in the flat opposite is doing yoga. I watch her disappear and reappear from the window in different poses – downward dog, tree pose – and she sees me, sipping my badly made tea, watching her. I don't care. I control the urge to shout at her: 'YOU'RE BAD AT YOGA.' It's 7.32 a.m. and I have a night shift today. I need to do something and see someone today, anything, anyone.

I list the former friends I've had in my head. Nice people, sure. Girls. I could text one of them. But if I do that I will have to talk about Hannah, how Hannah died and exactly what I've been doing since. The girls couldn't handle it, how extreme it was, it is and will always be.

List of what I talked about
with former friends:

- Celebrities we don't like
- Picnic plans that will be affected by the weather

- What little we know about politics but that's OK
- What little we know about global warming but that's OK
- Sixties retro hairbands on Etsy
- Thighs and upper arms
- How long is too long for oral sex
- The optimum amount of water to drink a day without needing to wee every five minutes
- Do we know any chefs?
- Getting married or not getting married but still having a big party anyway
- Trying for a baby
- Not trying for a baby
- Psoriasis
- Hating our jobs/applying for jobs/how cool our jobs are
- Siblings

The last one was my typical topic. I talked about Hannah and her life because it was reliably interesting and more eventful than mine. If I met a friend today, what would I talk about if I can't talk about my sister?

They would text me in those first few months, various iterations of the 'I'm so sorry' bullshit, not understanding that their texts made it even worse, because the texts made it more real. They came to the funeral and memorial and I don't remember their presence at all because I was looking down.

When I didn't reply after a few months, they stopped texting. At first I was glad, but now I resent them even more. I don't know what I would do if a friend lost her sister but I know I wouldn't send a text saying, 'I'm so sorry <sad emoticon> xxx', and then two weeks later ask them if they wanted to go to a gig as if everything was OK again, as if everything was normal.

There's no back to normal now, bitch.

Top three former friends:

1. *Maria.* She tried the hardest. She texted me four times, but all of the texts were just, 'Thinking of you.' I resented her because she still has her sister, one she is close to. A few times the four of us met up and went to watch a bad film. Just the thought of only three of us meeting up now makes me shout, 'NO!' over and over again and punch through a wall. No. I never want to see Maria again.
2. *Sarah.* She thought I would open up to her because her grandma died recently.
3. *CeeCee.* In her first text after Hannah died she wrote, 'I cannot imagine the colossal loss.' I googled 'colossal': extremely large or great, monstrous, towering, elephantine, gargantuan. I replied, 'Yes, CeeCee. Yes.'

Two weeks later she texted me again, and I hoped she'd give me another new word I could relate to and write down in my notebook. But it was an invite to her twenty-ninth birthday party at a place called Ballie Ballerson in Shoreditch. I googled the bar:

*Guests frolic in pits filled with over a million balls at this night spot serving retro cocktails.*

Fuck you, CeeCee. Fuck you. No, I don't want to frolic in a ball pit meant for toddlers.

I tried meeting a few of them some months after the funeral, for brunch. They asked me how I was and as I looked into their eyes I could tell that they wanted me to say I was getting better, that the pain was easing – because then it would make them feel less scared, and they could go back to believing that such a thing was unlikely to ever happen to them. I left the brunch place abruptly and decided to never brunch again.

I pour the rest of the tea in the sink and wash the cup. I stare at the single cup on the draining board, and think about taking a sleeping pill but when I check the cupboard I have none. So I put on my swimming costume under my Adidas tracksuit, swig some mouthwash and get out of my flat as quickly as possible. I don't understand the sudden urge to exercise, but I'm going to go with it. I don't take my phone or even check it before I leave which feels like an achievement. I'm bagless and it feels odd. All I have in my pocket are my keys and a ten-pound note.

I decide to walk all the way there, to the pool at Ironmonger Row near Old Street. This is the pool Hannah and I had swimming lessons in growing up, even though it was on the other side of London. Our mother chose it because she could use the thermal spa while we swam. I choose some vaguely familiar back streets, without following a route. Soon I find myself outside Hannah's Portakabin, PaperbackKids, with a 'FOR SALE' sign stuck on the window. It looks so sad. I've completely neglected it, forgotten about it. The gate is padlocked. Who locked it? Who has the keys? Who put it up for fucking sale? I blame my mum because that's always easiest. I go to get out my phone to text her before remembering I left it at home.

I claw the railings to try to look inside: the Quentin
Blake posters I helped Hannah blu-tack to the walls are
still there, but Hannah's bunting has fallen on one side
from the ceiling. I'm about to leave when I see something,
a paper note squeezed in between the railings. I pull it
out and open it to reveal a child's handwriting.

I miss you hana

Love jimi 🚣

He's drawn a little doodle of a boat. Rowan's tattoo. I
take the note with me and cry all the way to the pool.

★  ★  ★

The teenage lifeguard checks her phone and smiles to
herself while sitting on the high chair, twirling her hair
around her fingers. She looks distracted and conceited,
like she's got plans for the future and is sucking lots of
dick. Maybe she left someone in bed this morning. She's
barely doing her job, but I guess no one seems likely to
drown right now. The pool is full of adults, here to do
their early-morning lengths, making time for exercise
before their big important jobs in the city. I feel like a
fraud in the fast lane, but it's the only one available.

I swim as fast as I can for six lengths and then need to
stop. I hang on to the side of the pool, my knuckles
white, and I look up at the gym. People are running on
the treadmill looking over the water. Hannah used to be
one of those people. I waved, she waved back. After
swimming she'd announce how many lengths I'd swum,
adding on two to be nice.

I would join Hannah in the gym sometimes when I didn't feel like swimming, walking slowly on the treadmill as she did sprints next to me. She would listen to empowering podcasts about businesswomen and I would watch *The Real Housewives of . . .* on the tiny treadmill TVs that freeze every few minutes.

I force myself to do another fifteen lengths, some fast, most slow, and then kill as much time as possible wading slowly underwater, coming up for air only when I absolutely need to. The preoccupied lifeguard watches me. She'd be the one to try to rescue me if I attempted to drown myself this morning. It's 9 a.m. and I could ruin her life.

There is only one shower free when I get out, and I find out too late that it's the one that's always cold. After the excruciating first ten seconds, I quite like it, I feel rejuvenated. Mum was right. I lean my head back to let the water run over my face, and I see Hannah. I see her drifting away underwater, but this time there are no scuba divers to retrieve her broken body. Maybe that would have been better, more dignified, lost to the sea like a mermaid. I turn off the shower.

Hannah once pressed her boobs against the shower glass to make me laugh. We'd use the shampoo she brought specially from home because she said the gym shampoo was just hand soap. We'd draw hearts on the steamed-up glass or write, 'Hey bitch'. I long for her to be here.

On my way to the changing rooms I very nearly slip on the wet floor. I manage to regain my balance until the floor gets wetter and slopes downwards and I slip again, falling and bashing my left thigh. I am thankful my thigh has got bigger lately, that there's more fat to cushion me. I brace myself to find a crowd laughing at me. But

249

no one is there when I turn around. I get up and walk as normally as I can to my locker, where I'm confronted with two huge breasts in the changing room, so gigantic it's impossible not to stare. Their owner is aggressively talcum-powdering her feet, sitting down with a towel wrapped around her lower half. Her boobs suggest that she's about forty-five. Droopy, but nice, likely used for feeding multiple children.

Hannah's always going to be beautiful; she died young. I'll rot, deteriorate and droop.

The bruise on my thigh is already making headway. I imagine what she would have said about the talcum-powder lady's boobs.

I forgot to bring a towel, pants or bra because I'm a fucking idiot, so I take my clothes into a cubicle and stand inside flapping my arms up and down to try to air-dry my entire body. The flapping doesn't work, so I give up and sit naked on the bench in the cubicle. After a while I put my Adidas tracksuit on top of my swimsuit again, and the wetness creates deep uneven patches of colour. I leave the cubicle and dry my tracksuit with the hairdryer, leaving my hair wet. The three pounds I have left jingle in my pocket as I tip my head down.

I gaze at the snacks in the vending machine, like I did when I was six. Snacks after swimming were – are – the best thing about it. I can't decide between a Twirl and a bag of Maltesers for breakfast, but I can't afford both. The prices have increased since I was a girl. I go for the Twirl and head up the stairs to the observatory, the same stairs Hannah walked up two, sometimes three, times a week to go to the gym. Along with my life, our weekly routine has been obliterated.

I sit in the same spot I sat in when I waited for her to

come and find me after the gym. I'm ready for her head to pop round and tell me off for eating a Twirl. The lifeguard checks her phone again and I wonder if she's still going to be a lifeguard in five years, if she will lead a happy life after the age of twenty. I watch the swimmers, focusing on the bad ones – it's nice seeing people try.

# 47

2002

We took the headscarf off the telly and started clearing a space on the coffee table for our bowls of mixed cereal. It was a Saturday morning, maybe a Sunday. There were the usual few strangers sprawled on our living-room carpet. Hannah started banging pans together in the kitchen while I stood over them, with my menacing eight-year-old smile. It worked and they left pretty quickly.

The house phone went and we heard Mum scream upstairs, but didn't think anything of it, accustomed to her vocal warm-ups. She came downstairs ten minutes later wearing a scarlet off-the-shoulder summer dress, beaming. She shouted eagerly for us to get ready, we were going out to celebrate, and that she'd laid out our 'fancy clothes' and hair bows on the beds for us. Dad came downstairs sleepily, already dressed, as we went up. I looked at them as they met at the bottom of the stairs and Mum did a giddy jump into his arms, like a girl, like I'd never seen before.

We got in a black taxi to Regent's Park. Mum said she had packed a picnic, but when we laid it out on a rug, it was only champagne and crisps. We sat down and waited for Mum to tell us what this was all about. She got up and did a cartwheel, which made her dress fall over her face, displaying her white lace knickers and matching bra. Dad almost choked on a crisp. She straightened her dress and made her announcement.

Mum: I'm going to be in a film! The one I've been waiting for!

My dad lifted her up and twirled her around; she was beaming. I'd never seen them both so happy at the same time. We watched in disbelief as they moved their kissing to the picnic rug. Hannah watched while eating almost all the crisps, and I moved my attention to some boys playing football nearby who weren't wearing shirts. I'd never seen that before either. Suddenly, out of nowhere, the football hit me, hard on the top of my head. I fell back onto the grass, dizzy, seeing spots.

Hannah got up, without checking on me, and charged for the footballers, shouting all the way. She picked up the football and kicked it as far as she could to the other side of the park. It flew over our parents, who were still kissing despite the commotion, above my dizzy head. I watched it flying in the sky.

When I was able to sit up again, Hannah motioned for me to come with her, quietly. We ran away and hid behind a tree. We watched our parents until they eventually realised we'd gone. We saw them begin to panic, and we waited until they looked genuinely concerned, enjoying their despair. Then we ran back to them. By the time we reached them they had fallen to the ground laughing. I tried some champagne for the first time.

The film was never made, but that day was nice.

# 48

The Mediterranean
The first day of the last holiday

We were helped with our suitcases to the room. Hannah
took one look inside and shook her head at me. I knew
this was my cue to stay outside – she was on a mission.
She walked around the room confidently, checking the
bathroom first, then inspecting the sheets, then the view.
She came out and spoke charmingly in Italian to the
concierge. She got us moved to a much nicer, bigger, lighter
room within half an hour. I waited patiently in the lobby
while she handled things. I felt taken care of, special.

We got into our fancy new room, and each did a
celebratory fall onto the bed, face first and laughing. She
patted my head and scuffed up my hair, like I was her
little pet. Then we got changed and walked down the
hill to the beach.

Her: One day I'm going to live by the sea.
Me: What will I do?
Her: You'll come with me.
Me: But what if I don't want to live by the sea –
Her: We're sea people, Ruth –

She enjoyed saying we were sea people when we were by the sea, country people when we were in the country, cool warehouse people when we were in a cool warehouse. She made me feel like we could have been anything. She ran down the last bit of hill gleefully, with her arms wide open. I ran after her.

I saw a man lying on the sand getting help from a lifeguard after being stung by a jellyfish, and a family of four applying sun cream to each other's backs in slapdash circles. The father drew a smiley face with his finger on his son's back. We found two empty deck chairs underneath a giant umbrella and ordered a plate of watermelon and a bottle of white wine from the beach-bar staff. Hannah went into the sea while I waited for the snacks. I watched her flinch as the cold water hit her feet. She turned back to me and smiled. I was about to take a photo of her but the beach waiter arrived and said something I didn't understand, so I beckoned Hannah back. He needed our room number. She flirted with him and I got annoyed. Only a little, though.

That night we ordered room service even though we were in one of 'the food capitals of the world, with delicacies waiting for you on every street corner', according to a travel magazine that Hannah had read on the plane. We just wanted to be together, not waste time walking around trying to find a place; we wanted to save our energy for the week. She let herself cheat on veganism when we were abroad, so we had lobster and chips and watched a dubbed episode of *Friends*. She passed out asleep, snoring happily. I tucked her in, put her phone on charge and noticed three unread texts from Rowan. I knew her pin, but didn't read them, in case it started a fight the next morning.

I kissed her cheek and went to sleep next to her. I wish I had stayed up for longer. I wish I had watched her sleeping, I wish we'd had one more chat about nothing or one more episode. I wish I had known.

# 49

I arrive at Storage Etc., hair now dry from the walk. I feel anxious without my phone, and keep reaching into my pocket. Has he texted me? Will he be waiting for me to text him?

No one is behind Reception, but I hear shouting. I try to see what's happening, peering into the room behind the front desk. It is bare, with just a boxing bag hanging down from the ceiling and a square marked out with tape on the floor. Mickey is skipping and his father is filming him on a phone, shouting out encouragement and numbers in an angry way. One hundred, two hundred, three hundred. He skips faster and faster until he trips up and bends over to get his breath back.

As I'm waiting for the lift, Mickey comes up behind me and makes me jump. He smiles.

Him: All right?
Me: Yeah.

The lift doors open and he gets in with me, out of breath. I press the button and the doors close. His stomach is shiny and his breathing is loud. He keeps staring at me. I don't know where to look so I look down.

Him: You smell of chlorine.

We creak slowly upwards and look at each other briefly. Do I like him? The lift doors open and he runs away, towards the toilets in the darkness. I walk the other way and the lights wake up as I reach the door. It's locked so already I know that Rowan's not in there. I get inside, lock the door again, and smell him on the pillow as I punch it.

The bloodstain on the bed is now a shade of brown. I strip the sheets, getting more and more worked up as I go. The blood has soaked through to the mattress.

I stare at the piles of her possessions in big Ikea bags I tied up with string in a panic. She loved bedspreads and pillows and would only get really good-quality sheets. Whenever I slept in her bed I would run my hand along them in awe. She kept all her 'fun' pillows on display during the day and at night took them off one by one. In the morning she did the pillow dance all over again. I told her it was ridiculous.

I unleash the contents of one of the bags and twee little cushions scatter out onto her bare bed. They don't know that she's never coming back, at least they can't feel this. I decide to take one pillow home to my flat, and give the rest away. It's a pillow which says, 'YOU GOT THIS!' And I was horrible to her about it.

I lie back on the pillows. Two hours till work. My mouth is dry, I feel foggy. I check for water in a tote bag I left here, momentarily confusing myself for someone who remembers to carry water. All I have is gum.

I feel depleted and hollowed out, but I blow a bubble I'm proud of and sit by the piano. I play the only tune I know, 'Yankee Doodle'. I play it ten times. I stroke the keys and consider keeping the piano for myself, in my flat, but I know it's not meant for me. I used to watch Hannah dust the insides. I open the lid to look at the strings; I've never looked inside a piano before.

I see that there's a Polaroid, stuck on the inside. It's Hannah, in only a bra and pants. She's smoking on her balcony, hair wild and loose, in front of the black night sky. The flash has made her eyes red and she looks unfamiliar to me. This is someone else's Hannah.

I stick the Polaroid back and close the piano lid, chewing harder and harder and harder.

# 50

I'm on the Tube to work and reunited with my phone.
I text my mum.

Me (text): Who put the Portakabin up for sale????

Although I know the answer is my dad, I don't want
to text him today. I read my book on death, flicking
through for any advice specifically on how to cope with
waiting for a text.

I arrive at the airport hungry with just half an hour
before my shift starts. I remember to buy some sleeping
pills from the fairy godmother for after work, avoiding
the bomb-tattoo boy. I buy a tube of Pringles from the
WHSmith self-service machine, plus a Crunchie, a diet
7 Up and a bottle of water. I can't remember the last
time I had a proper meal with vegetables, real food.

In an attempt to get me to cook more for myself,
Hannah once ordered me an kitsch wooden spice rack
and a collection of seasonings. I never used them. I never
even put the spice rack up on the wall, it's still just sitting
in my cupboard, next to some nails and a hammer. I walk
around the airport, chewing the Crunchie and sipping
the 7 Up. I see Sal, sitting where I usually sit to watch

the planes. She's not eating, which is unusual. I down the bottle of water, stuff a few Pringles in my mouth and go to sit next to her. She doesn't notice me at first, she just looks wistfully into the distance. I nudge her and offer up a Pringle. She accepts.

Her: Ready for the long night?
Me: Kind of. I don't mind night shifts.
Her: Me neither.

We watch a load of passengers going up the pull-out stairs to board their plane. They all look so tiny from a distance. I see the last people in the queue, a couple, taking a selfie as they stand in front of the plane at the foot of the stairs. They get told to hurry up by an airport worker in a fluorescent orange jacket. Sal's feet start anxiously tapping and it reminds me of Rowan.

Sal: Where's this one going, do you think?

Her voice is shaky, and she looks very sad. She doesn't look at me but keeps staring ahead at the plane.

Me: Are you OK?

She shakes her head and starts crying, so loudly that strangers stare. I've never really thought about how old she must be, I just assumed that she's older than me. She seems much younger right now, as she wraps her arms around herself and hangs her head down. I freeze. I want to touch her arm or something to show that I'm not a cold person, but I can't and I don't and maybe I am a cold person. She rubs her eyes. Her blue mascara has run and the darkening blue sky outside matches it. Her lips are chapped and she keeps biting them.

Me: What happened?

The plane switches on its window lights and we see people in their seats. Sal looks out dramatically, yearningly, like she's in a scene for a student short film, having just said goodbye to her love. Has she ever been in love? I don't think I have. I eat another Pringle.

Sal: My cat died.

She begins crying harder and heavier and louder and people stare. Snot drips out of her nose and she wipes it with her hand. I want to slap her.

Me: Are you fucking joking?
Her: What?
Me: Are you fucking joking? About your cat?
Her: No. Why? She died last night – she was very
    old but still –
Me: That's even worse. An old cat –
Her: Ruth –
Me: I thought something terrible had happened to
    you –
Her: It is terrible –
Me: It's a cat. My fucking sister died eight months
    ago.

She goes silent and stares at me as my secret disperses into the air around us.

She looks shaken, ill-equipped to respond, as she should be. I want to shout the horrible sentence again, to make a point – my sister died, my sister died – but I just eat another Pringle, two more, three more. I stare at the plane again. It begins to move. The pilot is probably making his not-quite-funny announcement by now. After a few long minutes of silence and one airport security announcement about sharp objects, Sal straightens up and turns to me.

Her: I'm so sorry.

I offer her another Pringle. She accepts, but doesn't eat it.

Me: What was its name? Your cat.
Her: Squiggle.
Me: Squiggle?
Her: Yes.
Me: OK. I'm sorry.

I'm now trying really hard not to laugh. I'm not really sorry about her cat, and even less so upon hearing its stupid fucking name, but I smile and take a sip of 7 Up and it tastes so good. I feel lighter. Sal looks shellshocked and weary of me, but that doesn't stop her talking.

Her: What was your sister's name?
Me: Hannah.
Her: Oh, I like the name Hannah. Were you close?

She eats the Pringle and takes hold of my hand, putting it on her lap. I want to answer that question with something that's a million times more than a 'yes'. A billion times more, a trillion. But all that I can muster without crumbling are those three letters.

Me: Yes.

The plane we're watching starts to take off.

# 51

I wake up the next day and it's Friday evening and my time to go to the launderette. Thanks to a sleeping pill, I've killed a day. I check my phone, hoping there will be a text from Rowan, but I only have one frustrating message from my mum.

Mum (text): Breakfast tomorrow?

I buy some new liquid tabs and fabric softener and stain remover on the way, thinking about the four remaining liquid tabs I'm saving from Hannah's flat. They're in the storage unit in a little plastic bag. A crowd is outside the art school pub when I arrive at the launderette, drunkenly singing 'Happy Birthday'. It's my own birthday soon. Fuck.

I put my three sets of uniform, the bloody towel and Hannah's sheets into the huge washing machine. I like putting an extra liquid tab in because that's what she did and her things always smelt so nice. I put all my clothes into another washing machine, then I find the perfect spot to watch people exiting and entering the pub.

There's a paper on the bench next to me, one of the tabloids I haven't read since they reported on Hannah so grossly. I've avoided the news for so long now that I'm curious, so I pick it up. The front page is splayed with a story about the inquest into the death of a young fireman who was killed by a group of teenagers. They were driving over the speed limit after picking up one of the group who'd shoplifted, and their car hit the fireman as he turned a corner. He'd just gone out to get milk, to make tea in the morning for his new wife before he went to work.

The story is heartbreaking and there seems to have been a public outcry, which is still going on even though this happened eighteen months ago. I put the paper down and go outside. I pace back and forth outside the launderette and wish I had something to do, or that I smoked. Three women are outside the pub rehearsing a TikTok dance, having balanced a phone on a ledge, and they look utterly insane. I watch them, trying to make them notice me, to make them feel even the tiniest bit self-conscious, but they don't give a shit about how silly they look. The dance and the 'likes' are more important.

I shouldn't have picked up the paper. I'm jealous of the fireman's story, the wife's public and beautiful grief, the sustained coverage. There was no outcry for Hannah. There was her funeral and a few Instagram posts by random people, but that's it. People have forgotten, they aren't still angry, like me. To them Hannah was just an irresponsible person who took a risk and paid for it.

I go back inside and look at the photo of the fireman's wife again. The paper has been folded a few times so her face is wrinkled. When I smooth it out in my hands, I read that she's still really young, only twenty-five. She looks pretty, made up for the cameras, but I can tell she's destroyed. I begin to cry for her and suddenly, I feel relief. Relief that I can cry for someone else.

I turn the paper over and find the Sudoku page. I get a pen from my bag and write all the wrong numbers and decide which random, ominous but ultimately silly message I can leave for a stranger. Today I go for, 'I STILL KNOW WHAT YOU DID LAST SUMMER.'

# 52

I open my new notebook and write:

Need to make friends.

I'm sitting in a place called Ozone Roastery in East London. It's one of these super-cool coffee and food places run by super-cool Australians who act quite serious one day but are overly friendly the next. My mum and dad will be arriving any minute. This will be the first time I've met them both together for a meal like this. Alone, without Hannah.

From what I can gather by the high-pitched shrieks, there's a bridal brunch party in the booth opposite me. One of them is wearing a white floral hairband with a mini-veil and a white summery dress. She's not wearing 'L' plates, but I can tell she is the bride-to-be. With the heat coming from the open kitchen, they look like melting wax sculptures, all with too much bronzer and highlighter on their cheeks. They take a group selfie, and then get a waitress to take a photo of them. They check it and then yank her back to take another, sucking in their cheeks and pouting for a 'funny one'.

There are eight of them. Eight friends.

I can't imagine having eight friends. The bride side would be practically empty at my wedding. Though I'm sure that I can't ever get married now, knowing that she won't be there. I have no one. I had her and she was my gateway into social activity. I was lazy, I was arrogant. I thought I didn't need anyone else, because she would always be here.

My cappuccino arrives. It's tiny because it's proper coffee in here, so I order another straight away and the waitress seems to understand why. She smiles at me and I feel better. I like her energy. I want to be the type of person who has a nice energy. I watch the cooking in the open kitchen: bacon sizzles and eggs are cracked. Hannah and I came here a few times, and each time I would get a full breakfast, Hannah some variation of avocados. I liked to remind her that as a teenager she used to eat bacon with her fingers, greasy with fat dripping down her chin. She said she didn't miss bacon, but I know she was lying.

My parents enter. Together. Even from afar it's odd to see them walk somewhere as a unit. They don't hug me, or kiss me, and they look neither happy nor sad. My mum looks pretty. Youthful even? She must be fucking someone new. Her hair is freshly coloured, almost the same colour as mine, and she looks like Hannah. When they have taken their seats, we accidentally have a silent moment, addressing the absent.

I order bacon; they order eggs. We talk about random things to avoid the most obvious one.

List of things we talked about to avoid
talking about how Hannah is dead:

Where Dad got his shirt from
Why he likes grey shirts so much

269

Why Mum is quitting Pilates because of a rude
   teacher

The difference between a flat white and a cortado

Something the prime minister did, something the
   president did

How Mum might get a particular breed of spaniel
   even though she isn't a dog person

Dad's painful tooth

Once the bill is paid, by my dad, we endure another silence. I decide to go to the bathroom and scream into my thighs as I sit on the toilet. I realise that it hurts to wee and choose to ignore it. When I get back upstairs, they are arguing as quietly as possible while my mum looks steely-eyed into her compact mirror, the same one she's had for ever, applying lipstick. It has an image of Marie Antoinette on it. He looks pained, and she seems emboldened, if only by the make-up. Something is about to happen.

I sit and exhale. Mum places her hand on top of mine. She's about to say something big, like she's telling me she's got terminal cancer or is eloping with a twenty-year-old understudy. Either way I think it's unlikely I will be able to feel anything. I just want to get back to watching the waitress with nice energy and writing my lists.

Mum: I'm going to take over Hannah's flat.

Me: Take over?

Dad: She's going to move in. We're not selling.

Me: Oh.

Dad: At least until the housing market is better.
   Personally I think it would be better to rent it out
   but your mother needs a place to live.

Mum: And it would be nice to be closer to you, darling.

As she says that she takes her hand off mine. My dad looks uncomfortable. He's wearing the same suit jacket that he wore at the chicken restaurant. It looks shabbier in the daylight.

Dad: I'm going to go back to the States for a bit. I have a friend who's letting me stay at his place. I think my book will go down better over there anyway.
Mum: Oh, of course, the book! Have you finished it yet?

He takes a sip of water. She waits with her punishing blue eyes for him to answer. His back straightens.

Dad: Not quite.

I wish Hannah was here playing her usual role of 'mitigator'. My need to talk about her bubbles up. Do they blame me? Do they think about her every second like I do?

Me: I don't mind about the flat, you know I didn't want it to be sold.
Mum: Good.
Me: I care more about the Portakabin –
Dad: What about it?
Me: I want to reopen PaperbackKids –
Mum: Why?
Me: Because Hannah worked so hard building it –
Mum: Let's discuss it another time, darling.

She's ready to go, she's already gone.

Dad: I'll think about it.

I don't have the energy to push them any further. Mum smiles a fake smile and Dad looks downcast. She squeezes his forearm, like she used to.

Mum: Come on, now. Don't be sad. I'm doing a
    rehearsed reading at the Old Vic next week. Only
    a small part, but still, the Old Vic!

My dad feigns a small smile. He's always found my mother's optimism for their unforgiving industry astounding.

Dad: I'm going to be leaving quite soon. I'll stop
    by at the airport, Ruth. See if you're there.
Me: Or you could just text me? To check?
Mum: Yes, do that. Text her, Michael.

She stands up, agitated. My dad stands too, leaving a tip of coins, but it's nowhere near enough and I suddenly feel sorry for him. I see my mum eyeing up the air outside, and I feel sorry for her too. They wait for me but I stay sitting. I try to be honest:

Me: I don't think I'm ever going to be OK again.

Their faces change. I've obliterated the facade.

Mum: Don't be silly, darling.

I think she tuts. Then she kisses me on the cheek, leaving a lipstick mark, and as she picks up her bag I see tears in her eyes. She leaves quickly. My dad looks at the ground and drifts away. The bridal party are leaving and walking behind him one by one, so he awkwardly moves to the side. He smiles at a bronzed, shiny young woman in a lime-green dress. Then he looks back at me without looking in my eyes, nodding like a horse as words fail him again. He walks out of the place with sloped shoulders, trailing behind the future bride, teetering and tottering in her stupid fucking heels.

The nice waitress comes to clear the table.

Waitress: Would you like anything else?
Me: A doughnut, please.
Waitress: We only have Cronuts, which is half-croissant, half-dough –
Me: I'll have one, thanks.
Waitress: Good on ya.

I stare at balloons left behind by the hen party. Three lettered balloons spelling 'HEN'. The H is drifting slightly towards my booth and I want this to be a sign: this balloon is Hannah and she likes the waitress too. But I know it's just the air con. I watch the hen party attendees get into two huge cars outside, giddy with pink champagne and talk of happily ever after.

I want something awful to happen to one of them. Today. Even though that thought makes me feel so ashamed, because it's so evil, that thought is there. I just need someone to know what this feels like, but no one ever could. Not even my parents. Mum's pain, dad's pain. Rowan's pain. Leila's pain. Sal's pain. It's all different. They

273

could never know mine, and I could never know theirs. All I do know is that no one in this world had a sister like her.

My phone vibrates and I get excited. This must be him; it must be? But it's from Fred. I don't open it. I have no need.

My Cronut arrives but it can't save me. I look up at the waitress.

Me: Do you think I could have the H balloon?

# 53

Two months after the funeral, before the inquest, there were these five days when my mum said she needed to stay with me. I didn't understand why she wouldn't stay at Hannah's, which was much nicer, and my mother likes nice things, but I didn't say anything. I thought this could be a rare opportunity for us to bond.

She told me to meet her at the station at 3 p.m. She's always been late, so when I got there at 3.05 I was surprised to see she was already there, tears in her eyes, wearing one of her five good dresses. She wears them on rotation, all of them designer and bought decades ago, which she has altered and mended over the years. She likes looking the part, even when she's not playing a part.

Her: Vera Lynn's died.

She walked fast and talked all the way about how she had sung 'We'll Meet Again' at her drama school audition. She started humming it and sounded like Hannah. I felt disorientated and was short with her.

Me: How old was she?
Her: A hundred and four. Isn't it incredibly sad.

I did the maths in my head. A hundred and four (Vera's age upon death) minus twenty-seven (almost my age). Seventy-seven. If I was to die at Vera Lynn's age, I would have seventy-seven years left of living without my sister.

We walked back to mine with Mum humming all the way. To avoid a fight, I told her that she would be sleeping in my bed, and I'd be on the sofa. So she plonked her vintage suitcase down in my bedroom, the same postbox-red suitcase she's had for over a decade and will stubbornly use for ever despite me suggesting she gets one with wheels – and went straight to have a shower. She emerged from my bedroom an hour later in another of her dresses, face full of make-up.

She said she was going out for 'milk'. I knew what that meant.

Me: Don't bring anyone back, Mum. Please.

She raised her eyebrows, and I could see she had a few more lines than she'd had before, which shocked me.

Her: Don't be silly, darling.

She went towards my door and I saw her check her figure in the mirror, avoiding her face, sucking in.

Her: When I come back I have something to show you. You've got clean sheets on your mattress, don't you?

She didn't wait for my response and trotted away in her heels, leaving the door open. A power play. I guess her calling it a 'mattress' was accurate but it's not exactly right. It's my bed, which is on the floor and has no frame, but it's still my 'bed'. As I stripped it I remembered Hannah helping me flip it over once, after I told her I'd never flipped a mattress. She fell over and the bed almost crushed her. Probably once a week she tried to get me to buy an actual bed frame. I never saw the point.

By the time I'd finished making the bed Mum arrived back, a little wobbly and carrying a bag from PC World. I could tell she'd already had something to drink. With an unlit cigarette in her free hand, she sat on the sofa and signalled at me for a lighter.

Me: I don't have a light, Mum –
Her: But you smoke?
Me: No. Hannah smoked. Used to smoke.
Her: Oh. Get me some scissors then.

I went to the kitchen to fetch some scissors and while I was in there I stood and put my forehead against the cold wall and closed my eyes. She shouted.

Her: Come, come.

She pulled a box out of the PC World bag and revealed a DVD player. I handed over the scissors and she knifed the box open. She started setting it up under my TV, suddenly an expert with wires, bum in the air, her skirt riding up to reveal a flash of her reliably lacy knickers peeking through her thin tights. Then she sat back down on the sofa with a satisfied thump. I wondered if they were her special-occasion knickers, and if they were then why did she get me to change my sheets.

Me: Mum, I don't need one of these, no one does
— there's Netflix and —
Her: Put this in.

She handed me a blank DVD. I felt uneasy as I looked
at the shiny disc, which was reflecting the trees from
outside. I put the DVD in and perched on the sofa, which
I had put a blanket over in honour of her visit to hide
my takeaway stains. The screen lit up with footage of my
mum, much younger, in high-waisted jeans and heavily
styled bouffant hair. She stood next to a little Hannah,
aged about five. I jumped up from the sofa and turned
my back.

Her: Sit, sit. Ruth. Sit!

She grabbed my hand and pulled me down again.

Me: I don't want to watch this —
Her: Listen. She's about to tell us a story —

I forced myself to look at the TV, tears springing
uncontrollably, as my mum on camera whispered something to Hannah and then walked away, blowing a kiss
as she sauntered off-screen. I heard my dad off-screen
too, who must have been holding the camera, giggling
with a youthfulness I didn't recognise. Smoke from his
cigarette wafted in front of the lens. I remembered the
kitchen wallpaper.

Hannah climbed up to stand on the kitchen table. My
dad moved in closer with the camera. Hannah drew a big
intake of air and started telling a story with a sweet and
squeaky voice. Hair in pigtails. A Teenage Mutant Ninja

Turtles T-shirt. She was reciting the story of the three little pigs, with her own special additions.

I looked over at my mum, who was beaming. She gripped my hand and pointed at the TV, urging me to keep watching. Then a baby somewhere in the background started crying, interrupting Hannah's story. Me. Hannah jumped down confidently from the table, and the camera followed her as she picked me up from a Moses basket into her arms. My mum took me from Hannah and told her to get back up on the table – 'Keep going, darling' – but Hannah didn't want to. She just stroked my baby feet. My dad said, 'OK, that's that, then' and then turned off the camera. The TV screen went blank.

I put my head in between my thighs. Mum stroked my back – only a couple of times, but she did it and it felt nice. When I sat up I saw that her eyes were dry, in fact she actually looked – happy. She kicked off her heels and stood up on my coffee table to do an impression of little Hannah. It felt as though I was watching a horror film; my reality was warping. She laughed manically at my dismay and jumped down.

Me: What are you doing, Mum? It's upsetting, can't you see that?

Her: It's not upsetting – she's not gone in this, is she? And look how amazing she was! Such a natural –

I escaped to the kitchen. I put the empty kettle on to boil, and tried to focus on the funny sound. I opened the fridge and closed it. I heard Mum pottering around, shouting to me.

Her: But wasn't she amazing, Ruth? I got all my
home videos put onto DVD. Plus all my adverts
and show reels and things — so we can look at
them later.

I couldn't think of anything worse that watching Mum's
showreels that evening. I looked at her from the kitchen,
prancing around in her bare feet. She was still agile and
girl-like because of her daily stretching and dance classes.
I reached my emotional limit as she did a pirouette.

Me: Do you remember when we came to LA to see
you?
Mum: Hmm?
Me: We tried to help you with lines for an audition,
in your hotel room. Remember?

Mum shook her head, but I knew she remembered.

Me: You could have told Hannah she was amazing
that day. Instead you chucked us out. Ignored us
even though we'd travelled across the world to
find you.

Mum said nothing, she just kept prancing about, though
with slightly less flair. I opened the window which she
had closed only a moment before and held my tongue.

Her: Do you have any gin, darling? Or wine?

I shook my head, even though I did have wine and
gin. I just didn't want her to drink near me. Mum looked
back down at her new box of DVDs and held up the

disc. She put it on her finger like a ring, spinning it round and round.

Her: She'll live for ever in these.

Then she came towards me and took my hands and made me dance with her, twirling me around, humming the Vera Lynn song again. I let her lead me. As we danced I could tell she was planning her escape, planning her night.

I drank my wine after she left and fell asleep on the sofa. When I woke up it felt like the middle of the night, but it was light outside and birds were tweeting and I could smell bleach. I heard something in the kitchen and I walked towards it, a little scared. I found my mum on her bare knees, scrubbing my floor with a J-cloth, wearing one of Hannah's big T-shirts and nothing else. She kept scrubbing harder and harder until she saw me. She was startled but tried to smile. I didn't say anything, I just dropped down to my knees and hugged her. She began crying and crying and crying, like I'd never seen before.

We went to my bed together and fell asleep. When I woke up again hours later, she was gone.

# 54

Fred lies me down gently on his bed, even though I'm telling him to fuck me hard. Everything has been rearranged since I was last here; he's got a new sofa I've seen advertised so much on Instagram that I know its exact price and that he must have ordered it ten to twelve days ago. A new, spotless shaggy cream carpet lies under his pristine bed.

He takes his shirt off, button by button. It's boring to watch but I like that he thinks I'm enjoying it. I take my tights and knickers off functionally, and lie on my back, ready and numb. I keep my black Lycra dress on but I wrestle my boobs out of it so they're pushed up. I need him to make me feel something, but instead of getting his dick out he gets a pillow for his knees and starts kissing my inner thighs. I try to pull his head up towards me, but he nestles it in deeper. His newly trimmed facial hair tickles me and I give up the idea of being aroused. I lie still and wait for him to be adamant that he's done a good job. I can hear the clock ticking on his bedside table, sitting next to some reading glasses, a philosophy book and a glass of water. I see vitamins for hair loss in his open bedside drawer, the same drawer that used to house his drugs.

When he re-emerges I turn over onto my front for him, ready. But he just lies down on the bed next to me, takes a sip of the water and wipes his chin. He smiles at me and I don't know what's happening, who he's become. Where is his collection of dirty coins and lighters? Or the wine bottles he used as candle holders that almost started a fire every time he fucked me so hard they knocked over?

Him: Do you want anything? A cup of tea?

He's never made me a cup of tea. Part of me wants to see what kind of cups he's got, but I shake my head, push him down and straddle him.

Me: Do you not want to?
Him: What?
Me: Fuck.

He touches my leg, which I shaved a few hours ago, for him. Why did I do that?

Him: I never noticed you have a cute mole on your
  inner thigh.

Cute mole? I want to throw up all over the shaggy carpet. I slot my boobs back into the dress and get off him.

Me: New carpet too?
Him: I'm doing the ad campaign for this brand.

I rub my toes in the carpet and like how soft it feels. I'm now more attracted to the carpet than him.

Me: It's nice.

Him: It's a nightmare to hoover, though.

He works in advertising and hoovers now. I don't want to be here, I want to run all the way home, but then he smiles at me and I remember why I liked him in the first place. He's trying so hard with me and I don't know why. If he feels guilty for how he treated me before, it's too late, I'm a different person now too. I pick my knickers up off the carpet and put them on with my back to him, not caring that he's seeing the inelegant squat I have to do to get tight things on.

Him: You're not going.

I like the lack of question in his tone. I want to be told what to do, and not be held responsible for my own decisions and mistakes. I lie back down next to him, flattered to see that he's still hard. He turns the lights off, goes on top and fucks me like he really actually likes me, which is unsettling.

I wait until he's asleep and then I look around the room. I pretend I'm in one of those pick-your-own adventure books I used to read as a kid. I could pick this room, the man, this life. I've got him now.

I look at the label on the carpet on the way out.

# 55

On the plane

Free magazines and papers are piled on her lap, and she yawns and unbuttons the top of her skirt, like I knew she would. She sees me judging her and smiles back widely, showing me all her weirdly white teeth. I'm mystified by how white they are. I'm sure she's had them professionally bleached but she denies it.

I look out of the window as subtly as possible, trying not to crane my neck and annoy the woman sitting next to it. She's staring straight ahead at the blank TV screen, solemnly. I can see tiny little people on the runway in fluorescent orange jackets. I don't like being in the middle seat, but Hannah drinks more water than me so she says she has to sit by the aisle. Hannah seems restless. I put my feet on hers to stop them from tapping incessantly.

Me: Stop!
Her: Rowan does it, sorry.

I'm annoyed that his presence is apparent even when he's not here. The air steward does the safety announcement, and I pretend to listen, but all I can think about is where

I would hide if there was a terrorist on board, how hopeless I'd be in any emergency situation. She squeezes my
hand and I squeeze back.

Her: I'm so excited.
Me: Me too.

She closes her eyes for take-off and her eyelids shimmer
with gold; some has speckled onto her cheeks and I
wipe it away. She doesn't like me touching her face and
flinches.

Her: You'd better have clean hands.

Once we're up in the sky, I'm settled.
She falls asleep pretty quickly, with her hot head resting
on my shoulder and her hoop earrings digging into me.
I raise her head gently and take them out one by one,
put them in my pocket to keep them safe. She sleeps for
the entire journey, which is unusual. Her snore is hilarious
and louder than I've ever heard it. So loud that people
are starting to whisper about it; some are laughing, some
are pissed off. I scowl at all of them. The woman sitting
adjacent to Hannah across the aisle keeps glaring at us
and complains to the air steward, who then tries to wake
Hannah by touching her shoulder.
I flip.

Me: Don't fucking touch her —
Air steward: Please don't use that kind of language —
Me: Well, don't touch my sister then?
Air steward: Would you please try to reposition her.
    Passengers are complaining.

Me: She can't help her snore. It's a medical condition.

A serious medical condition –

Air steward: Of course, I'm sorry, miss.

The woman stops glaring after hearing 'medical condition' and I feel guilty for lying. I worry that Hannah's sick, or will get sick, and I've tempted fate, but then forcefully remind myself that fate is bullshit.

As the plane prepares for landing she wakes up and smiles at me. Everything is perfect again, as she puts her hoops back in.

# 56

It's a full moon. Perhaps that explains why I've found myself wandering the streets wearing too few clothes and with stinging legs, having shaved too harshly before seeing Fred. As I stumble shivering in the dark, slightly lost on unfamiliar residential streets somewhere off Holloway Road, I think about how Hannah was right about Fred all along.

Of course she was right.

I walk as fast as I can towards my destination with the help of Google Maps, finding ways to distract myself from flashbacks of Fred's head burrowed between my thighs. I look through strangers' windows, trying to gather if the houses are rented or owned from the evidence on their walls.

My theory is that if stuff is in frames, the place must be owned. I peer into kitchens, and spot four different kinds of blender. I try to guess the age of the kids living in one house from the artwork on the fridge. If I ever became a mother, would I keep every drawing?

I stop at another house where a couple are watching TV on the sofa, their faces lit by the screen and the fairy lights they've stuck to the walls with tape. Renters. Over her stomach, the woman is clutching the same 'YOU GOT THIS!' pillow that Hannah had.

I wonder if they'll have sex when they go to bed, if they brush their teeth together whilst they look at each other in the mirror, toothpaste foam dripping down their chins.

I don't see any of these pillows, blenders or frames in my future.

When I get to Storage Etc., Mickey is shadow-boxing in the reception area. His father is smoking and filming him again, and they're joined by a girl in a neon tracksuit who sits on the abandoned sofa, crushing the 'TAKE ME' sign with her back. I wait outside until Mickey sees me, and his dad puts the phone down. He pretends to punch the door before opening it, which scares me, even though he's doing it in jest.

Mickey: Late night?

I don't say anything and get in the lift, paranoid they're going to laugh about me as soon as I'm out of earshot. Maybe they even hate me? The lift slowly travels up, until it suddenly stops and makes a louder screech than usual. I am sure that this is their doing, that they're trapping me. They'll keep me in here all night as a sick joke, and this is where I'll die – but then the lift starts moving again.

I walk down the corridor and in the few seconds before the lights wake up, I notice light creeping out from under the door to our unit. I don't let myself get excited – it must have been me forgetting to turn them off – but the door is unlocked and I push it open and he's there, resting his head on the piano lid, asleep. One of his eyes is bruised and swollen. His white T-shirt is dirty; there are little splatters of blood around his neck. I leave the unit and get straight back into the lift and out of the front doors, back past Mickey, who's now being straddled by the girl on the sofa.

I run to the small twenty-four-hour newsagent's near the storage unit and there's a man dozing behind the till. His beard is long and there's a band around it under his chin. I've seen this front ponytail from a distance and it's been enough to put me off coming into the shop until now. I don't trust men with beards.

The bell rings as I enter and it jolts him awake. As I buy some frozen peas, water and paracetamol, I stare at his front ponytail with a level of fascination that I reserve for wildlife. I pay with cash, which he puts straight in his pocket. He says, 'Thanks, little lady,' sleepily as I leave and I like it, which is pitiful.

I head straight back. Towards him. I'm neither excited nor upset. I just want to look after somebody, to rectify something. When I get back into the unit, he's fallen to the dirty, hard floor. Still sleeping soundly, drunkenly. He smells of whisky, he's drooling and doesn't look like himself. I kneel down and pull him to Hannah's carpet. I put the bag of frozen peas over his swollen eye and hold it there for ages, until I become immensely tired. I turn him onto his side in case he vomits, with the peas still propped up against his eye, and walk towards the bed. I fall asleep instantly.

When I wake up hours later, he's next to me. The peas are soaking the bed. I get up, head pounding from the expensive but disgusting wine I drank at Fred's. I walk over to Hannah's sofa and take two paracetamol and down the water, leaving some for him. I can't sit on her sofa, it feels wrong. So I pace around and open a box.

It's full of A4 plastic folders, which at first I assume is

another box of her work papers, university papers – stuff I won't understand and don't need to keep. But one file catches my eye; it's red and has a label: 'RUTH BEST'. I open it and see that it's all the drawings and birthday cards I've ever done for her. She's meticulously labelled them according to dates and months. I look through some of my drawings and can't believe that I did them. They're quite good. I put the file in my bag, feeling tingly.

She fucking loved me. She fucking loved me.

Next I open a box I've labelled 'ALL OF HER BAGS'. She used to take a tote bag and a handbag to work, and had a few different combinations, some of which were disgusting (she had bad taste in bags) and I don't mind throwing them away. In each tote bag I find a tub of Carmex, and a half-eaten pack of gum. I decide to keep them all. In the last bag (the one she used for groceries which has an illustration of two avocados high-fiving each other on it), I find her car keys. I clutch them close to my chest and collapse back onto her carpet. I need to find her car, which is another thing I've avoided doing.

He snores so gutturally that he wakes himself up, and I turn to face the bed. He opens his eyes expectantly, like he's known where I'd be sitting, knows what I've been doing, knows I've been here all along.

# 57

The Mediterranean
The day after the accident

A fly lands on my leg. I have my eyes closed and I'm sitting on the balcony floor. I slam my hand down on it, knowing I've killed it, and I feel guilty.

Hannah hated insects and creepy crawlies; she was an expert killer. It would shock people if she did it in public. Once we were walking along, not realising there were a couple of schoolgirls trailing along behind us, and she stamped on a snail with full force, twisting her heels to make sure she really fucking killed the thing. The girls looked terrified. Whenever I said anything about how odd it was, her unfounded hatred of any form of small creature, she would say, 'It doesn't mean anything.' I told her she was going to get put in prison one day.

I open my eyes and I see that I haven't actually killed it. The fly is still half-alive, with one wing trembling. I scrape it off my leg and drop it over the balcony. My legs are still smeared with her blood. I touch my scalp; it's burnt from being outside so much yesterday and it stings. The balcony door opens and without looking behind me,

I see Rowan's bare feet walking out. His toenails are thick, a tiny bit too long, and he leans on the rail, looking out to the sea. He has no T-shirt on, just rolled-up jeans. I stare at his spine.

Him: We should check out soon.

I don't say anything. I don't remember when I last used my voice, other than in the torment of my non-sleep last night. It feels like I have screamed all night. He holds up some papers without checking that I'm looking.

Him: They gave me some forms to fill out. About how to get her − um − body home.

She's already just a body now? I want to un-fill the fucking forms, I need to un-fill them. I would if I could move. My throat hurts, everything hurts. He turns to me and I close my eyes again because I don't want to be looked at. I'm still in my swimming costume and my whole body is numb and stiff, skin dry with salt.

Him: You've been out here a long time, Ruth. Come inside.

I feel stupid for not even considering throwing myself off this balcony yet. That would have been the most logical option.

Me: I can't move.

He reaches out his arms. Once he's pulled me up, he lets go and I'm light-headed.

Him: You need to shower now. Then we need to
   go home.
Me: I can't go home.

He leads me back into the hotel room. He's packed for both of us, and laid out clothes for me on the bed. He turns on the shower. I stare at him while he stands at the door, willing me to go in. So I do. He closes it carefully behind me once I'm in, but not all the way shut. I get into the shower, and my scalp stings from the water. I sit down, and watch her blood and mine wash away.

I must be in there a while because he comes to check on me. He turns off the shower, getting partially soaked. He wraps a towel around me as I stand motionless and stare in the steamed-up mirror. He's packed all of our toiletries, and I want to ask him where her moisturiser is, her conditioners, but I can't speak. He walks me in the towel, and because it is wrapped around my arms too, I waddle like a penguin.

I begin to laugh as I waddle and he looks confused. My laugh gets louder and louder until I'm wailing again. He watches me silently and puts a T-shirt on. When I'm done making sounds he hands me my dress, which I put on over my swimming costume. I see he's laid out pants and a bra too.

Him: Sorry, I didn't know if I should –
Me: I can't leave this room.
Him: We have to.

I haven't looked at his face yet. His voice is low and robotic.

He opens the main room door and waits for me in the corridor, with his suitcase and ours. The balcony door is still open, the breeze from the sea is making the thin curtains flutter in and out of the room. I think of the breeze yesterday. If she had jumped one centimetre to the right, or left, she'd still be here.

Suddenly I sprint up to the balcony door, ready to jump – and in those few seconds I realise he's not trying to stop me. I get scared. I falter, and in my rage try to slam the door shut but it's a sliding one. So I slide it as forcefully as I can, so much so that it bounds back open. I'm pathetic, I feel exposed.

Rowan watches and waits. I make more sounds I don't understand as I crouch down by the door. He just watches and waits.

In the lobby, which is too cold, I stand next to Noè, who I'm told is taking us to the airport. I watch Rowan checking us out. He tries to hand over his card but the lady behind the desk stops him. It seems we're getting a free stay, something Hannah was always angling for on every single one of our holidays by being so nice to everybody.

I can't bear it. She's not here. She should be here. Why isn't she here? As I try to storm out of the hotel, I have to hold the door open for a woman arriving with her designer suitcase. I wonder if she'll be checking into our room.

We drive to the airport in silence. Rowan sits in the front seat, I'm alone in the back.

Noè takes our bags out of the boot when we get there. Rowan tries to tip him but Noè doesn't accept. He just shakes his hand for a long time. Noè's a big man and I want him to hug me, but he simply puts his hands on both my shoulders, hangs his head down, too sad to look into my eyes, and gets back in his car. We watch him driving away, past the palm trees.

# 58

King's Cross

Her car isn't where she normally parked it. We've walked all the way to Hannah's street, and her car is nowhere to be seen. I worry I've forgotten what it looked like, what colour it was – silver or grey? Rowan reassures me in his monosyllabic but comforting way. It was grey, of course it was grey. We walk up and down the streets parallel to Hannah's, and I try to think back to when she would have last driven.

The week before we went on holiday we drove to Columbia Road flower market. She wanted to buy some big plants and didn't want to carry them back on the Tube. I told her it was a bit hypocritical, to be buying plants to oxygenate her London flat, whilst also polluting the planet driving the plants around. She got so angry and uninvited me even though I was sitting in the front seat and we were already on our way. I called her bluff, I pretended I was getting out by unbuckling my seat belt and opening the car door. She got so scared I was about to jump out that she swerved and almost crashed.

She was furiously silent until we approached the market. When she saw all the happy hipsters in their knitted hats, cradling their eco-coffee cups and plants – there were so many of them – she muttered, 'What is it about hipsters and plants?' She decided she didn't want to go after all and that I was right – if we were going to use the car, we should make it worth it. We spent the day driving round London, listening to pop songs and waving at landmarks. Tension was still in the air, but she'd forgiven me by the time we reached Big Ben.

Rowan starts walking faster, ahead of me, with new motive.

Him: I know where it is –
Me: Where?
Him: We went to get petrol one day, because we
     were planning to go on a road trip when we got
     back from – when you both got back from –

I help him as he stumbles with the pain of a new memory.

Me: Let me guess? She felt guilty about driving to
     a petrol station and so insisted you walk back –
Him: Yes. The logic being, one less car journey.
Me: She was so silly sometimes.

We stop for a second. I try not to think about how I just said 'she was'. He smiles softly and as we continue to walk, we don't talk about where they would have gone on that road trip, we just talk about nothing. The trees. The road names. How it's quite hot for this time of year, look at those leaves, how hungry we are. When we find her car, it's covered in bird shit. Completely covered. She parked under a tree. We stare at it for a while.

Him: Isn't bird shit meant to be lucky?

He takes the keys out of my hands and unlocks the car.

Him: Come on.

He sits in the driver's seat and pushes open the passenger door for me. He seems at ease in her car, like he's driven it before, but I can't bring myself to get in. I see my empty bottle of Fanta Zero on the floor and think of how drunk I got after her funeral. Rowan waits patiently, staring ahead. When I finally get in and close the door, I smell her and the minty dice-shaped air freshener I got for her as a thank-you for being my personal taxi.

The car doesn't start. He tries again and again.

Him: It's the battery. I didn't think, sorry. I should
    have warned you.
Me: I don't understand —
Him: It won't start —
Me: Why?
Him: Because it's been sitting here so quiet for so
    long.

The way he says 'quiet' makes me want to scream. I feel stupid for knowing nothing about mechanics and crushed that her car is dead too. I abandoned it. He faces me and cups my face, dark eyes in a frenzy.

Him: Don't go anywhere.

He gets out of the car and just before he shuts the door, he speaks again.

Him: Do not leave this spot. OK?

I like being told what to do right now, though I'm confused. I'm also kind of thrilled. I watch him sprint away, down the road until he's out of sight. I close my eyes and put the car seat back, trying to calm myself down. I lie back and start counting leaves from the tree directly above the car. I reach 189 before my eyes get tired and I let myself drift to sleep.

I'm woken with a car honk. It's Rowan, in his own car, smiling madly. He gets out, holding two wires, one red and one black, and rushes to open the front bonnet of Hannah's car. He opens his bonnet too, and it looks like he's doing something illegal. Cars begin to build up behind his, as it's in the middle of the road. I have no idea what he's doing and he looks like he's got no idea either.

But before long, he's running to get in Hannah's car again and he's managed to start it.

Him: Yes!

He gets out again and rushes back to his car, closing the bonnet. He shouts as he leaves.

Him: I'll be back in one minute.

He drives off. I get out and shut Hannah's bonnet too. I put my hand on the warm metal and smile as I see Rowan sprinting back towards me, sweating and manic.

Him: I did it! I can't believe I did it!
Me: You did.

It would be inappropriate to make a joke about how sexy it was to watch him bring a car back to life, so I restrain myself. It feels so very wrong to be aroused in this situation, with Hannah strikingly gone. Though I can't help but feel terribly attracted to him, even more so now.

He drives us victoriously around the block to get the car 'going'. As he drives me up and down the same roads in silence my heart rate settles. Then he takes us to the petrol station, where there's an automatic car wash. We stay seated in the car. As it gets covered in water and soap, he reclines his seat and I recline mine again too. The swishing noises get louder and louder and it feels like we're being swallowed up. He puts his hand on my thigh and starts tapping, as though he's playing a piano. Finally he smiles, softly.

Him: Have you ever been in a car wash?
Me: No.
Him: Me neither.

I stare at the water crashing down onto the windows, I close my eyes and feel his tapping. I begin to cry, quietly. When I open my eyes, I see he's crying too, but he looks serene, with tiny tears rolling down his beautiful cheeks. I wipe them for him and we begin to laugh.

Me: What the fuck are we doing?
Him: I have no idea.

We grip each other's hands as the car wash completes. He starts the engine and lets go of my hand as we drive back into the daylight.

I think of us in the car to Brighton, how he kissed me on the beach.

Me: What about your car?
Him: I'll get it when I need it.

He parks in Hannah's usual spot by her flat. As we get out, I take out the dice air freshener and put it in my pocket. He locks it and then hands me the keys. She would want me to sell the car; I can't drive – it's a waste. She was planning to sell it anyway so she could feel even more environmentally superior to me. We approach her flat in silence again. He opens the doors with his keys, like it's important to him.

We get inside and it's empty. I go straight to open a window, because she liked having a window always slightly open. He lies down on the floor and closes his eyes. I copy him. For a while we both lie in starfish position on the wooden floor. All I can think about is how I laughed in the car. I feel guilty, immensely guilty, that I'm still able to laugh when she's gone.

I sit up and make him sit up too. His hands are cold and he looks as exhausted as I must do.

Me: Once you came to PaperbackKids after you and Hannah had just had a fight. What was it about?
Him: I don't remember. I wish I did.

He lets go of my hands and looks at me intently.

Him: Listen. If Leila invites you over for dinner, will you say yes?

Me: Fuck.

Him: She thinks you hate her.

Me: I don't hate her.

Him: It might be good. To be in a normal situation
   – for both of us –

I cover my face with my hands. He comes closer and uncovers it.

Me: OK, maybe.

He smiles. His eye looks so sore. She would hate seeing him like this.

Me: What happened to your eye?

Him: I got into a fight with a stranger. That happens
   occasionally when I drink whisky. Any more
   questions?

I have a thousand more. But I go with just one, even though it's the most painful.

Me: Do you think you would have got married?

He takes so long to answer I think he mustn't have heard me, so I get ready to ask again just as he hugs his knees and begins nodding.

Him: I think so.

He stares at the walls as he rocks back and forth.
I'm proud of these walls. We spent a weekend painting them a shade of white called 'Winter Moon' when she

first moved in, eating takeaways which rested on the tops of her unpacked boxes. We looked out of her windows and made predictions about who would be the most sexually active neighbours.

She had a housewarming party soon afterwards with so many people, friends I'd never even heard her mention. She didn't like it when I asked her if she had just hired them to make her seem cool, and was cold to me for the rest of the party. So I went into her bedroom and continued painting one wall we had yet to finish. She came in, very drunk, when everyone had gone home, and said she was sorry.

Her: I saw you come in here alone and I should have checked you were OK –
Me: I'm fine – you were having a nice time –
Her: I wish I didn't need approval from random dickheads but I do.
Me: It's OK –
Her: No, it's not. You're real, Ruth. You're just – you. I feel like I'm pretending quite a lot of the time –

When she saw that I had finished painting the wall, she cried. I tucked her into bed. She sleepily insisted that she take her make-up off – so I took it off for her with a face wipe as she fell asleep, her drunken snore already gearing up.

Rowan goes to the toilet. I hear him pissing. I get up and close the window again and wait for him by the door, ready to lock it, with my keys this time. It's dark when we get outside. As we pass Hannah's car, he puts his hand on the roof to say goodbye.

304

Him: Are you going to be OK tonight?
Me: Yeah. I'll be fine.

I pretend to bang my head on his chest and he pulls me in. He needs a shower.

Me: You should get some more peas.
Him: What?

I'm hurt that he doesn't remember about the frozen peas. I think of them still in the storage unit, defrosted and abandoned.

Me: Doesn't matter.

I watch him walking slowly away. I turn on the TV as soon as I'm home. *Newsnight.* I put it on mute and look out of my window. The glum woman across the road has a guy in her room. I can see his hairy knees. She's in just a bra and knickers, kneeling on the bed, trying to look sultry.

I put some bread in the toaster and look at the night sky, imagining she's a star now.

# 59

The Mediterranean
The day after the accident

Before I know it we're walking onto the plane, silently.
I don't have anything with me apart from a little plastic
bag containing her phone and one salvaged hoop
earring. I must have checked in everything else. We
reach my seat and he doesn't say goodbye, keeps on
walking to his. I sit by the window and the two seats
next to me are empty, which I've never had before. I
don't like the space. A few people are still filing onto
the plane, but it's not full at all. I look back to see if
I can spot him but I can't. I put in her hoop earring
for take-off.

When the air steward offers me pretzels, I ask for wine.
After an hour or so, once we're in the sky, I get up and
go to the toilet. On my way back I see him, asleep, on
his own in the middle of an empty row. I sit down next
to him and fall asleep too.

When I wake up we are landing. Our knees are
accidentally touching and I let them. The sun is rising.
I feel sick from the wine on an empty stomach. He

wakes up and looks at me, confused, and moves his knees away from mine. He must have thought I was her.

Him: Are you OK? You look –

I put my head between my legs and throw up all over my shoes. He holds my hair back. The few people around us make sounds of disgust. Everybody hates me but I hate myself more. The plane lands and the air steward gives me a few paper towels without looking at my face; she's angry with me too.

Me: Sorry, sorry, sorry, sorry –

The air steward doesn't say it's OK. Rowan helps me dab my shoes. I push him away, ashamed.

Me: I'll throw them away.
Him: Are you sure?
Me: They're destroyed.
Him: They're nice shoes –
Me: Not any more.

How can we be talking about shoes? I take them off and my socks too, as the vomit has soaked through.

We get off the plane last to avoid anyone seeing me. We walk through the airport, silent again, and are separated by a family of five in the queue at security. The mother has her baby in a baby carrier; the father holds the hands of two young children. They notice I'm not wearing any shoes and tell their father, who ignores them politely. I don't look back to Rowan, and he doesn't come to join me; he looks spaced out. If Hannah was here, she'd queue-jump and rescue me.

I show the man my passport and I expect him to ask me questions, to ask me about what happened, where is my sister, where are my shoes, but instead he just stamps my passport and I stagger onwards to the baggage reclaim. As I wait for my bag, Rowan finds me and stands next to me again. I still don't look at him. People glance at my bare feet – my hands are sticky and I want to die again.

Rowan's bag arrives before mine. As he leans over to pull it off the conveyor belt his T-shirt rides up and I see his lower spine protruding, even more than it did this morning, more than yesterday; he's hunched from the flight. He looks frail, so different to all the men she'd been with in the past. I think of Hannah's body, how she must have felt quite heavy on top of him, how he must have liked that, how the woman he loves is gone.

Him: Can you watch my bag while I go to the bathroom?

I nod and watch him walk away. I see our suitcase come towards me on the conveyor. The suitcase doesn't know that it's just me waiting and I feel bad for it. I'm light-headed as I lift it off. Dizzily, I walk out of the airport as fast as I can, leaving him and his bag behind, hoping I get injured by something on the street outside so I am forced to go to hospital and be sedated for a long time.

As I get in a taxi, I glance back and see Rowan looking around for me. Bewildered, I stare out of the window at the traffic jam of people leaving the airport, on their way home. She should be sitting next to me. She should be answering banal questions from the chatty driver as I rest my head on her sunburnt shoulder. I should be content and smug about my time away with her, looking forward to our next trip, wondering where she'll take me.

My bag vibrates from within the suitcase.

Rowan (text): Where did you go?

I switch off the phone, and try to switch myself off too.

I get the taxi to drop me at her flat where I stand in the corridor for a moment, fumbling with keys as her neighbour Joe bounds out of his door towards me. He's relatively handsome but quite bland; does too many weights.

Joe: Hey! How was it?

He gave Hannah a cactus last Christmas, so she was convinced he was in love with her. I see him staring at my bare feet. His question is my first test. Do I open up or pretend?

Him: You're back quick! How was it –

I choose to lie, but before I can, his phone rings. He motions that he has to take the call. I mouth 'sorry' and I don't know why.

I wait to open the door till he's got in the lift. Before I step in, I have to grip the door frame. She's left a window open in the sitting room. Everything is neat. Nothing in here knows. I close the door behind me and go straight to her bedroom, climb into her bed.

I take two paracetamol and two sleeping pills and I close my eyes and we're just back in our hotel room, getting ready to go out for dinner.

# 60

I'm first in the pool, though two muscular, irritated men are fast behind me. The lifeguard hasn't even climbed up to her high chair yet. I dive in and swim underwater all the way to the other side. I struggle, but manage and feel triumphant and it's only 6.41 a.m. I do twenty-seven lengths and get out as people are starting to queue because there are too many in the pool. Smugly I walk past, happy that I must look like I've got my shit together because I was here so early.

I feel my heart thump, my blood flowing; my cheeks are hot and I feel proud of myself. I am getting fitter. I am getting stronger. And today, I'm finally following through on my promise to Hannah to try acupuncture, even though I'm terrified of needles and ambient music.

I arrive at the clinic in Camden with wet hair. It's next door to a health food shop where I've just bought a bag of dried mango. The young girl at reception asks me my name and I say Hannah Rothwell. I like using her name for things. She ushers me into a waiting room with no sofas or chairs, just little cushions on the floor. There is a sound of running water which I realise is coming from a plastic waterfall with pebbles and flowers and a fake frog. Each wall is painted with a different mantra, and I chew the mango as I read:

*No matter what occurs around me I am centred,
balanced and in a state of well-being.*

Hannah loved this kind of bullshit.

The lollipop man at our primary school called me
Hannah, every morning and every afternoon. He ushered
children across the road like herding sheep, getting all of
our names wrong. When she said goodbye to me in the
playground, I would hug her and shout, 'Bye, Ruth!' as
I watched her skip towards her classroom, excited about
her day. She loved school, while I hated it. I wanted the
end of the day to come quickly so she'd hug me and we'd
be mistaken for each other again.

At secondary school, it was different. She was four years
above, so when I arrived in Year 7 she was preoccupied
with GCSEs and became so stressed, different to how
she'd been with me before. One day I found her in the
library during the lunch hour, crying hunched over her
coursework. I told her it doesn't matter, grades don't
matter. She suddenly got angry.

Her: This is my future, Ruth! It does matter!

I stare at the fake waterfall. Why did I dive first? Why
didn't she? The door opens.

Someone: Hannah?
Me: Yes.

I am led through to another room. A kind-faced woman
who communicates in gestures instructs me to lie on my
back and display my stomach. She looks at notes on a
clipboard and then finally speaks.

312

Lady: Fertility, yes?

Me: Sorry?

Lady: Fertility acupuncture, yes?

Me: Um, no – just plain, plain.

Lady: It says here you came for fertility six times –

Me: What?

Lady: Hannah Rothwell?

Me: Yes, well – yes. OK.

Lady: Welcome back.

She smiles, and turns on some fucking wood-chiming sounds.

# 61

I can smell how fresh the paint is. A navy-blue front door. Navy seems regal to me. I can't imagine ever being in a position to own my own place, to paint my own door, but if I could, I'd paint mine purple. I've liked the colour ever since a girl called Helena told me in Year 9 that purple means 'sexually frustrated'. I googled what the colour actually means recently and it said, 'If you surround yourself with purple you will have peace of mind.' Helena lied.

The first thing I see is a huge bump covered in a stretchy floral dress. I lift my eyes to observe the gold H necklace that's haunted me since I first saw it. She touches it with her alternating yellow and orange varnished nails. I'm jealous she can find it in her to have 'fun' colours on her nails. I haven't painted mine since Hannah died.

I imagine what Hannah would have looked like pregnant, what kind of maternity clothes she'd have worn. Would she have gotten super-fat pregnant the way some women do and expanded like a hot-air balloon? I'm still hurting that she didn't tell me she was having fertility problems but then I guess she never told me that she got her teeth whitened either. My sister was proud.

Leila: You look amazing, hon!

She kisses me on both cheeks which is awkward, and I dislike the happiness emanating from her. But I've made an effort. I'm in Hannah's red espadrilles. I used her leave-in conditioner and scrunched my hair up so it curls, like hers. The long peach halter-neck summer dress I ordered off the internet when I was half-drunk is having its first outing, an early birthday present to myself. The static from the dress keeps giving me electric shocks and I'm pretty sure I don't look amazing.

As I approach the age of twenty-seven, I thought I should try a halter-neck dress for the first time. It will be my first birthday without her, and in my books on death they say, 'The first is the worst.' As a result I've been slightly audacious online. Last night, at 3.42 a.m. precisely, I ordered a shaggy cream carpet, the exact same one as Fred's. The purchase was triggered by another text from him, asking what I'm 'up to' (his textual repertoire is alarmingly limited). Rather than shower, shave and traipse over to his flat like I've done so many times, I just ordered the carpet and didn't reply.

Leila is telling me not to worry about taking my shoes off as she leads me through her house, which seems bigger this time, with newly painted white wooden floorboards. I came here last year, with Hannah, and I don't recall it being so nice. Leila's Instagram must be serving her well. As we walk through to the kitchen, there are signs of the forthcoming arrival – a new shiny buggy ready and waiting, boxes of wet wipes, stacks of nappies. These things show such optimism.

Danny – who today looks strikingly similar to Rowan – stands in the kitchen. Same hair, same height, same bad

315

posture, but he looks a bit more − approachable? He hugs me and I feel bad that I only faintly remember meeting him at the funeral. She pours me a drink and Danny checks on what's in the oven. I look at the magnets and photos stuck on the bright green fridge. Although I'm far away, I can see a photo of Hannah.

Danny: Rowan is running late −

Leila hands me a glass of red wine as she sips from one herself.

Leila: Just a small glass, I promise. In France they
    drink throughout pregnancy −

My wine glass is massive and oddly shaped; the glass is so thin and fragile that I want to crush it in my hand.

Leila: Of course he's running late! He's always late!

I really do want to crush the glass now. I look at the fridge again. Did Leila know Hannah wanted to get pregnant? Were they planning to be pregnant together? I begin to remember when I was last here, and see Hannah next to me.

*Hannah's bare legs, not quite newly shaven but still smooth, graze against mine as I sit down at the table. She pours me a glass of wine and smiles, gold-lined eyes sparkling.*

Leila: He says he's been helping you −
Me: What?
Leila: Rowan. He says he's been helping you with
    Hannah's stuff −

Me: Oh. Yes. He has.

Leila: I know I don't have long left before the baby but honestly if you need my help – with anything –

Me: It's fine. It's almost done actually.

*Hannah fiddles with one of her bra straps. I can see it's too tight so I loosen it for her while Leila tells us about the food she's been cooking for us, which I know I won't like because it's vegan.*

Leila: He's seemed a bit sad lately.

Danny: Lately?

Leila: More sad, then. More sad than ever.

I feel hollow inside. I've made him more sad. My body, my mouth, my touch, my personality; it's all made him more sad.

Leila: How have you been, hon?

She strokes her bump. I want to tell her to stop calling me hon, but she's trying so hard to make me feel welcome.

*Hannah squeezes my thigh and mouths 'BE NICE' as Leila has her back to us, untying her polka-dot apron.*

Me: I'm fine.

Leila: It's your birthday coming up, isn't it?

Me: Um. yeah.

Leila: We should do something –

Me: No. I don't think so, no.

Rowan enters. I smell alcohol ever so faintly and – I hope I'm imagining it – perfume. He doesn't hug me.

He kisses Leila on the cheek, and hugs Danny, who hands him a bottle of beer. Why doesn't he hug me?

Rowan: Sorry I'm late.
*Hannah: I've started seeing someone. He's lovely. Different.*
*A bit of a hopeless artist but he's – well, he's amazing.*
Leila: I've made everything vegan, in memory of Hannah.

I finish my wine. God, I hate this. I'm not ready for sentences with 'in memory of' – fuck that, I'll never be ready. Rowan sees my shoulders rise and he moves closer to me. I tilt my head to the side to delay the tears. I try to look less hostile.

Leila: We have some news.
Rowan: Triplets?
Leila: Ha, no . . . We're getting married.
Danny: And having triplets.

Leila hits him playfully and they kiss and the kiss seems real. My quick analysis of these two human beings making another human together is that it will work out for them. They seem compatible, they even look kind of similar. Hannah told me once that if you draw a line down the centre of your face, and match it up with the half of your partner's face, and it's symmetrical – it means the partnership is good, and it will last, you'll live happily ever after. She showed me a photo of half of Jennifer Aniston's face and half of Brad Pitt's put together, to prove it. By this point they were divorced so the theory was clearly faulty. But she was adamant that they'd get back together one day, because they were perfectly symmetrical. Ever since, I've mentally cut couples' faces in half.

I see that Leila's ankles are swollen and it makes me warm to her. Rowan refills my wine glass and this time, I know I smell perfume. Why am I here? Why did he make me do this? I'm drinking too fast.

Leila: Your mum is coming to stay with us for the weekend, Ruth. Maybe you could come over for brunch?
Me: I don't do brunch.

She laughs, she thinks I'm joking. I stand up, unsteady on my feet, which feel like they've been replaced with bricks. Danny puts his hand on the bump and my rage is now visceral.

Rowan sees the look in my eyes and comes towards me; he puts his hand on the small of my back. Leila notices.

*Hannah opens Leila's fridge and sees the photo of her on the door.*
*Hannah: Is that me? I don't remember that day. My hair looks nice.*

They're faffing about with the memorial food. Rowan helps them. I down my wine, pour another and down that too.

Me: I'm just going to the bathroom.

I leave the house as quickly and quietly as I can.

# 62

Drunk by the time I get home, I put my bag on the side of the sofa and run a bath. The TV is on, ready for my return. *The Graham Norton Show*. I begin to undress unsteadily in the living room. The glum woman who lives opposite is smoking out of her window, and sees me taking off my bra. I don't cower, I don't care. I let my boobs hang down as I undress completely. I have marks on my hips from the thong I decided to wear. I remind myself (once more) never to wear one again.

I walk to the bathroom, naked except for the espadrilles, and it feels funny. I catch myself in the mirror and I like it, so I get in the bath with the espadrilles still on, quickly taking my feet out of the water so that my legs are resting on the sides of the bath. I close my eyes and wish I had a TV in the bathroom. I saw someone on Instagram watching *Love Island* in the bath, a classy white TV embedded into their bathroom wall, and I got so jealous that they could watch such trash and get clean at the same time. I listen to Graham Norton chatting to Judi Dench from the other room.

I look at the espadrilles dangling. The steep woven wedge seems so ridiculous.

I wonder if I will ever be the type of woman who is

comfortable in heels. Those women just seem stronger than me, somehow. Less afraid of going further afield to make the most of themselves, to look desirable. I close my eyes. I don't know what to do with her fancy shoe collection, which is sitting in a box in the storage unit right now.

I remember waking up one night, after falling asleep on her sofa waiting up for her to come back from a date, and hearing her singing in the shower. Her heels and clothes were discarded by the bathroom door. I thought it would be funny to get undressed and put on her heels, ready for when she came out of the bathroom. So I got fully naked, put them on and waited.

When she came out in her towel, I attempted a naked catwalk, but stumbled and couldn't walk in the heels so the overall image was quite tragic. She had to help me get out of them, and I sat on the side of the sofa, covering myself up with my hands and crossing my legs, feeling silly. Then she put the shoes back on and started doing a proper catwalk, trying to teach me, giving me tips in a really bad American accent on how to walk in heels. We were laughing so much her towel fell to the floor and then we were both naked on her sitting-room floor, in hysterics.

I open my eyes.

Graham Norton's voice has gone, and a dead fly is floating on the water next to me. I don't touch it as it drifts nearer to my body. I unplug the bath and stagger out with sodden shoes, watching the fly twirl round and round, until it is eventually sucked into the whirlpool and down the drain. I stay with it until it's gone. I dry my body and wrap a faded yellow towel around my hair, a family one that I was given when I first moved out. When

I was little Dad wore this towel draped around his hips. I asked him why he was wearing a skirt.

With the espadrilles still on, I totter around the flat naked, trying to build up to a catwalk, trying to remember Hannah's advice. I hear her laugh. I gather confidence, my walk sexier and stronger, until I see the glum woman in the flat opposite staring at me. I wave at her as she closes her curtains.

My phone vibrates.

Rowan (text): I'm outside.

I quickly unwrap the towel from my head and put it around my body. I go down to let him in. I know I should get dressed, but part of me also wants him to see me like this. I rehearse the movements in my head – he'll come in and lean over to kiss me as my towel falls, accidentally on purpose. He will have no option but to find me alluring.

I backtrack on my allurement plan – even in my drunken state I know it's far-fetched. I run back to get a big T-shirt and pants. I try to take the espadrilles off but they are too wet and the stubborn straps are tangled around my feet. I give up and waddle downstairs. I open the door and the cold air makes my nipples go hard instantly.

He's holding a beer bottle and doesn't smile. I don't either as I close the door behind us.

He looks me up and down. I can tell he is confused about my outfit. We go upstairs silently, and once inside I become nervous about having him inside my flat. It feels different, here. He leans back on the sofa, which makes my bag fall. He doesn't attempt to pick it up, so I do. I am kneeling at his feet, putting my gum and snack wrappers back into my dirty bag when I see that the photo of Hannah jumping has fallen out of my notebook.

I look up at him, he hasn't seen it.

I unzip his trousers, to see if I can make this pain go away for five minutes. Just five minutes, pain free, just five minutes. I begin to pull his boxers down, but he stops me. I try again, he stops me again. Instead I rest my head against him. His beer bottle hangs down by his side and cools my cheek. I'm too embarrassed to stand up, so I sit back on the floor.

After a minute, he sits down with me and sips his beer, looking perplexed, swaying back and forth slightly. We are both so drunk. Tenderly, he helps me get the espadrilles off and rubs my feet. I think of the sand between my toes the day she died, the blister on my heel which I didn't look after for weeks and which has left me with a slight scar.

Him: I'm sorry.
Me: What for?

He shrugs. I shrug back. I don't know what more we can say or do.

Him: I think I need to go away.
Me: Me too.

He is rubbing my feet with his thumb, and it feels so nice.

Me: Where will you go?
Him: I don't know yet.
Me: Far away?

Him: I guess so.

He stops rubbing.

Him: You won't get rid of it?
Me: What?
Him: The piano.
Me: I couldn't.
Him: Will you keep it safe for me?
Me: Yes.

He looks at my chest and then looks away again. My wet hair has made the T-shirt see-through. I cross my arms.

Him: She wouldn't be angry with us, I don't think.

I begin to laugh.

Me: She would be. She fucking would be.

He smiles sadly. I stop laughing.

Me: But I think that's why we did it. If she's angry, it's like she's still here.

I go to the bathroom. When I come back, he's found the photo of Hannah jumping and he's crying. I feel guilty for never showing him that photo before now. But I'm also angry that another piece of her, our final moment together as sisters, now has to be shared.

# 63

Each part of my day is still so saturated in fear, and I can't help but see the worst in everything.

When I step off the train, I will slip through the gap to the tracks and no one will help.

When I go up the escalator, I will lose my balance and fall, killing other people on the way down.

When I eat this cracker, I will choke and feel humiliated as I die that I died via cracker.

When I cross this road, I will get hit by a speeding car and become paralysed.

When I have sex, I will get a rare incurable disease that destroys my vagina and my womb.

When I go to sleep, I might just not wake up – each sleeping pill could be a death pill.

When I next love someone, they will die suddenly, unfairly, quickly, oddly, suspiciously, horrifyingly, traumatically; they'll die in the worst way that someone could, and I will have to stand by and watch, take a photo.

The woman from downstairs is filling a bird feeder to hang back on the washing line. Her little girl stands nearby, and keeps shouting, 'Birdie, birdie, birdie.' The mother inspects the fence, which has caved in even more now and looks close to being dangerous. They go back inside and miss a beautiful sparrow gracefully landing to feed. I shout, 'Birdie, birdie, birdie,' but they don't hear me. I scream.

I'm on the Tube where all the other passengers have varying sizes of headphones in and look so stern. I see Hannah, as a teenager, blowing a massive Hubba Bubba bubble. The light is fading behind her and she looks like an angel. I scream.

I'm at the storage unit looking in a box full of hair-curling tongs and heated rollers that she kept hidden from everyone to keep up her curly-hair lie. I hug her special ion-technology hairdryer. I scream.

I'm in a health food shop standing opposite the herbal teas. Teas for pregnancy, teas for breastfeeding, teas for fertility. I scream.

I sort out clothes at the launderette and I can't remember which fabric softener she liked the smell of most. I scream. Into the dryer.

It's been one week since Rowan said he was going to leave, since I wore Hannah's red espadrilles, and I've started screaming. Screaming everywhere, screaming freely.

My only real witness so far has been a little boy in Terminal 5. He was watching the planes while his parents had a hushed fight nearby. The father was about to take the boy away somewhere, and the mother was panicking that the father wouldn't be careful. The little boy kept staring out at the planes, a brown teddy bear in his lap. The same shade of brown as Hannah's skirt, the one she wore on our last flight together. Only the boy turned to look at me when I screamed. The parents kept hush-fighting.

After each scream I feel better, and I wish I'd started doing this months ago. I've realised that most people are so focused on themselves and their day that barely anyone notices.

On a break at work, Paloma chats to me with her mouth full again. She's dyed her hair acidic orange, which only highlights her eyebags. I've just seen her eating two Costa paninis in one sitting. She tells me she's now in a relationship with the bouncer from Secrets, and that he likes bigger women, so she's eating more. I don't know if I'm happy or sad for her.

During the eerily quiet shift when nothing seems to be in the sky, she invites me to Secrets to have a free drink tomorrow night. I accept but not as keenly as I think she would have liked. I suspect there must be an ulterior motive. Maybe she's been told that if she brings customers into the club she gets a bonus or something. She tells me she's invited Sal too, to cheer her up.

Paloma: Sal has been so quiet lately.
Me: Squiggle died.
Paloma: Oh, no! Not Squiggle!
Me: Yes. Squiggle. Dead.

Paloma bursts into laughter. I laugh too, and although it's not quite a real laugh, it feels nice.

On the way home, my phone vibrates. For a split-second, I think it's her. It must be her, it must be her. Please be her.

But it's him.

Rowan (text): Can we meet at the unit tonight?

# 64

My phone has run out of battery and I don't have my book on death. I fear Tube journeys without these two things – so I decide to draw the most unusual face I spot in the carriage.

I've almost filled my notebook. This will be the first one I will have begun and finished in the time since she died. Sal asked what I was 'doing' in the notebook the other day. I panicked and said, 'Poetry,' thinking that would be enough to put anyone off asking further questions. Unfortunately she said she loved writing poetry too and got out her cat-themed notebook and started reciting one of the many poems she had written 'in memory of' Squiggle.

Sal: Grief makes you more creative in a way, doesn't it?

She went on to recommend her grief counsellor. I lied and told her I already had one.

I exit the Tube station and realise I'm walking behind Mickey. He's in his gym kit and has boxing gloves slung over his back. I see a young woman in a stupid beanie stare at him and I get slightly jealous. I walk quickly to catch up with him.

Me: Hey.
Him: Hello.

He stops walking for a second and takes in my Costa uniform.

Him: I'll have a latte, please.

I can't help but smile. He smiles too and his gold tooth shines at me. As we walk to the storage place we engage in some small talk and I think I enjoy it. We talk about our days, his dad, my favourite coffee, how tired we are, and I do – I do like him. I wait for him outside the newsagent's and he comes out with two Lucozades, one for me and one for him. I see that the man with the front ponytail has had it trimmed slightly. Mickey and I wave goodbye as I get in the lift at Storage Etc. and I feel empty again.

I unlock the storage unit and turn the lights on. Moths fly around. They have multiplied. A new wave of urgency hits me – I need to get us out of here. I don't anticipate Rowan's arrival any time soon – I am sure he will be late – so I begin sorting with a sense of finality. I confront boxes I've avoided, I don't let myself cry.

When he finally enters the room, he doesn't say anything. He sees the moths too. He's wearing a grey T-shirt, his black eye is mostly gone but there's still a faint shade of green, and his hair is wild. I don't like the silence any more, it's unsettling.

Me: You OK?
Him: Not really.
Me: Have you decided where you'll go yet?

He doesn't acknowledge my question but comes closer.

Him: I've missed you this week.

I wish I believed him. I wish we weren't here in this dark, dirty room. I wish we were in a fancy hotel, maybe in Paris. I've never been and up until this moment I've never fantasised about going. I watch him and realise it would be completely creepy to ask him right now if he's ever been to Paris, or if he planned to take Hannah, who was taken to Paris by every single one of her boyfriends.

I want someone to want to take me to Paris.

He goes to the piano and starts stroking the lid. I want to know if he stuck the Polaroid inside. I go up to it and play 'Yankee Doodle' for him. He laughs and some tension dissipates.

When I get up, he stands so that we're facing each other.

This will be the last time. Neither of us has to say it. I don't know what to do other than let myself forget for a second, let myself go.

He takes off my top as I take off his. He kisses me and it's different to the other times we've kissed, though we've kissed so very little. The sex is different; it's slower and more considerate. I look into his eyes and he looks into mine, as if for the first time. We move down clumsily to Hannah's expensive carpet. It's prickly, not as soft as it looks.

She'd be annoyed about my new shaggy carpet which will be arriving soon, and how much nicer it is.

He's on top of me and his weight feels good. He sucks my right nipple, and I come quickly, too quickly. At one

330

point, just before he finishes, I think I see her in his eyes. I have a moment of ecstasy before we catch our breath and separate onto two different-coloured Home Bargains pillows and it's over.

We are both without her in that infinite way again. Regretful and panting.

I get a towel from the 'TOWELS AND FLANNELS' box and wipe my stomach clean as he falls asleep. I decide to throw all the towels away. They will remind me too much of him, of what we've done, the blood and the come. They will remind me of this space, the dark space we've created together, and I don't think I want to remember.

I get back into bed and turn onto my side, facing him. He snores quickly and looks peaceful.

I can see why she loved him, I can see it so clearly.

When I wake up he's gone, but I'd expected that.

As I get dressed I see he's left a Post-it on the piano: 'You're wonderful, Ruth.'

I pick up the Post-it, not knowing what to do with it, unsure what it means. I stick it back and look around the sad room. I push the sofa so it's nearer to the door and begin to roll up the carpet. I put it on the sofa, ready to be taken.

It's time for these things to be looked after by someone else.

I walk home, finishing the Lucozade Mickey got for me, looking around for signs of her. The sun is bright, oddly bright after yesterday's grey.

A plane crosses past another and they leave an 'X' mark in the sky. Maybe that's worth writing down in my new notebook?

# 65

I get up early and put on my swimming costume straight away. Last night I packed a bag of pants, a bra, a towel and face cream. I leave straight away despite being hungry, walking all the way to Ironmonger Row. I count eight people. Eight people who walk past me on their way to work, groggy and mindless and holding coffee cups. Three of the coffee cups are from Pret, two from Starbucks, three unknown. It's raining slightly which wakes my skin.

As I approach the PaperbackKids Portakabin, I notice that there are loads of boxes lined up outside the fencing. I open one to find that it's full of children's books. New donations. I walk away without closing the box, knowing that the rain will ruin them, but I'm upset. Upset that my subconscious made me walk this route. Now I feel awful when I was feeling fine, I was feeling OK, I was organised this morning.

I get to the pool and see people swimming through the window and I feel incredibly thirsty. I go to the vending machine to buy some water with contactless payment, and remember going to vending machines when we were kids, having been given the exact amount of change by Dad. Wheat Crunchies for her, Monster Munch for me. We would eat half the pack and then switch. I down the water and run out of the building, all the way back to the boxes of books in the rain, which is coming down harder now.

I stack the boxes on top of each other, which takes a while, and order an Uber. The driver arrives quickly, his name is Mo. Silently he helps me load the boxes into the boot. He's wearing very smart shoes with tracksuit bottoms. He smiles at me in the rear-view mirror while he speaks on the phone, headphones in. When I'm home he helps me get the boxes out of the car and all the way up to my front door, still speaking on the phone. I tip him £5, the first Uber tip I've ever given. I take the books out stack by stack and lay them on my floor to dry.

I leave my flat again and walk back towards the pool. I text my parents. The first group text we've shared as a three.

Me (text): Is now a good time to discuss PaperbackKids? Can I take over the Portakabin?

I feel bad that I wrote 'the' instead of 'Hannah's'. Hannah's Portakabin.

I don't expect them to reply for a while. I doubt they will let me. I've never proven myself to be reliable or responsible, to handle anything even moderately adult. But I manage to swim thirty lengths, my personal best, and I stare at my red cheeks in the changing room afterwards as I regain my breath. At the vending machines I buy a protein bar instead of a Twirl, wishing it was Monster Munch. I sit in the gallery, in our usual spot, and watch the swimmers.

On the Tube to work, still with no reply from my

parents, I panic that all the photos of her will disappear somewhere in the cloud thing and I won't be able to find them. I have 647 photos of her on this phone. But what about my old phone, and the one before that? If I put them all onto a hard drive, what happens if I lose it?

How can I rely on a hard drive to remember her, to not break?

One photo sticks out and I can't stop looking at it. She's in a blue dress, on her way to a work dinner exactly two years, one month and three days before she died. Her hair is in loose 'natural' curls, and she's holding an empty jam jar full of orange juice and vodka. I remember how annoyed I was that night, because she was going somewhere fancy without me and she looked so beautiful. The world was at her feet and I was staying home again. I told her, as I took this photo, that she looked like a 'slutty milkmaid'. That's why she's laughing.

I look at the photo – that was my sister. I look at the photo – I can't even believe that I had a sister. I look at the photo – I had a sister.

I had a sister.

I begin to feel light-headed and short of breath, staring, unblinking at Hannah in the blue dress until she's swirling around and around and her head is off and she's dead again, I'm watching her die again, she's on the rocks and blood is everywhere.

I google 'PANIC ATTACK' because I think that's what's happening.

When the doors open for Heathrow, I sprint all the way to Costa. Sal sees me arriving and follows me into the back room.

Sal: What happened?

I can't speak, so I put my head between my knees, clutching my phone, hyperventilating. She sits down next to me and rubs my back, which I don't particularly like but I don't push her off.

Sal: Breathe in, breathe out. Breathe in, breathe out.
Me: I can't – I want to scream –
Sal: Scream then, scream.

So I scream. Paloma rushes in.

Paloma: What the fuck is happening? Did someone die?

Sal looks at me, wanting my permission to say, 'Yes. Someone did die.' But I don't let her.
I can't make a joke, I can't smile, I can't be honest. I just breathe in and breathe out. After a minute, maybe ten, I feel better.

Me: Sorry.
Paloma: I'll get you a snack.

I don't want one, but she wants to do something for me. Sal goes to get me a tissue. I've forgotten how nice it feels to be taken care of. Paloma comes back in with a bag of crisps for me. Salt and vinegar.
Maybe I do want a snack.

Paloma: Oh, I forgot to say. Someone dropped something off for you. A man. Quite handsome, older. I put it in your locker.

She fetches it for me. It's an envelope marked 'FOR RUTH'. I open it to find a set of keys and a note: 'Portakabin keys. It's yours if you want it. Dad x'

Me: When was he here?
Paloma: About half an hour ago, just before you arrived.

I should be upset that he didn't wait for me, say goodbye to me, didn't even text me, but I'm not. He's given me what I need.

For the first time in my life, I have a plan.

# 66

I've already downed a couple of double Malibus and Coke.

The day has been difficult. I dropped Hannah's clothes off at a charity shop. All of her fancy power-suits and dresses and her box of horrible heels (except the espadrilles, I'm keeping them). I needed to find a charity shop that had a nice energy, and it took me quite a while. I really don't like them the way she did, they kind of creep me out. In the end I chose one near Angel station which is friendly but also very cool. Hannah once bought a *Lion King* T-shirt from there which was way too small for her, making her boobs look so ginormous that it distorted Simba and Nala's faces.

The trendy shopgirl, who was extremely short and skinny, gladly accepted her clothes and immediately put on Hannah's scarlet power-suit jacket and checked herself in the mirror, rolling up the sleeves and taking a selfie. She didn't realise how insensitive she was being, but the way it swamped her tiny frame made me smile. I walked out feeling lighter, knowing my sister's things will be worn and enjoyed and lived in by other people.

I'm now sitting in a dark purple cushioned booth with Sal, who is sipping a 'sex on the beach' cocktail. I'm really nervous. Secrets is very quiet tonight, or at least quieter than the last time I was here, stalking Paloma. The music is loud and the dancers' movements seem more enhanced in the emptiness of the room.

Paloma, currently at the bar, wears a silver mini-dress, and I notice new fat spilling out of the sides, so she looks like a roll of tin foil that has come to life with frosted pink lipstick. She seems so happy to have us here, which puts the pressure on but is also nice. It seems she has no ulterior motive and I feel bad for doubting her, for being so suspicious.

They've really dressed up, heels and everything. I'm wearing a long-sleeved black leotard thing, which Hannah said made me look like a Mormon, and a skirt that has a Sudocrem stain. Paloma arrives back with the drinks and we all silently note that I'm the one who's struggled with the outfit part of 'girls' night out'. I can't help it but I long to be at home, watching shit on TV. I try to picture Paloma and Sal on my sofa, but I can't, I can only picture Hannah.

I want to know where Rowan is and exactly what he's doing, if he's thought about me at all, if he's booked his tickets, where he's going. I smile as they chat and joke about their bodies compared to the dancers'. They talk about people from work, fondly and not fondly, names I recognise but can't associate with faces, because I just don't care.

I wait for Sal to bring up her cat. I feel it coming, her eyes are getting glossier by the second as the alcohol seeps into her system. I don't want to talk about anything; I shouldn't have come. Paloma's boyfriend, the bouncer, is on a break in fifteen minutes apparently. She wants me to meet him. I smile and get up to go to the toilets. They're thankfully empty and I go into a cubicle and scream. Once I'm finished I sit on the toilet and read some fresh new writing on the toilet door. 'CALL 4 ANAL'. Who brings a Sharpie to a strip club?

When I open the door of the cubicle, Sal is standing in front of me.

Sal: I heard you scream again.

She hugs me. I hug back for a bit and then feel awkward. She goes to the toilet. As she locks the cubicle door she starts talking but I don't listen. I want to have sex. I want to feel nothing.

I reapply my lip gloss and make the decision to do something stupid.

★　★　★

I want to capitalise on the confidence from alcohol, so in the Uber en route to Fred's, I text him. Inspired by the cubicle writing in Secrets, but tame by comparison, I do my version of his 'You up?' having never sent a text like this in my life.

Me (text): I want to see you and your dick right now <siren emoticon>.

He doesn't reply, but maybe he's asleep. In my head I try to choreograph my 'sexy wake-up, Fred' routine for when he sleepily answers the door. When I arrive outside his flat, I can see his lights are on as my Uber drives away. I think about texting him again, something slightly deranged but funny, like 'I can see you' – but then I recall that Fred doesn't really have a sense of humour.

I now know he's up, because I can see him wandering around in bright yellow button-up pyjamas, which remind me of Paddington bear in his raincoat.

I don't want to have sex with this man. What am I doing? I don't want to see his dick, I take back the siren emoticon.

However, his lack of reply is spurring me on and making me feel worthless. I'm sobering up by the second.

I keep watching his windows. After a minute I see a woman pass by, wrapped in a towel. Her hair is wrapped in a towel too. Fred probably ran her a bubble bath with his expensive new oils and candles and other fancy bath things. I'm not surprised. Nor am I angry.

Hannah would have predicted this.

I order another Uber. Eight minutes away. So I spend eight minutes looking at him and her get into bed and watch something together on his phone. Probably a dog video, he fucking loves dog videos. He's seen my text. Maybe she has too. He knows I'm waiting for a reply. I text him as the Uber pulls up.

Me (text): Nice pyjamas.

# 67

Hannah is in front of me, leaning against the bathroom wall waiting for me to dry my hands. I know I'm dreaming and it's horrid but I don't want it to end, because if I do I won't see her so clearly.

She applies Carmex and her lips look so full. I notice there is blood on her skirt, which is slightly too short and as usual too tight. I know that she's dead, but Hannah tells me not to worry, time to go, let's go! I follow her out of the toilets and she tries to get her phone to turn on but it won't. I tell her it just needs charging. She holds my shoulders and shakes me hard.

*Hannah: It's so good to see you.*

I know we haven't seen each other in a long time, the longest time in ever for us, but I also feel like I've been with her constantly, and I'm confused. She strokes my cheek and her hand is cold. I stop a passer-by who has a postbox-red suitcase just like my mum's.

*Me: Please – can you see her – can you see her?*
*Stranger: Yes! Don't be silly, of course I can see her.*

I'm so relieved I hug the stranger, who feels warm. Then I hug Hannah but she's so very cold. I ask the stranger to check Hannah's heartbeat. She holds Hannah's wrist and searches for the pulse, then shakes her head and smiles.

*Stranger: It doesn't matter! She's here, isn't she?*

Then she walks away. Even the way she holds the suitcase reminds me of Mum.

*Me: Where have you been?*
*Hannah: I just went to get food.*

I see there are piles and piles of food next to her. She doesn't touch any of it. I understand that she cannot eat, that her body doesn't need food any more. So I begin eating it for her, eating and eating, and when I turn back to Hannah she is gone.

I open my eyes. The hangover is pounding. I'm angry that I let myself go back to sleep. I woke up hours ago and checked the time – 6.30 a.m. – and knew it was risky because that half-asleep zone is when the truly awful dreams happen. I walk unsteadily to the kitchen. I can feel a throbbing pain in my womb. At least, I think it's my womb. I don't understand bodies, or where organs are – it's something I was always grossed out by at school and have managed to avoid learning about in adulthood. The pain is low down and doesn't feel like a UTI. I am usually disciplined with how much I google symptoms because I know the result is mostly just 'DYING', but this morning I go for it. Google gives me the verdict:

*Most likely: Sexually Transmitted Disease.*

It makes sense. My body deserves some reckoning. I text him.

Me (text): I think I have an STD.

He replies instantly.

Him (text): Me too.

I want to send a plethora of inappropriate emoticons but I control myself. I want to send them somewhere though, so I send them to Hannah. A red exclamation mark appears, indicating that the text is undelivered. I try again and the same thing happens, and then I remember that I only paid for her phone to be continued until the end of her contract, which was up last week.

I scream.

★   ★   ★

Two hours later, I'm holding a flat white in each hand and waiting outside a coffee shop in South London. Fourteen minutes late, I see Rowan walking his bicycle towards me, looking tired. He hugs me with one arm and I can tell he's in a bad way again. My heart pangs. He sips the coffee, and I take his bike from him as we walk, as if I've done this before, as if I know how to handle a bike.

Me: You OK?
Him: Not really.

We don't say anything as he gets his lock from his backpack. I remember Hannah telling me she bought him a bicycle lock because he didn't have one. Simple metallic blue. We walk into the clinic. It's not as busy as I thought it would be.

The last time I was here, she was with me. She made me get tested after she thought I'd ended it with Fred.

Her: This can be your new start, OK?
Me: This sexual health clinic is my new start? Is there a job going?
Her: You know what I mean.

It wasn't my new start. I kept sleeping with Fred, kept taking the risk, kept lying to her.

Rowan and I take a form and a biro each and sit in the waiting room. I look over as he fills in his form and I see he's ticking boxes I'm not ticking and I feel utterly stupid and scared and cheated but also – nothing. It doesn't matter any more. None of this matters. We hand in our forms and we sit back down in silence as the waiting room begins to fill up. Lunchtime rush? He gets a text. I don't look. He puts his hand on my thigh. I feel nothing.

Him: I would never put you in danger intentionally, you know. I just –
Me: I know. Me too.

I feel hurt that he needed to feel better without me, or couldn't feel better with me, but then I don't feel better with or without him either. It could be either of our faults.

A woman's name is called and she walks towards a

doctor, limping slightly, in pain. I wonder if the pain is because of her tiny red thong, which I can see peeking over the band of her jeans. Or maybe she's just been injured by a massive, massive dick. I begin to laugh like a child, and then laugh more when I see one of the posters advertising femidoms and another poster with blue bubble writing: 'Syphilis is back!' Rowan looks at the poster and then smiles too.

Me: Sorry. It's just that – sometimes – doesn't sex
    seem so fucking silly?
Him: You're funny, you know.
Me: I'm not. She was the only one who found me
    even slightly –
Him: You are.

I regain composure and the silence between us comes back. I can tell he's scared.

Him: Do you think she'd forgive us?
Me: I don't know.

I don't want to answer that question truthfully because there's no point; there's no going back and there's no way of going forward together.

He hugs me and I hug him too and it feels like we're hugging for the first and last time. People look at us as if we've just received some awful news. They don't know that they're watching an actual ending.

## 68

I stand in front of the self-service printing machines at Snappy Snaps, hoping I don't need help. I turn on Hannah's phone. I waited until I was in public to do this, so that I'm less likely to break down. I charged it last night, and stared at the ceiling whilst I went over the plan in my head again and again. I need to make this as painless as possible.

I tap the photos icon, and search for pictures she took of PaperbackKids and the poster she designed for it. I'm going to print them out, and maybe get them laminated so I can attach them to trees, and hopefully achieve my goal of getting out of here without crying or screaming. I avoid looking for too long at the screensaver, which is of Rowan, not me. I plug her phone into the machine, and wait for the photos to load so I can start scrolling through, but I stop immediately, and stare in shock at the last photo she took. It's of me.

I'm jumping off the cliff, suspended in mid-air. She didn't tell me she'd taken this – she knew I didn't want a photo.

Snappy Snaps lady: Hello again, would you like any
    help –
Me: No. No.

She nods at the screen, sees the photo.

Snappy Snaps lady: Just printing the one again?
Me: No. Please. Fuck off –
Snappy Snaps lady: Excuse me? That's not acceptable
    language –

The Snappy Snaps lady goes to the counter and speaks to a colleague, who then tries to make me exit the shop. I become desperate, my voice is panicked.

Me: My sister died. My sister died jumping off this
    fucking cliff. So please – please – can you leave
    me alone while I try to print some photos, please?

The Snappy Snaps lady looks shocked and walks away; her colleague backs down. I should swear at strangers more. The adrenaline pumping through my body feels sweet, and gives me the energy to keep going with this dreadful task. I select the photo of me, and I scroll back quickly, past selfies of her in random toilets, past shots of Rowan in bed, of us in bed making silly faces with inane filters.

I find the PaperbackKids poster, and a few other photos from the last session she held – there's one of her and little Jimi, with me in the background. I select them all. Once they're printed, I put them into a little pouch thing and go up to the Snappy Snaps lady, who's now behind the desk.

Me: Please can I get five of this photo laminated?
    A4 size?

She slides a piece of paper over the counter, with an email address on.

Snappy Snaps lady: Send the photo here, they'll be ready to collect in an hour.

I pay for it all and walk towards the door, unsure what I should do with the free hour that lies ahead of me, scared of having the time to think, to look at her phone. As I open the door she comes up to me.

Snappy Snaps lady: I'm really sorry about your sister.
Me: Sorry for swearing.

I turn Hannah's phone off, because I know if I start looking through it, through her life, I'll see all her secrets. And I don't think I want to any more.

\* \* \*

2013

Hannah once texted me early on a Saturday morning, saying she was outside my flat in her car. It was 8.32 a.m. She started honking the horn, and sent ten more texts, telling me to hurry up and get dressed. I got in the car sleepily, still in my pyjamas.

Me: What's happening?
Hannah: We're going to Newcastle.
Me: Why?

She started driving and told me she'd found a white anorak she wanted from New Look, but they only did it in her size at a branch in Newcastle. I suggested she order it online, but she wanted to get it in person, today. In my half-asleep state, I didn't think to question her mysterious motive or logic; she was on a mission and needed my help.

She was twenty-four and between boyfriends. Because she was a serial monogamist and used to routine male validation, her common sense in these rare single periods went a little astray. She was still highly functional and practical at work, but she possessed this raw crazy-girl energy on the weekends – searching for something to tide her over until the next man came along.

We stopped for coffee and crisps at the first service station on the way. She bought us some water and raspberries from M&S while I went next door and secretly bought her a keyring with her name on. I told myself I would give it to her if we didn't find the anorak. I fell back asleep in the car and woke up as were entering the car park of a shopping centre in Newcastle.

The anorak was nowhere to be found in New Look. Hannah rushed up to three different people who worked there and asked them if they had it in stock, showing them pictures on her phone. They shook their heads and Hannah was defeated.

Me: Why don't you get it in yellow or blue?
Her: Because I wanted white.

She was chewing the insides of her cheeks, trying not to cry. On our way out someone ran up to her smiling, holding the shiny white PVC anorak. Hannah practically

349

hugged it and the New Look employee. The anorak was nice, but nothing special.

She tried it on in front of the mirror near the entrance. She suddenly had a mischievous look in her eyes, as if she might just run out of the shop in it without paying. I guided her towards the tills, and she drove us home wearing it.

I never saw that anorak again.

# 69

I sit on a beanbag and wait. There's definitely a mouse problem which I need to sort out, but for now, it's looking quite good.

It's Wednesday. PaperbackKids day. I imagine that this nauseous feeling is similar to one you'd get if you were throwing a party and waiting for people to turn up. I've never thrown a party so I can't be sure. The place looks nice, just as if she had done it herself. I've brought my speaker, which is playing music that I think the kids will like. I've brought her plants from the storage unit, whose stubborn will to live despite my horticultural ineptitude has surprised me. I've even blown up balloons and tied them to the railings outside. The balloons say 'HANNAH'.

I've spent the last few days, on the way back from work, tying the laminated posters around trees in the Old Street and Shoreditch areas, and cleaning the Portakabin. I've emailed all the local schools. I know Jimi wore a red school uniform so I worked out the school and put a poster up outside it. It felt a bit weird, trying to track down a kid.

I've stuck back up the posters that had fallen to the

floor in Hannah's absence, and made a collage of the photos I got printed for the wall too. I've opened the windows and the door and bought a fan to air the place out. I've washed the beanbags with special fabric wet wipes. I've rehung the bunting.

The volunteers who previously worked with Hannah are here, and they are eagerly waiting outside for the first children to arrive. They were quite cautious at first, especially after seeing the balloons, but they've relaxed now. My mum is here too, very dressed up in heels and one of her five special dresses, and she's with Leila, who looks even more pregnant if that was possible. I'm worried she's going to go into labour dramatically and steal Hannah's thunder.

Leila: It looks so nice, Ruth, well done.
Mum: You look nice too, darling. What have you been doing?
Me: I've been swimming. I'm also on antibiotics for chlamydia, do they give a glow?
Mum: Some do, actually.

Leila laughs and I'm grateful she doesn't realise I'm not joking. Mum doesn't flinch. I watch her lower herself onto a beanbag and once she's down she looks like she might never be able to get back up. Hannah would have been staggered that my mum is here, on a second-hand beanbag.

Mum: Do you have any drinks?
Me: It's not a party, Mum.
Mum: So people bring their own drinks?

Me: The kids might bring a water bottle if that's
    what you mean.
Leila: I can pop to the shops if you want? I'm craving
    a Diet Coke. Do you want one, Han – I mean,
    Ruth?

Leila is mortified. Mum hasn't noticed.

Leila: Sorry, God. Baby brain –
Me: It's fine. Honestly.
Leila: I'll be back soon.

I'm beginning to like her a bit more, I guess mainly
because she's not given up with me, with us. Mum checks
her phone. I see a few children pacing outside, unsure if
they are allowed in.

Me: Mum, can you stand up, the kids are here –
Mum: Relax, darling. It's just a party –
Me: It's not a fucking –
Mum: Pull me up then.

I pull her up, almost toppling over in the process. We
stare at each other for a second, like we could hug, but don't.

Mum: I had it last year. Chlamydia. Not fun.

I laugh a little as she goes to the window and peers
out. I open the gates, searching for Jimi in the queue,
but I can't see him. A parent comes up and squeezes my
arm, tears in her eyes, acknowledging the Hannah balloons
which is nice, but I refuse to cry today.

Me: Are you guys ready to come in?

The kids do a mumbled but keen 'yeah'. I let the parents know they can stay outside on the little deck chairs I've cleaned, but most of them leave, to go back to work or to have a few hours 'off' parenting. The kids rush in and dive onto the beanbags. I assign the volunteers, who are barely more than children themselves, to read with them. My mum joins a few of the remaining parents outside for a smoke. She looks as though she's from another time, clutching her handbag like the queen, smoking thin elegant cigarettes outside a Portakabin in Old Street. She immediately starts chatting to them, more at ease with strangers than me.

I go to turn the music down as the *Frozen* soundtrack comes on. For a minute I just listen to the music and the kids' voices, their stilted sentences, the cool facts they're sharing with each other –

Boy: Do you know gorillas eat poo?
Girl: Neptune is my favourite planet.
Boy: If I had a dog I would call it Bingo.
Girl: Olaf is my favourite but I like Elsa too.

And then I see him arrive, little Jimi, with a girl I assume is his big sister. She leaves as soon as he's through the gates. He's taller than before, and he sees me through the window and heads straight for me. I want to hug him but before he reaches me, he is seized by a friend, and I can tell he is conflicted about whether to come straight up to me or him. He goes to his friend, and I follow, with a few books. He smiles shyly at me then sits down on the beanbag, still wearing his oversized backpack.

Me: You came back.
Jimi: Yeah.
Me: You've grown.
Jimi: Two centimetres since my birthday.
Me: Wow, that's amazing.

This little boy has grown two centimetres and Hannah will never see him again.

Me: Here are some books – you can take these home too, if you want.
Jimi: Thanks.

He can't quite look at me. I walk away, not wanting to seem uncool in front of two eight-year-olds. Then I'm tapped on my back and it's him.

Jimi: Hannah died?

His eyes look so open, ready and waiting to be altered by whatever I, the grown-up, say. I desperately want to lie to him. But I can't.

Me: Yes. She did.
Jimi: Are you really sad?
Me: Yes.

He nods, and looks a little confused. He walks back to his friend. When he sits down again on the beanbag he looks back at me, and I try to smile. I turn away and see that my mum has a little girl on her lap, reading to her happily, doing all kinds of voices and accents like she used to do for us. She catches my eye and goes even bigger with her performance.

I watch her, not just because I want to but because she needs me to.

# 70

Tomorrow is the first of the month and the payment for the storage unit will not be leaving my account. Today, I've almost emptied it. I'm saying goodbye.

I look out of my kitchen window. The fence is being fixed. They had to break it apart, putting each bit of broken wood into a pile and replacing it with brighter, newer fence planks. Before they closed the gap, I saw the two little girls wave to each other from their gardens, maybe even seeing each other for the first time. After a minute or so, their mothers called them back inside because: 'It's dangerous.'

At the station, I get some cash out for the removal men. A homeless girl sits nearby and asks me so directly for money that I give her £10 in the hope that it brings me good karma. I've never given anything other than carrot cake to a homeless person before and it feels quite nice.

Yesterday I watched as her small pink velvet sofa was put into the back of a stranger's car. I didn't know her name, just that her username on Freecycle is ilovehalloween33. I felt sad as the sofa was put in, with its legs taken off, but also glad that ilovehalloween33 was so excited to be taking it off my hands.

Mickey is outside Storage Etc. when I arrive, doing sprints in the car park. His dad is timing him, smoking. They don't notice me as I go in, so I leave a note on the front desk: 'I am vacating today. Thanks. Ruth.' I'm glad it's not the type of establishment that asks too many questions.

It hurts me to see how bare it looks upstairs. Just the piano and the bed. I open the piano and unstick the Polaroid that was hidden inside and put it safely in my notebook alongside the cliff photos. I walk around the space and notice a huge spider's web. No spider. The door knocks and I jump. It's Mickey, holding rolls of bubble wrap.

Mickey: Thought you might need help, Ruth?

He looks so sweet I want to cry.

Mickey: You'll want to bubble-wrap the piano. It looks like a good one.

He puts his hand on the piano and I flinch, worried that another person's touch will change it somehow.

Me: Thanks, that's really nice –
Mickey: You take this side –

He rolls out the bubble wrap and we begin to smother the beautiful thing.

Mickey: Where will it go?
Me: I'm not sure.
Mickey: It's yours?

Me: No. It's my sister's.
Mickey: She didn't want it?
Me: She died.
Mickey: Oh, fuck.

I begin to laugh.

Mickey: That's fucking shit. I'm sorry.

He doesn't ask how and I'm glad. I can't say how she died out loud without sounding like I'm joking. When we've successfully bubble-wrapped it, along with its stool, he comes closer to me.

Mickey: It's safe now.
Me: Do you think I should do the bed?

He looks over at the stripped bed, he must see the bloodstain. I'm not embarrassed.

Mickey: Nah. The bed will be OK. It's sturdy.
Me: OK.
Mickey: Let's get some air?

We go down in the lift together, out into the car park, and sit on the bench outside. It's getting darker and I can feel the heat coming from his skin, sweaty from the sprints and the bubble-wrapping. He drinks a bottle of water in one go and crunches it up in his hand, which I find weirdly impressive. I check my phone.

Me: A man with a van called Francesco is arriving in five minutes, apparently.

359

Mickey: I've got to get back to training.

Me: Thank you.

Mickey: No worries.

Me: No, thank you for saying it's just shit. No one really says that.

Mickey: Well, it is shit. Really shit.

Me: Yep.

Mickey: Life is pretty shit for everyone, most of the time.

Me: God, that's depressing.

Mickey: Yeah – but you can make the most of the shit, you know?

He smiles. I like his gold tooth.

Mickey: Listen. Do you want to go for a drink sometime?

I attempt to smile but I think I frown.

Mickey: Just think about it. You know where I am.

I feel relieved that I don't have to answer now and safe that I do know where he'll be if I need to find him. He goes back to his sprints. I watch him, stunned.

Five minutes later, Francesco pulls up outside in a black van and beeps his horn. He jumps out with open arms.

Him: I'm here to rescue you!

He's tall and muscular with a thick Italian accent.

Him: Have you been waiting for me?
Me: No, you're on time –
Him: I know. I'm always on time.

I smile, though I can't tell if this man is real, and lead him into the storage unit Reception. Another man waits in the van, on the phone, smoking out of the window. I can hear Mickey now boxing in the back room. I feel anxious about what to say on my own to Francesco, so I press the lift button again. Once we are inside the lift and the doors close, he goes on his phone and starts humming loudly.

Him: So we have a bed and a piano, is that right?

I nod.

Him: The piano has wheels?

I shake my head.

Him: Lucky I am extremely strong. They call me the Hulk.

He gets down on his knees and pretends to weightlift. He lets out a huge grunt to be more manly and impressive, and I giggle. My stupid real giggle. When I unlock the door again, the room looks gutted out. Have I been too brutal with her things? Would she be angry that strangers will be wearing her power-suits, using her plates? Francesco assesses the bed and piano and then opens the door again.

Francesco: I get my friend and then we move. I'll
    be back in a minute, OK?
Me: OK.

He does a funny grunt to make me laugh again and
leaves. I wait for a moment, until I'm sure that he's gone,
and then I drop to the floor and scream. Francesco rushes
back, panicked.

Francesco: What happened?
Me: Nothing, sorry. Fine. I'm OK, thanks. Sorry –
Francesco: But you screamed?
Me: Yeah, it was just, um – nothing.

He goes. This free time feels dangerous. What would
Hannah have done if it was me who died that day?
Would she have put my stuff in this exact storage room,
would Rowan have helped her? What would happen to
my shitty little flat, would she have kept it? My skin
itches.

I put my hands in my pockets so I can't hit myself. I
have a bunch of coins in one pocket. I yank them out
and throw them against the wall. The sound of them
rebounding off the bare walls and onto the hard floor
doesn't seem loud enough so I pick them up and throw
them against the wall again, harder this time. I see the
coins rolling on the floor and begin to pick them up in
a frenzy. Pathetically I realise that I will need these coins
for food, that they can't be spared.

I pick a moth to stare at until the door opens and the
men come in. They take the bed out, ignoring the
bloodstain, as I stay sitting on the bubble-wrapped stool.
They must have seen plenty of bloodstains along the

way. I rest my head against the piano and think about the day we got it. She said she would learn how to play songs I loved, but I couldn't think of a single one I really loved. I want to bang my head into the piano as hard as I can, but I'm scared of the pain, even if it's bubble-wrapped.

I think of Rowan. I think of the Diet Coke lid which fell to the floor, the pizza we ate, the dirty toilets, my vomit, his dick that was actually beautiful.

They come back in and I have to get up and the room is suddenly empty, no piano, nothing. It's just me in here. Me and the moths. I sit on the filthy floor, where her carpet was, and say her name over and over again.

★ ★ ★

As I sit in the middle seat of the van next to Francesco's friend, whose skin looks sunburnt, I regret only double-bubble-wrapping, not triple-bubble-wrapping, the piano. Hannah would definitely have triple-wrapped. The sunburnt man is smoking again, hand dangling out the window like he doesn't give a shit if it's cut off. Francesco drives too fast. Magic FM is blaring and Hannah's bed and piano are knocking about in the back. I want to ask him to drive slower but I can't.

We arrive at my flat and they start unloading the bed. I run ahead of them to open the door, and I see the little girl from the flat below in the lobby, helmet on and riding a mini-scooter skilfully. Her mother is on the phone, as usual, and doesn't look at me, or avoids me, as usual. So I stop in front of her and make her look at me, make her look up from her phone.

Me: The fence is fixed. That's good.

Her: Um, yes. Sorry – was it bothering you?

Me: No, not at all. I liked it actually.

Her: Oh.

Me: I'm Ruth.

Her: I'm Sandra.

The little girl smiles at me and scooters away. Sandra runs after her, putting the phone in her pocket.

Her: OK. Bye, Ruth.

The removal men arrive at the door and I lead them awkwardly up the stairs. When we get into my flat, I lead them to the bedroom and show them my bed on the floor.

Francesco: We take your mattress?

I see now that it is just a mattress. They take it out and I watch them through the window, chucking it into the van like rubbish. I don't mind.

I pace around until they come back up and I watch them put Hannah's bed frame back together again. I consider offering them a cup of tea, but I offer them a cracker, which they decline. I wait for them to bring up Hannah's mattress, staring at her naked bed frame. It makes my little bedroom look instantly more grown up, more sophisticated, less studenty.

They put her mattress on the frame and it feels like we are all staring at the bloodstain as I stress-eat cracker after cracker. As they leave to go back down to get the piano, I have an idea and run after them.

Me: Can we actually drop the piano somewhere else?
    I have more cash.

We are now driving towards Hannah's flat. It's nice to
see the street names again. The sunburnt man is driving;
he has nice forearms which are hairy compared to his
shiny head. He has a tattoo on his wrist: 'Loreen'. It's
fading and the ink has gone kind of greeny-grey and it's
a horrible font but still, it must mean or must have meant
something. He loves or loved a Loreen.

I lead them out of the lift towards Hannah's door. My
hands shake as I knock, something I've never had to do
before. After the second knock, Mum finally opens the
door, in a dressing gown. She looks disturbed and I hope
to God she doesn't have anyone in here with her.

Me: Hi, Mum. This is Francesco and –
Sunburnt man: Paolo.
Me: Sorry, Paolo. Francesco and Paolo. And we're
    dropping the piano round for you. Can you just
    show them where you'd like it?

My mum smiles gamely, but she eyeballs me as if to
say, 'What the hell are you doing?'

Mum: I'd love it over in the corner, by the windows,
    boys.

The men nod and she waits until they are in the lift
to drop the smile, suddenly looking severe.

Her: What's going on?
Me: I think you should keep something of hers.

Her: I have lots of her things –

Me: That's bullshit, you don't. Most of her things are now in charity shops or the dump or at mine. You should have something.

Her: I'm living in her flat, aren't I?

Me: Yes, but everything of hers is gone now. You can't just erase her –

Her: I'm not –

She starts rubbing her arms and her body slouches, eventually dropping to the floor.

Me: She'd like you to keep it –

Her: I don't want it –

Me: But you can use it. Play it. You could sing to her. Like you did when we were little.

I move closer to her.

I look around the flat; it's still mostly empty. She's got a small sofa and a telly. Posters from plays she was in during her twenties are in frames on the floor, yet to be hung up. Posters that I grew up with. Her first headshot which she got blown up sits next to them. I want to see how she's done the bedroom but the door is closed. We hear the lift doors open. She gets up quickly and wipes her face. Her mascara has run, and I wonder why she is wearing make-up when she's in her nightwear. She composes herself, and puts on a show.

The men look at us for direction. Their hands, gripping the piano, pop some of the bubble wrap. I go and stand where the piano was, where Hannah chose for it to go.

Me: Over here, Mum?

Mum: Yes, thank you, boys. Let me give you some –

She doesn't look at the piano being placed and fumbles around with her handbag. Her hands are shaking as she pulls her purse out. I see that the fake leather on her purse is peeling. I put my hands over hers.

Me: I've sorted it, you don't need to pay them, Mum.

They begin taking the bubble wrap off, making squeaky sounds. I hand them the cash in the corridor. Paolo presses the button for the lift, while Francesco hangs back and looks at me, kindly. I'm starting to think that strangers are generally quite nice.

Francesco: You OK?

I shrug and smile. As he walks away, I want to know everything about him and tell him everything about me. If he's married, if he cheats on his wife, if he still goes down on her, what telly he likes, if he has kids, what their names are, his favourite food, if he thinks I look pretty or destroyed. I close the door to leave me and Mum alone. She walks over to the piano slowly, popping some of the bubble wrap on the floor with her toes on the way.

We stand by the piano together for a while, looking at the engraving.

'H & R'.

# 71

It's my twenty-seventh birthday.

It's almost the end of my double shift, which I took on intentionally to avoid this day. My mum's texted to say she has dropped round a present, and my dad has forgotten, but he never thought birthdays were worth remarking upon. I haven't drunk coffee for hours so that I can fall asleep as soon as I get home. I haven't thought about what she might have got me, or where we would be going for dinner. I don't want to wake my brain up and realise what a horrible thing it is to be a year closer to the age my sister was when she died, or that in three years' time I'll be older than she ever will be.

I don't want today to mean anything. But, of course, it does.

I serve a customer who orders an iced Americano with coconut milk and a brownie. She's got a pixie haircut, which makes her look like Tinker Bell with a nose ring. Her T-shirt has the Powerpuff Girls on, a cartoon which Hannah and I loved, and she looks tired. As I turn the iPad towards her to pay she asks if she can use cash. This is rare. I say yes and she hands me some coins, but she's short by over two pounds. She watches me count it and waits for me to ask her for the remainder.

She looks so nervous that my heart breaks for her and I try to be nice.

Me: Where are you going today?
Her: Home. I hope.

Her accent is pretty. I hand her the brownie on a plate and watch her wait for her coffee, made by Paloma, whose hair is now blue. The girl mouths 'thank you' as she goes to sit at a table.

I think of Hannah when we were last here together, at the railings on the phone to him.

Paloma taps me on the shoulder and says she needs me to come to the back room. I ask Michelle to take over from me. I've just learnt her name even though she's been here since before I started. Michelle has very warm hands all the time, which leave the iPad warm when she hands it over and I like her. Before I follow Paloma into the back room, I put the coins in my hands and take them over to the Tinker Bell girl. I place them down on the table next to her half-eaten brownie and smile.

Me: Good luck.

The girl looks like she could cry. I go into the back room and see Paloma holding a bunch of balloons and Sal holding a little pink cake with one candle lit.

Sal/Paloma: Happy birthday!
Sal: I made the cake –
Paloma: But the little party was my idea.

I don't want it to be my birthday, I don't want it to be my birthday. But they're trying so hard to make me happy.

Me: Thank you. It's really nice of you, both of you.

I blow the candle out. They wouldn't be doing this if they didn't like me?

Sal hands me a plastic Costa knife. As I cut the cake, I don't make a wish, and we eat the cake in silence. Paloma's legs are bare and it's obvious that she's not shaved in a while, they're covered in really long dark hairs. She sees me looking and shrugs.

Paloma: I just stopped caring for a bit and it feels nice.

We all smile with mouths full of pink cake. It's not as sweet as it looks and it's really nice. Sal gets a tiny little pink frosting moustache.

Sal: I have some news! I'm getting a new kitten.
Me: Squiggle Two?

Paloma laughs so hard at my basic joke that a small bit of cake shoots out of her mouth and lands on my lap. Sal starts laughing too, aware that we're making fun of her but enjoying the attention. There's a tiny little slice of cake left.

Paloma: You should go home, Ruth, you look awful.

I'm getting used to Paloma's rather brutal sense of humour. I want to be more like her.

Sal: Get some sleep.

Me: I guess. OK.

Sal: Do you want to take the balloons?

Me: No, thanks.

Paloma: I'll take them to the club later. The strippers can use the balloons.

Me: Really?

Paloma: Men like props.

I try to hang on to my laugh, make it last longer than it probably should. They hug me. I'm too touched to hug back. I want to remember that it is possible to feel this way. Sal wraps the cake in tissue carefully for me. They go back to their stations and I walk away, through the airport.

I love it in here when it's dark outside. I plan to go and watch some planes take off into the night sky before I'm ready to go home. Then I see him. His back, crouched over one of the Costa tables, his feet tapping away. He has a suitcase with him, a big one. I stand in front of him.

Me: You're here.

Rowan: I'm in the wrong terminal but I wanted to say −

His voice is shaky.

Me: You don't have to say anything −

I see Paloma looking at us quizzically from the coffee machines.

Rowan: Leila had the baby.

Me: Oh, wow − that's nice.

371

Rowan: I just wanted to say goodbye — and that
   I'm —
Me: Which terminal do you need?
Rowan: Four.
Me: That's a nice terminal. This one's the best but
   Four is pretty good too —
Rowan: Ruth —
Me: What's the baby's name? Or are they gonna
   wait —
Rowan: Ruth, I need to say something to you. Before
   I go.
Me: No, please don't —
Rowan: Just let me say it.
Me: I'd prefer you not to because then I need to say
   sorry too and I really fucking hate saying sorry.

I don't want to ask where he's going. He stands up and
I can tell he's about to hug me. I back away slightly to
put him off because I don't want to cry right now, I don't
want to miss him. He picks up his suitcase.

Me: I've given the piano to my mum. She's living
   at Hannah's now.

He looks sad.

Me: But you can come and play it, you know. When
   you come back, maybe. Also —

I get my notebook and pull out the Polaroid from the
piano. I give it to him and as soon as he looks at it I
know that he's seen this photo before. He took this photo,
the photo was always his. He puts it in his front pocket,

and goes in for a hug, ignoring my frosty stance. I'm engulfed in his long arms for a long minute. I dig my fingers into his back.

When he pulls away he notices the cake I'm holding.

Me: Oh . . . it's my birthday. Some, um, friends –
    they made me a little cake.
Rowan: Oh. Happy birthday.
Me: Do you want it?
Rowan: No, no.
Me: Take it –
Rowan: I'm fine, thanks –
Me: Please?

I really need him to take the cake and I don't know why.

Rowan: OK, thanks.
Me: Eat it on the plane.

He hugs me again briefly and I begin to back away as we wave. Both of us swallow tears. I turn and feel him watching me walk. When I look around it takes a second to spot him but there he is, already tiny and far away.

I sit for a long time in Departures, surrounded by silent strangers on their way somewhere. I can't help but sit there and imagine Rowan and me living together, some-time in the future, in a normal house, being a normal couple, pretending we haven't been thrust together by grief. Maybe our cute kids are at school and we're sitting on our stained sofa. Maybe we have a picture of Hannah on the mantelpiece that we have to dust every week but sometimes forget and feel guilty but don't say anything about how guilty we actually feel. Maybe we have different haircuts and we're still sad but capable of being happy in our manufactured domesticity. I let the fantasy play out naturally, and I'm relieved when an airport announcement pulls me back. To the real world and to the end of that not-quite-there version of Us.

I get home much later, half-asleep, and there's a washing machine outside my front door with a huge pink bow wrapped around it. A Post-it is stuck to the side: 'Happy birthday darling. Love Mum xxx'.

I don't remember telling her my washing machine was broken.

# 72

Today I finally sold her car on WeBuyAnyCar.com. I got £350 for it that went straight into my account. It made me feel dirty, so now I'm sitting in the shower with my legs crossed, trying to gauge if it's been three minutes yet. That's how long the conditioner needs.

Hannah wanted to me to look after myself better, take care of my body, my hair, so I'm doing this for her. Three minutes seemed like such a waste of time for me and my hopeless hair. And of course it makes no real difference to how my hair looks, but I like doing the things that she wanted me to do, even though she isn't here to witness the (lack of) results.

My shaggy cream carpet arrived this morning. It takes up most of the floor space in my tiny sitting room, and is the most expensive thing I have ever bought. I don't regret it yet. Without my constant witness, I am left to my own devices. I yearn for her to be here still keeping tabs.

Sometimes I wonder if I should just become a new person, move to a different country, change my name. Be a boxer or a banker or a chef.

I have no strings.

The three minutes is up. I found it strangely therapeutic.

I turn the shower back on and watch the conditioner rinse out and down the drain. Then I turn the temperature up so my back begins to burn.

When I get out of the shower I scrub the steam off the mirror so I can see myself for a second to put on her moisturiser, before it steams up again.

I get dressed. I write a list while I cook my dinner.

How to be more ~~of an adult~~
~~be better~~ like my sister:

Get my own lamps
Pay the rent on time, don't do IOUs
Hoover
Use a real bin, with a proper lid, not just a plastic bag
Recycle
Close the curtains at night, and open them in the
    morning
Use fabric softener, bleach the toilet, floss teeth
Write shopping lists before you go shopping
Wash my hair more
Use condoms
Finish antibiotics
Descale the kettle
Don't judge people for their tattoos or cat names
Only have sex with people that like you
Only have sex with people that you like
Don't send texts after midnight

Ketchup on pasta. I have no sauce so I make myself a meal suited for a five-year-old. I eat it quickly in the kitchen, looking out of my window at the starry sky. I can't actually see any stars but I know they must be there.

I consider buying a telescope on Amazon, but then I don't think I would suit a telescope, and I don't want the glum woman opposite to get any ideas. I hear my mum's voice – maybe I accidentally pocket-dialled her, but I look at my phone and I haven't.

I realise her voice is coming from the television. I go into the sitting room and see her face, filling the screen in an advert for Tetley Tea. She's sipping from a mug, looking directly into the camera and smiling. She looks glorious. My eyes have filled with tears by the time the advert is over. Why hasn't she told me she finally got a TV gig? Maybe she's embarrassed. It's an advert, not the Shakespeare or BBC prime-time drama she dreams of. Still, I text her.

Me (text): You look great in the tea advert, Mum xxx

I don't expect her to reply but she does, straight away.

Mum (text): Thank you, darling. I'm trying to be less proud.

I want to reach through my phone and hold her hand. Instead all I can do is send a smiley face, disappointed by how quickly I resort to emoticons when it comes to meaningful moments.

# 73

I stand nervously in front of the navy door. There's lots of mail poking out of the letterbox, and it seems as though no one is home. But I look through the window and see Leila, asleep on her sofa. A Moses basket is beside her on the floor and what's in it scares me. I have second thoughts – it's stupid to have come here.

I decide to leave the box I've brought for her on the doorstep, which contains all of Hannah's vinyls and cookbooks. Rowan's guitar mug is in there too, for when he comes back. I begin to make my way to the gate when the door opens.

Her: Ruth?

When I turn around, I'm surprised by how awful she looks. Though she still looks cool in an oversized basketball shirt and tiny black cycling shorts.

Me: Hey, sorry. I didn't want to wake you –
Her: I wasn't asleep.
Me: Oh –
Her: Did you come to meet the baby?
Me: Um, well –

The baby starts crying and Leila charges back inside, leaving the door open for me.

She turns on the lights in the sitting room and the baby's cries get louder. She sits down to feed it, not embarrassed at all about pulling her boob out in front of me, which is almost double the size of the tiny little baby's head. She puts some calming music on from her phone and tries for a while to get the baby to feed, but it won't. It keeps thrashing itself all over the place. Leila hangs her head and sighs.

Me: Are you OK?

She stands up, agitated, and gently thrusts the baby into my arms, leaves for the kitchen. I hear her clunking about as I sit down with the baby and do some amateur shushing.

Leila comes back a minute later with a small bottle of baby formula and a glass of red wine.

Her: No one told me it would be this fucking hard.
Someone should have told me, right? He won't take my boob. He won't sleep.

I make it clear that I'm struggling with the baby, having never held one before now. But Leila doesn't move, she just keeps sipping the wine, making no attempt to get the baby back into her arms.

Her: Try bobbing up and down. He fucking loves bobbing.
Me: I thought you were having a girl?
Her: Me too. I wanted a girl. I know I shouldn't say that but it's true.

She offers me some of her wine and I shake my head. The baby keeps screaming and so I pick up the bottle of formula and pretend I know what I'm doing. The baby sucks and is calmed and I feel like I've done something good.

Me: Oh, wow –

Leila tries to smile but looks strangely dead-eyed and despondent. I've never seen her like this before.

Me: Sorry I haven't sent a present.
Her: I really don't give a shit about presents. I just want to get some sleep, get him to eat from me.
Me: Where's Danny?
Her: He's on a work thing for another week. I'm glad he's managed to escape. I've not been a lot of fun.
Me: You're not meant to be fun right now, are you? You just gave birth.
Her: Yeah but still. We've packed in a lot of stuff in less than a year. I think he's terrified.
Me: Do you have any other help?
Her: My sister, I guess. But she's got her own shit going on, she's a nightmare.

She must sense the way I prickle at the mention of a sister, a sister who's still alive, a sister she can still bitch about. I look down and focus on the baby, this beautiful baby boy, whose eyelids are starting to flutter with exhaustion. Leila softens.

Her: You know, what you and Hannah had – you were so lucky. It was more than just – blood. You actually liked each other.

My eyes fill with tears but I don't want to cry on the baby. I look around at this house that was so pristine when I came here last. It's a tip. Nappies on the floor, laundry everywhere. Dirty dishes. I want to help her. The baby stirs and begins to cry again. Leila leaves for the kitchen and I follow, worried I'll drop the baby as I walk. She busies herself with anything but taking him back – folding a tea towel, pushing in a chair, scraping some crumbs off the table onto the floor, sweeping them up. Opening her fridge, closing it again.

I look at the Polaroid of Hannah on her green fridge as I bob and sway the baby, unsure if I'm doing it right, scared I'm doing it wrong. I look into his eyes and he looks back quizzically, analysing my face. I see Rowan's face.

Me: He looks a bit like Ro –
Her: I know, right?
Me: Did he meet him?
Her: Yeah. He was really good with him, oddly.

I love the weight of this little thing in my arms. The baby calms down because of my bobbing and Leila visibly relaxes.

I want to ask Leila if she knew about the acupuncture? But I can't face the answer.

Me: I'm going away for a bit.
Her: Where?

I don't want to tell her the truth.

Me: I'm not sure.
Her: Maybe that will be good for you.
Me: Maybe.
Her: What about PaperbackKids? Who's going to
    run it?

I feel so guilty that I haven't factored PaperbackKids
into my plans. Jimi will be waiting for me, just as he's
still waiting for Hannah.

Me: Oh, God –
Her: Can I? I'd like to. It would make me feel like
    I'm doing something other than feeling sorry for
    myself –
Me: Are you sure?
Her: Yeah. I really want to.

I get the keys out of my pocket and try to get the
Portakabin ones off my keyring but struggle. She helps
me. She puts them on the kitchen table and then hugs
me.

Me: Thank you.
Her: It's nothing –
Me: It's not nothing. Can you tell Jimi – can you
    tell him –

I hate that this child knows about death already, that
life can be so mean.

Me: Just – can you tell him I'm sorry.

We stop hugging. She ushers me back to the sitting room and we sit on the sofa. She lies back, positioning one pillow underneath her boobs and one between her knees. The baby's eyelids begin to flutter again; he's falling asleep with a content look on his amazing face and I feel a tiny bit victorious.

This baby knows nothing yet. This baby is safe.

Me: I can watch him for a bit while you rest.
  If you want.
Leila: No, it's OK. You don't have to –

But we both know that she really means yes, yes, yes. She puts her head on the arm of the sofa and closes her eyes, with a slightly pained smile. I keep holding the baby. I even hum for a bit. Once he's asleep, I kiss his tiny cheek and gently put him down in the Moses basket. As I begin to leave Leila turns to me sleepily.

Her: I miss her, Ruth. I just miss her.

I can't say anything because it hurts too much, so I kneel down to stroke the baby's cheek one more time. I turn the lights off as I leave, hoping I'll be back soon.

\* \* \*

When I get home, the TV is on like I meant it to be, ready and waiting for me. I leave no time for silence, no time for changing my mind. I get undressed, and turn the volume up while I clean my teeth with Hannah's electric toothbrush.

I get my laptop and climb into Hannah's bed, with my

freshly clean sheets. It smells different, not like me or her. I don't mind it. I book some flights, using the money from WeBuyAnyCar.com. Afterwards, I force myself to look at her urn in the corner of my room, wrapped with the fairy lights that I now always leave on. I google 'HOW TO TRANSFER ASHES SAFELY' and watch five YouTube tutorials.

I wake up a few hours later, lights still on, laptop on my stomach, annoyed that I won't be able to get to sleep again. I stare at the pile of books and airport magazines I've been avoiding making a decision about. Keep or throw. I can't bring myself to throw away her crime novels. At the top of the pile is what she was reading on our last holiday, one of two books she bought at the airport. I pick it up. Maybe tonight is the night to get into crime novels. A piece of paper falls out.

List of what not to forget:

Sun cream. +++
Hats
Tell Ruth to bring her own headphones
Mosquito spray
Adaptors
Almonds for Ruth
Tell Ruth to pack two swimming costumes
Tell Ruth to double-lock her door, close her windows
    (pigeons)
Condoms for Ruth
Folic acid
Paracetamol +++

I get into bed, clutching the list like it's lost treasure. A moth flies onto my bedside lamp. They have followed me from the storage unit, and I'm glad. I turn onto my side to face the moth as I turn off the light and don't feel silly speaking out loud:

Me: Goodnight, Hannah.

# 74

It's early and the sky is bright and almost totally cloudless. I take out the rubbish as the glum woman who lives opposite takes out hers. We don't say anything to each other, but we both know that she's seen my boobs multiple times in a non-sexual capacity and it feels unequal. I smile at her regardless as she scowls, unlocks her bike and cycles away in heels, her long grey skirt pulled up around her knees. No helmet. Fucking idiot.

A delivery van parks outside the building and I wait to see if the courier buzzes my door, which she does.

Me: Ruth Rothwell?
Courier: Yep. Sign here.

I sign my name and she hands me an A4 package. I don't want to go back home so I put it in my tote bag and begin the walk to the station. No Disney Princess soundtrack. No noise.

Hannah used to say the same set of words any time I became quiet. We could be in a crowded room, at a party, on the Tube in a tunnel, or in the Topshop changing rooms. She usually said it when she sensed I was stressed, or in bed late at night even though it was dark and she couldn't see my face. She would say it quietly and hold my hand:

*Everything is going to be all right.*

The plausibility of being all right, even being close to all right, has been so far away since the day she jumped. But as I look up at the clouds, wheeling my suitcase and holding a tote bag full of snacks I've been organised enough to pack, I do feel all right. For the first time in months, I feel all right.

I don't even think seeing a single magpie right now will make me think I'm going to die today. I don't want to cram a French baguette down my throat to stop me from feeling anything. I won't throw a boiling-hot lasagne out of my window, or fuck a man I don't like, or lie about what my name is.

Right now, in this moment, I am all right.

These secure, composed moments are happening more and more – or is it me who's making them happen? I know it's usually just down to the rush of adrenaline that comes from shouting, 'FUCKING IDIOT!' at a bitchy neighbour, a caffeine high, an orgasm or having just read an inspirational meme about grief on Instagram, but when they come – in those few seconds of feeling all right – it feels as if she's hugging me.

Even so, when I reach the station, I get into the empty lift and scream. Not for the same reasons, but because it's incredibly rare to find oneself in an empty Tube station lift in London. The scream wakes my voice up; I feel cleansed. The platform is empty too. I have three hours before my flight. I open the bag of Percy Pigs from my tote bag and stuff a couple in my mouth as the Tube arrives. It's 6.01 a.m.

On the journey I get to the last few pages of my book

387

on death, the fifth one I've read so far. I remember buying the first one, two weeks after I came back alone from our holiday. I was walking everywhere, for hours at a time. I found myself outside Foyles in central London and somehow had the wherewithal to know that I needed instructions on navigating this kind of pain. I googled 'best books to read about death' and asked the woman behind the tills if they had the top five. They had them all, so I bought them and carried them home, heavy in my arms.

I read till I fell asleep each night, and I'd wake up on the sofa with the book having fallen to the floor, TV still blaring. I wish that the books had said something practical like, 'It won't get better, it will hurt as much for ever, so get really good at Tetris for when you need to stop thinking for a bit.' I regret not getting into video games.

I feel in my tote bag for the Percy Pigs, and the back of my hand brushes against the plastic bag full of Hannah's ashes. The task ahead of me starts to sink in, and I think about it more realistically than I have until now. I have to be brave, something I've seldom been. I become increasingly scared with every Tube station that passes towards Heathrow. I let the feelings of panic come and go with each breath. I stare out as we enter a black tunnel; the lights become harsher and my feet start tapping beyond my control. I think of Rowan. I wonder if he's fucking someone new already, if he finished the course of antibiotics.

I take out the plastic bag of her ashes, and place it on my lap. I cover her with both hands. No one is sitting near me, not that anyone would care. I just have to keep her from falling to the floor. I have to protect her. She's just coming with me, she's coming with me.

The Tube arrives at Heathrow Terminal 5 and I put her carefully back in my bag. I walk my usual route through the station into the airport. I like the smells, I trust this place and its clockwork nature. I go to Boots and buy some paracetamol from the Fairy Godmother, who seems happy to see me. I stand in front of Costa, hoping to see Sal or Paloma, but it's their day off. No one else working recognises me, and I don't mind. I'm just a passenger today, a consumer, somebody in the queue.

I order a mocha with an extra shot, like I did when I was here with Hannah. I sit down at a table and drink it quickly. Have I remembered everything? Will anyone miss me? I scrunch up a Costa napkin in my hand and think of the doodles Hannah and I did of each other on napkins when we were last here together. I think we just left them on the table. I wish I'd kept them.

A surge of longing runs through my whole body which I don't want right now – it won't help me get on my way – so I look around. The tables are full and the place is a tip. I can tell that they're understaffed already, or have been overnight. I quickly gather up all the discarded plates and cups, without being noticed, and put them where they're meant to be. I go into the back room and sit on the stained chair, which is probably going to stay here for ever. I get out my notebook and do a drawing for Sal and Paloma. I write underneath: 'Thank you both for being so kind to me. We'll meet again. Love Ruth x'

I rip it out and slide the doodle into Sal's locker.

My mind becomes totally consumed with getting though security: will she be taken off me, mistaken for drugs? So I open my suitcase and slide her down inside, to the middle, so she's cushioned by my clothes. I sip the dregs of my sugary coffee, even though I can't really taste it. I feel sick. I get the plastic folder out of my bag, which contains Hannah's passport and mine, like it always did. I take one last look around the back room as I leave to go to Check-in.

When I've put the suitcase on the conveyor belt, I get down on my knees and hug it, not caring if I look mad. As I stand back up, the airport worker holds my passport out to line up with my face, probably studying how much older and sadder I look since the photo was taken, two years ago in a booth at Baker Street station. I want to know if my eyes are a different colour, or if they just look darker to me now. She hands me back my passport and presses the button for our suitcase to be sent on its way. I watch it until it's gone. I hear Hannah.

*Her: Once we're through Security, we can relax.*

I speed-walk up the escalators to security, as if the quicker I am, the sooner the plane will leave, and the sooner I will get the suitcase back and she'll be safe again. I get in the queue behind a couple who keep touching each other's bums and I want somebody to tell them to focus on taking off their fucking shoes. The queue is taking for ever. As I watch the couple graduate from bum touching to whispering in each other's ears, I finish the bag of Percy Pigs.

I remember about the package from this morning. To pass the time and just in case it contains something I could get arrested for, I open it. It's my dad's manuscript, and a note: 'Just a first draft. Also, belated happy birthday. Dad x'

390

# 75

Once I'm through, I'm struck by how different the atmosphere is up here.

Downstairs, around Costa and Check-in, the air is tenser, colder. People are worrying about making their flight, the weight of their bags, how much money they are about to spend, how much it's already cost them. Everyone has rushed here, set an alarm, adrenaline is high. Up here, relieved of our possessions and liquids, with conveniently small bags and sunglasses on our heads, the holiday actually begins. For most of them, anyway. Some of these strangers are going on business trips, some are visiting family. I imagine very fancy conferences with fancy sandwiches in dull conference centres, and *The Godfather* gatherings around a sickbed. I'm travelling for a different reason.

As I wash my hands in the toilets, I look at myself in the mirror, in between two women who are applying make-up. Since I used up all of Hannah's reddening conditioner, my natural mousy colour is beginning to show again. One of the women applying make-up begins to glue some fake eyelashes on, while the other sucks in her cheeks and rubs on a cream blusher. They both look so pretty I make a note of the brands they are using, because I know Hannah would want to know.

I check I have her list of what not to forget in my pocket as I walk onwards. I contemplate buying a book, one that's not about death or a depressing memoir. An actual work of fiction. I glance into WHSmith and can't help but see Hannah at the self-checkout tills, buying her two crime novels. I see me, begging her to buy me a bag of Haribo. I stay watching them – the sisters – for as long as possible. I don't want to go in as the new me and make the old us disappear.

I pick up the free papers and magazines on the walk to the gate, and take the travelator as an act of rebellion because she always made me walk. But standing still on this thing, despite technically moving forward, feels unbearably slow – my heart palpitations come back and I begin to sweat. This all feels wrong. It's wrong that she's not with me. I brush past people, and begin to run.

At the gate area, I find a seat facing out to the planes, out of breath. I have over an hour to wait before the flight starts boarding, an hour to get brave.

I see two little boys across the terminal from me, jumping around, hyper, about to embark on an adventure with special little Disney-themed suitcases, sun hats attached to the handles. Is this their first holiday? I see an old couple, reading their books already, with deep wrinkles and saggy chins that suggest years of contented-ness. His hand rests on her thigh, which she moves off occasionally, but he keeps putting it back. I wonder who will die first.

We are all going to the same destination.

I buy a Diet Coke from a vending machine and when I sit back down I get out my phone and brace myself. I want to prepare myself mentally for my arrival, so I don't collapse as soon I get there. I search the location of my destination on Instagram to reacquaint myself visually. Lots of photos come up of the beach and hotels on the island. I scroll down and down, until I see a couple, on the cliff. I instantly recognise them; this is the couple Hannah took a photo of. I zoom in and see my pink flip-flops in the bottom-left corner.

I sip my Diet Coke and get out my photos. The one of her jumping, the one of me jumping. I hold them close and try to focus on breathing until the plane is suddenly boarding and I want to scream:

But it's not time yet. I'm not ready.

# 76

What happens on the plane:

Katy Perry's 'Roar' plays too loudly as everyone takes
   their seats.
I sit by the window for the first time ever.
Read a text from Sal just before take-off, 'Hope
   you're ok xx' with a picture of her new kitten.
I eat two bags of pretzels.
Drink one gin and tonic.
Hold in a wee for ages because I'm scared to ask the
   bitch next to me if I can go to the toilet.
Worry about getting cystitis.
See shapes in the clouds: a rabbit, Hannah's lips, a
   sword.
Pregnant lady (who happens to be the bitch sitting
   next to me) forces her husband to feel the baby
   kick – he does so reluctantly while staring at his
   phone.
I think of Rowan's fingers on the piano.
I think of Fred's shaggy cream carpet, I think of my
   shaggy cream carpet.
I think of the way Paloma eats paninis, how Sal eats
   bananas.

The pregnant lady clutches her bump as we land –
she's scared and I feel bad for calling her a bitch.
Katy Perry's 'Roar' plays too loudly as everyone leaves
their seats.

As I exit the plane I google, 'Has Katy Perry had her
baby yet?'
Hannah would want to know what it was called.

# 77

The conveyor belt gets slowly emptier and my legs are shaking. The baggage-less people start looking at each other with the first inklings of fear seeping in. They want their belongings back. I feel like I'm about to throw up with panic just as I see it. My suitcase – our suitcase – scuttling down the slide and slivering its way towards me. I stand very still until it's right in front of me, then I grab it and roll it, as close to me as possible. I head for the taxis, but I can't find them. I never had to think about directions before; she would have it all sorted and taken care of, like I was her child.

Lost, I stand still for a second, the airport swirling around me. I see the same palm trees outside, and the familiar smell of them hits me in waves as the automatic doors open and close. Eventually I find the taxi stand and I remember getting in the queue with Hannah. She asked for my passport so she could keep ours together in her plastic file; she checked the address of the hotel and gave it in perfect Italian to the driver. When we got off the motorway and onto a beautiful winding road she put her head out of the window, closed her eyes and screamed with joy.

Her: We're here!

I get in the taxi after gracelessly pointing to the address on my phone. He offers to take the suitcase and put it in the back but I shake my head, and I sit with it next to me, one hand on top of the plastic label which says 'HANNAH & RUTH' in her handwriting, the same elegant handwriting she's had since she was a teenager that I was always jealous of. I'm not strong enough to see the sights, so I look down at my knees for the whole journey. When I feel the car going up a hill, I ask him to stop. I know where we are. I pay him silently and begin my walk.

Very quickly I am out of breath and need a break. I need food, I need coffee, water. I need her. I put my head into my thighs and cry as I sit on the suitcase on the side of the road.

*Her: Come on, you can do it.*
*Me: I can't –*
*Her: You can, think how amazing it will feel when you get to the top –*
*Me: Think how amazing it would be getting in a taxi.*

I get back up and don't stop until I reach the top, red-faced and drenched in sweat. The suitcase has a broken wheel, my flip-flops need Sellotape. I am greeted by a young girl outside the hotel. I don't recognise her. She opens the doors for me and I see the concierge across the lobby. Noè. I remember every bit of his face. He doesn't see me and I'm glad. The lady behind Reception checks me in as she speaks on the phone, smiling apologetically. She passes me my room key. Room 228.

I consider asking for a different floor; we were in 224 last time and I don't want to walk past it. But I don't. I don't want to draw attention to myself, don't want sympathy. I just need to get into the room. I decline help with my suitcase and get into the lift, alone at last. Hannah took a selfie of us in here when we arrived, on the way up to our room. I was snappy with her because I thought I looked awful and told her to delete it. I wonder if she did.

The lift doors open and I see the sign on the wall: '220–224, turn right. 225–228 turn left.' I turn left without looking back. I reach my room, and it's similar to our last one, but the bathroom is on the other side. I put the suitcase on the bed, and open it up to find the bag still safely tucked in the middle. I hold her to my chest and then place her gently under my pillow. I lie down, just for a minute. I close my eyes, just for a minute.

A couple of hours later, I wake up and I'm shivering from the air con. I turn on the TV, and listen to the news in Italian as I empty my tote bag onto the bed. My keys, deodorant, lip balm, notebook, my phone and Dad's manuscript. I take the photos out of my notebook and look at them both, side by side on the bed. I pick up her ashes and the photos. Time to go.

It's late afternoon as I leave the hotel. I walk down to the beach, which is quiet. It feels odd walking about in just my swimming costume, with no bag. I am confronted by a couple of seafront hotel workers, who want me to sit and have a drink. They direct me to a deck chair, one of two. They ask if I am waiting for a partner. I shake my head. They quickly fold up the deck chair next to mine and take it away. They hand me a menu and I point to the iced coffee drink I had last time. I hope that it will not taste as good as it did before. I watch the waves. In and out. I see a surfer walking with his board back to the shore, dripping. His chest looks a bit like Rowan's.

My pretty little shot glass of iced coffee, cream and sugar arrives. I down it, and of course, it tastes fucking amazing. Maybe even better than I remember it tasting.

As I walk towards the cliff, someone jumps off. I wait to see if they come up again. They do. Friends cheer from the top. Do they know they're lucky? I trace her name again and again in the sand with my big toe.

I keep walking up and up and then, when I'm close to the top, I find the ledge where I stood to take the photo. The last photo. I sit with my legs dangling off the side of the cliff, and find her name in the sand down below.

HANNAH. HANNAH. HANNAH.

Me: Let's just stay here for another minute and watch
 the sun go down –
Her: It's gone, Ruth. But there's always another one
 tomorrow.

I kick my flip-flops off the side of the cliff one after the other, and watch as one crashes down onto rocks beside the sea. The other makes it and bobs up again, lonely in the water.

I think of the way she smiled too much when she was lying, how she always kept a little flannel in her bag for when sweat formed on her upper lip in the summer, how she wore tight bras that gave her a bit of back fat that spilt out and sometimes she would ask me to 'tuck it in' on Tube escalators, how she hugged me when I was annoyed, how she hugged me when I was happy. How funny she found me. How sad she'd be for me.

I look at the photos and kiss them both, before letting them go. They float down to the sea. Together.

I climb to the top of the cliff; the wind is not blowing and it's quiet. I notice that the sign which was fading before has been freshly repainted. It's standing up straighter, no longer wonky.

'*PERICOLO DI MORTE*'. I now know what it means; these words can't be ignored. Danger of death.

I've read stories about choking on your loved one's ashes as you try to scatter them.

I don't feel scared as I look down.

I don't feel like I'm ready to die, either.

I go to the edge.

I hug her ashes to my chest and then I open the bag, tipping it upside down.

The ashes fly. She flies.

Some of her goes down towards the sea and some of her goes up towards the orangey-pink sky, towards the setting sun.

I jump and follow.

★　★　★

Things about my sister:

She's bigger and better than me in almost every way.
She likes spiders and jumping queues.
She swears so elegantly you almost don't notice.
She has bird-like ankles but strong thighs like an
    MMA wrestler.
She wears slightly too much gold eyeliner every day.
She's a positive person but likes negative people, like
    me.

She snores loudly and sings beautifully.

She eats big meals and nothing in between, she's got willpower of steel but once a month eats a whole box of Crunchy Nut corn flakes and every single scrap of food that remains in her flat.

She plaits my hair too tight.

She has disgusting taste in carpets, heels and bags.

She uses her big boobs like ammunition, always wears a night bra.

She loved me and even though she's gone now, she'd want me to be all right – she'd fucking make sure of it.

## END

# ACKNOWLEDGEMENTS

I want to thank my sister Bebe, who I wrote this for. My amazing baby sister, who I wished for on dandelions every morning on the way to school until one day, she was here. She makes me laugh like no other, I fight with her like no other. My best friend. She helped me edit the book in the early, shaky stages and without her I would not have been able to write it nor have had the strength to. I am at my happiest when watching her work, and I can't wait to see what she goes on to create.

I want to thank my parents, David and Debbie. Growing up I was encouraged to do whatever I wanted to do as long as I worked hard. They gave me the freedom to be creative, which is something I never take for granted.

I want to thank in particular my mum for her beautiful sewing for the cover and for generally being my creative partner in all ways, on top of looking after my kids so that I can work. A lot of the writing was done during national lockdowns and when there was no school. So we have all learnt from the best mother in the world. I am in awe of her.

I want to thank my boyfriend, Alfie, for letting me be 'a nightmare' whilst writing this. He is the first person (outside my family) to ever make me feel loved and to know love. I've finished it, don't worry. Now I will force you to write your book and I will let you be a nightmare too. Almost every day I think we are so lucky to have met.

I want to thank my children, Donnie and Margot, who I hope (one day) will read this story and be reminded of how lucky they are to have each other to play with and to fight with. I love you both more than you could ever imagine.

And I need to thank the baby who was growing inside me for a large proportion of the writing process. I was writing before him, I was writing with him growing and I was still writing after he was born too. My writing sidekick, Tiny Tennessee; who was conceived when I was so heavy in my new grief for Ben and who helped me focus on what I still have to be incredibly grateful for. This book and this baby mark a new beginning. You will never know Ben but I will make sure he is remembered.

I want to thank all three of my brothers. Robbie, Ben and Jamie. I am so proud of you all, even if I don't show it. I will try to be a better sister.

I want to thank my brilliant agents, who have all helped me so much in different ways. To Debi Allen – thank you for sticking with me and being such a kind person as well as fiercely supportive. To Millie Hoskins – your professional enthusiasm is so uplifting. And finally I want to thank my publisher Jon Elek, who gave me my first chance.

\* \* \*

This book is in memory of my wonderful and magical brother Ben who died tragically in an accident in 2019. He was just twenty-seven. I miss him every second. We all do and will do for ever.

Here is a poem he wrote:

> It's very easy for people to slip into an easy
> existence, a numb life.
> Add weight to every moment.
> Don't try to defragment the code
> to find a logical meaning behind
> all things that seem inexplicable.
>
> Be filled with awe and passion.
> It's how you make things matter.
> By going on instinct and finding the beauty
> before you.
> It's how you find a purpose, a story.
> Otherwise what the fuck are you here for?
>
> Make these moments and kill the fickle
> transience of life
> by carrying them with you and letting them shape
> who you are throughout time.
> They last for ever within you and live far beyond
> your fragile morsel of a life.
>
> All our choices and decisions end up nullified in a
> meaningless universe
> with no rhyme or reason for anything.
> Most of us believe we have a special purpose
> or are constantly fighting against the realisation
> that we have no purpose.

True joy and love and passion can be found
though, despite ourselves.
We can make our own meaning
as we reconcile with pointless, inevitable death.

Ben Cave

# WELBECK

PUBLISHING GROUP

## Love books? Join the club.

Sign up and choose your preferred genres to receive tailored news, deals, extracts, author interviews and more about your next favourite read.

From heart-racing thrillers to award-winning historical fiction, through to must-read music tomes, beautiful picture books and delightful gift ideas, Welbeck is proud to publish titles that suit every taste.

## bit.ly/welbeckpublishing